THEY WERE AFRAID BUT
"THE FOXHUNTER" HELD THEM . . .

this runny-nosed army of boys and withered men. They ran like hell cursing him and died in the dust for him, the gangling, gray-eyed giant of a general.

In brigades they deserted him, stealing off in the night. In brigades they fought with him, laughing, sobbing, dying impaled like pigs on German bayonets.

Of his private agony they knew nothing. They froze with him, starved with him, followed him into unspeakable horror.

They ascended the heights of glory with him, with foul-mouthed wondering, "Washington—who in all hell ever heard such a name?"

"If there is any better historical fiction, bring it out!"

—LIFE

Books by Howard Fast

CONCEIVED IN LIBERTY

THE UNVANQUISHED

FREEDOM ROAD

CITIZEN TOM PAINE

SPARTACUS

MOSES, PRINCE OF EGYPT

THE EDGE OF TOMORROW

THE WINSTON AFFAIR

APRIL MORNING

MY GLORIOUS BROTHERS

THE LAST FRONTIER

THE AMERICAN

CLARKTON

A PLACE IN THE CITY

TORQUEMADA

Published by Bantam Books, Inc.

HOWARD FAST
THE
UNVANQUISHED

BANTAM BOOKS · TORONTO · NEW YORK · LONDON

To Sam and Peggy

*This low-priced Bantam Book
has been completely reset in a type face
designed for easy reading, and was printed
from new plates. It contains the complete
text of the original hard-cover edition.*
NOT ONE WORD HAS BEEN OMITTED.

THE UNVANQUISHED
*A Bantam Book / published by arrangement with
Crown Publishers, Inc.*

PRINTING HISTORY
*World Publishing Company edition published 1942
Modern Library edition published 1945
Bantam edition published March 1967*

Published simultaneously in the United States and Canada

*Bantam Books are published by Bantam Books, Inc., a subsidiary
of Grosset & Dunlap, Inc. Its trade-mark, consisting of the words
"Bantam Books" and the portrayal of a bantam, is registered in the
United States Patent Office and in other countries. Marca Registrada.
Bantam Books, Inc., 271 Madison Avenue, New York, N. Y. 10016.*

PRINTED IN THE UNITED STATES OF AMERICA

CONTENTS

PART ONE: BROOKLYN

1. THE FOXHUNTER   1
2. THE BATTLE   10
3. THE MARBLEHEAD FISHERMEN   17
4. THE RETREAT   29

PART TWO: MANHATTAN ISLAND

5. THE ARMY OF LIBERTY   39
6. ONE TERRIBLE SUNDAY MORNING   47
7. THE GRACIOUS MRS. MURRAY   64
8. VIEW HALLOO   71

PART THREE: WESTCHESTER

9. LET FREEDOM RING   85
10. HOW THE FISHERMEN WERE NOT AFRAID   98
11. HOW OTHERS WERE AFRAID   110

PART FOUR: JERSEY

12. THE FORT CALLED "WASHINGTON"   119
13. HOW THEY WENT INTO JERSEY   140
14. HOW DESTINY SAT ON GENERAL LEE'S SHOULDER   153
15. HOW THE FOXHUNTER BECAME A DICTATOR   170
16. AND HOW HE CROSSED THE DELAWARE A SECOND TIME   185

* * *

AN AFTERWORD
196

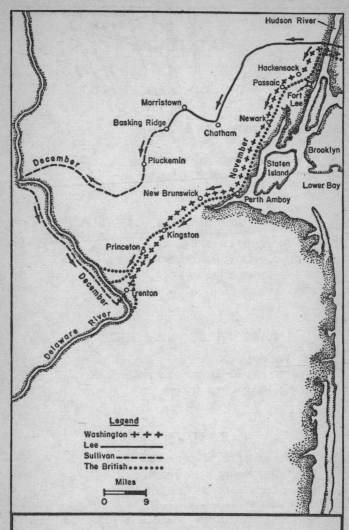

Legend
Washington + + +
Lee ————
Sullivan — — — —
The British • • • • •

Miles
0   9

Retreat through the Jerseys
Aug. 27, 1776 — Dec. 25, 1776

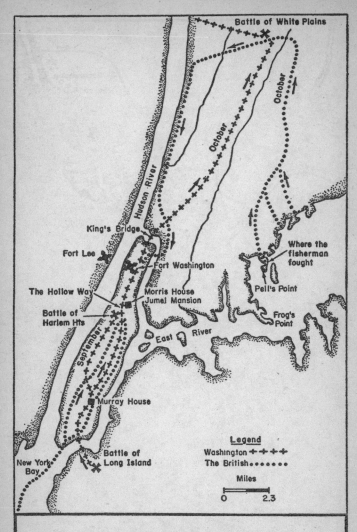

Battle of White Plains

Hudson River

October

October

King's Bridge

Fort Lee

Fort Washington

Where the fisherman fought

The Hollow Way

Morris House
Jumel Mansion

Pell's Point

Battle of Harlem Hts.

September

East River

Frog's Point

Murray House

Legend

Washington +++

The British ......

New York Bay

Battle of Long Island

Miles

0   2.3

Retreat through Manhattan and Westchester

Part One

---⊰{ BROOKLYN }⊱---

1

THE FOXHUNTER

With the heat running like warm water from the sides of
the room, backed by three closed windows and a closed
door, he slept badly and restlessly, waking up, closing his
eyes firmly, dozing, prodded into consciousness, fighting
consciousness because he was a man who slept well most of
the time, rolling over from a wet spot on the pillow, dreaming, recalling, forgetting, finding a painful ache in all the
packed, broad, slab-like pictures that went to make up his
memory.

While the night candle next to his bed burned, dim under
its sooty cover, he could look at his watch and mark the
hours, one o'clock, half past one, two o'clock, surely five
o'clock, ten minutes after two, until the candle burned down.

Sometime during that night, awakening, he became
afraid, and his sweat turned cold. He shivered and trembled
and sought reassurance in the deep pockmarks that covered
his face. His eyes searched the unending dark, but there was
no object, no end, no faint trickle of light through the tightly
sealed windows. His fingers traced out the pockmarks, nose

and chin and mouth and forehead and thinning hair and back to the pockmarks; and in the dark his sense of objects drifted away, the pocks deep holes, the nose a monstrous thing, the chin an ungainly wedge.

He rolled over, threw off the single blanket that covered him, and groaned, "Patsy, Patsy." Then he buried his face in the wet pillow.

The grey dawn crept into the room and revealed him. He was awake and sitting up in the tangled disarray of his bed. His linen nightshirt had wrinkled and twisted itself up above his knees, and his long bony legs stuck out like the props of a scarecrow. He looked haggard from lack of sleep, older than he was, and incredibly thin.

He rolled over to the edge of the bed and shuffled his almost grotesquely large feet across the floor, seeking his slippers. When his toes found the soft caves of felt, he stood up, crouching for a moment with the instinctive gesture of a very tall man. He stretched and yawned before he went to a window and threw it open. The air outside was a little cooler, and he breathed deeply of it. It was still only half morning, still too early to know whether the day would be fair or foul, roofed with a blue sky or with angry clouds; but hot it would be with the sickening wet heat that was the prize of New York City and no other place in all the land.

After a few moments at the window, he told himself, "It will rain," for out of the east came the faintest rumbling and grumbling of angry storm clouds; and he was sleepy enough to think no more of it than that, storm clouds, rain, mud, rubbing his eyes with his enormous hands, shuffling around the bed and sitting down in a spindle-legged chair.

As he sat, the thunder came again, but different, in staccato bursts that forecast ruin instead of rain; and the big man leaped out of his chair and lurched toward the window, losing his felt slippers, leaned out of the window and called, "Billy! Billy! Billy!"

He hadn't a big voice, but he could make it snap like a lash. Pulling his nightshirt over his head, he stamped around naked, calling, "Billy! Billy!"

He was skin wound on bones, with broad shoulders and broader hips; clothes would cover his lankness and give his huge frame an impression of strength. When a colored man came running into the room, the first words were for clothes.

He was calm suddenly, dressing himself with the aid of the colored man. He sat on the edge of the bed, pulling on his stockings, his buff breeches, his high black boots; and as he wore the clothes, he became a different man, stronger, wiser, vaster. His long, skinny body assumed more human proportions as the huge knobs of bone disappeared under the broadcloth and linen. His thin red hair was combed from its disarray flat back against his head. Only his tired grey eyes remained to tell of the sleepless night.

He washed in a white china bowl and then got into his blue jacket. If he heard the rumbling thunder now, the fears and apprehensions it evoked were tight-locked under his uniform.

"Shave you, sir?" the colored man asked.

"Later."

"Two gentlemen waiting," the colored man said.

"How long? Why didn't you wake me, Billy? Haven't you more sense than that?"

"Just a few minutes."

"How long is a few minutes, Billy? You have less sense every day."

"Maybe five minutes, sir."

The big, bony, stooping man, fully dressed now in a buff and blue uniform, left the bedroom. As he entered another room which he called his office, he straightened up and threw back his shoulders with a visible effort.

That same buff and blue uniform had made a stir in Philadelphia something over a year ago. A tall, tall man, long-faced, shy, but very well dressed, had sat down with the Second Continental Congress, wrapped in his buff and blue and in the deepest mantle of silence, and had sat and sat and sat without ever saying a word. His silence became something physical and alive; everyone else wanted to talk, and everyone else did talk. Things were moving; it was revolution, and the world was dropping into pieces, and the pieces had to be sorted out, and when someone suggested a humble and dutiful petition to the King of England, John Adams roared, "Oh, the imbeciles! The fools! The damned, damned fools, with their talk of petitions!"

And in all the crazy riot of talk, the tall man in buff and blue said nothing, heard everything, and kept his quizzical grey eyes fastened more or less intently upon the meeting.

"Who is he?" a member from Massachusetts asked.

"Nobody important."

"In that uniform?"

"Well, he's nobody important; he's a farmer from Virginia. His name's Washington."

"Washington?"

"Wash-ing-ton."

"Who ever heard of a name like that?"

"That's *his* name. He's rich."

The member from Massachusetts nodded, a merchant himself, putting the uniform at forty pounds, the lace at three, the shoes at four. "He never speaks?" he inquired.

"No."

"Just sits there?"

"Yes."

"Washington—" the member from Massachusetts said thoughtfully.

And John Adams told his cousin Sam, "I like him."

"Why?"

"He knows how to keep a still tongue."

"Maybe he's got nothing to say," Sam suggested.

"No—people who have nothing to say spend all their time talking about it," John said. "That man Washington, he's said nothing and he's chairman of four military committees. Nobody ever heard of George Washington of Virginia, but they look at the uniform and they look at the way he holds his head and they hear how much money he's worth, and then they vote for him without thinking any more about it."

"How much is he worth?" Sam asked.

"As much as any man in America."

Sam grinned and said, "Commander in chief?"

"Why not? Look at the way he wears his uniform, the way he sits on his horse."

"Some won't like it," Sam Adams said slowly, thinking of a people's revolution, but also of what it meant to be as rich as any man in America.

"The North won't like it, but the South will. We already have the North, and now we need the South, to be more precise, Virginia."

"I wasn't thinking of that," Sam said. "I was thinking of Hancock. He wants like all the devils in hell to lead this business."

"You want it too, don't you?" John Adams asked, squinting at his cousin.

"I can't wear a uniform," he replied sourly. "Still there'll be hell to pay for Hancock."

"Let it then. I'm going to nominate this Washington."

And now, nominated, appointed more than a year, this tall, forty-four-year-old planter, foxhunter, farmer, still found it difficult to think of himself as a general.

With a curt nod he greeted the two men who were waiting for him, and nodded for them to speak. They hadn't slept either; their eyes were red and their faces were dirty and their clothes were limp with sweat. They were from General Putnam, they told him.

"Billy," he said, "get these gentlemen something to drink." And he told them, "Sit down, gentlemen. You've come a long way and it's hot. Sit down."

His judgment was quick and certain and damning, because they were afraid, one of them a boy of eighteen or nineteen and the other a sallow man in his thirties, but both of them afraid and dirty and tired, dressed in old homespun and linen shirts that had once been white but were now muddy brown. The big man thought: "What am I looking at? A lieutenant and a captain, or a major and a colonel?" His army! They were Yankees with clumsy movements and nasal New England accents, and he had to cover his contempt by staring at the grained wood of the table where he sat. He had a physical abhorrence of physical fear; it was something twined in and out of the whole fabric and pattern of his life. He had always been a sickly man, and he had the sickly man's intimate knowledge of death; fear to him was real and black and terrible, and for that reason, being almost without the habit of introspection, he despised fear in others.

In these two, the messengers from General Putnam, fear was as hot and wet as the day itself. It slid from their lips as they poured out their story. They had come over from Brooklyn.

How had they come?

They stared at him amazed, not comprehending how his mind needed details, hundreds of little details for him to piece together, meaningless details when the world was falling apart.

They had rowed across in a skiff. They couldn't get a boatman. The younger one began to blubber; you would think with a message from General Putnam, they could get someone to row the boat.

"When was that?" the big man cried. "When did it start, you fools? Answer me!" He pulled out his watch; it was six o'clock.

That was what the younger one was trying to tell him, blubbering that they couldn't get a boatman, that they had to row themselves. The sallow man thrust out his palms in proof and showed the blisters. He had never rowed a boat before. He hadn't enlisted to row a boat; he wasn't a sailor. They had run all the way from the landing; well, he hadn't enlisted for that, to row boats and to run his fool head off.

"Get out of here!" the foxhunter roared. "Both of you—get out of here!"

He sat at the table while Billy brought in some breakfast, while through the open window came the distant rumble of cannon.

He shouldn't have lost his temper at those two, he told himself. His temper was a hot iron on hairsprings, an outpouring of all the inhibitions bound up so tightly inside of him. It was something he had wheedled and flailed and coaxed and beaten all of his life; and until he had come up here to the North to take command of the army, he had believed it under control, flung back, hammered down and tight in chains.

Before that taking of command, he could clearly remember the last time he had lost himself. It had been during a clear, glorious afternoon at Mount Vernon, when he sat in his saddle with the pack sprayed out in front of him, looking for game, a fox or a deer or a hare, with his horse's hoofs drumming sweet music and the smell of green things on the cool breeze. The pack raised a scent, but he reined in, his eyes on a flight of dark birds silhouetted in the sky over the Potomac. The picture was fixed and lovely until a shot from the river bank sent two of the birds twisting down in their death.

In that moment, like a taut thong snapping, he went insane with rage against the poacher who crouched in a canoe by the bank, a steep hill-slope away. The foxhunter put his horse over the suicidal slope of the hill, plunged down to the river, flung off his horse and rushed at the poacher, who was trying to get his canoe clear of the bank. The poacher, seeing this fantastically tall man charging at him, fired his gun in desperation; but the foxhunter crashed past, ripped the fowling piece out of the man's hands, and then deliberately beat the poacher to within an inch of his life. He dragged the poacher out of the canoe, through the water, up on the bank, punishing him all the way as a dog punishes a terrified rat.

The memory wasn't good. He hated poachers, but he hated no man enough to justify losing himself in rage. After that incident, for a long time, his temper had been carefully under control—until he came to the army, until he made up his mind that there was nothing else to do but fight. When that time came, he put on his buff and blue uniform of a colonel in the Virginia militia.

The pride of getting the command had lasted until he saw his army. The command was everything and all, and he remembered telling his wife, "Patsy, they've given it to me, all of it. I don't know why, but they've given it to me. To me, do you understand?"

Then he added, "I'm not the man for it, Patsy—why should they have given it to me?"

"Why?" he kept asking himself afterwards. "Why?"

But he was proud, no longer a foxhunter, but something else, so mighty in his pride, so big and strong and splendid that nobody, looking at him, could doubt that he was the right man, the only man, standing like a god, six feet two and a half inches with a broad impassive face, cool grey eyes, and because he said so little and had an air of knowing how things should be done. But like a boy, rewarded beyond belief or estimation, he told himself again and again, "They've given it to me," thinking of how it was that afternoon in the Congress when John Adams rose and talked about qualifications needed for a commander in chief, everyone taking for granted the fact of his speaking for Hancock, and Hancock himself flushing, moving with nervous little jerks, biting his lips, smiling sheepishly when Adams said something particularly lush, and then cocking his big head as Adams said:

"Gentlemen, I know these qualifications are high, but we all know they are needful in this crisis in this chief. Does anyone say they are not to be obtained in this country? In reply, I say they are; they reside in one of our own body, and he is the man whom I now nominate—George Washington of Virginia."

It fell like a bombshell, and Hancock's face suddenly became a lump of flesh, without expression and without features. The Virginian reacted more slowly; he had been staring at Hancock, and it was only moments later, as a memory, vague and poorly defined, that he heard his own name spoken. He got to his feet somehow, still staring at the suffering Hancock, and then turned and shuffled from the hall, as if he had done something unspeakably wretched.

Only afterward, bit by bit, the exultation came.

That was until he saw his army, New England men sprawled outside of Boston, besieging the British, picking their noses, bickering and complaining in their metallic, offensive Yankee twang.

After that his temper wore as thin as a piece of old and frayed cloth.

He read Putnam's message as he ate his breakfast. Sometime early this morning, the battle had begun, and things were going badly. Putnam didn't say how bad things were, but they were bad enough. He couldn't see much more than his own corner and everything was confused, but it was bad enough.

Putnam wanted more men.

The Virginian shook his head. How had it come to this? He sat here at the breakfast table, his body as inert and helpless as a bundle of wet rags, staring at cakes and honey, and over there in Brooklyn his army was fighting a battle, its first battle, the first battle of the Continental armies of the thirteen colonies. And he sat with nothing to do, no thoughts, no solutions, only the dreadful horror of a person caught in a trap of his own making.

He was not brilliant; even his dreams were formal things, and when he had made himself a picture of an army, before he had ever seen the army that was to be his and was to fight for the independence of the colonies, his picture had been a neat conception of many thousands of orderly men in orderly uniforms. They would wheel and march and attack and retreat and charge and fire just as an army should, and he in his buff and blue uniform would ride at their front.

And the Yankees outside of Boston hadn't a uniform to a regiment, and aside from eating and sleeping they were superlative at lying on their backsides and complaining.

Still, Putnam wanted more of them, more Yankees, for what they were worth. This was the real thing; this was a battle. Over, across the river, in Brooklyn, men were hacking at each other, cursing at each other, shooting their unwieldy, rusty firelocks, and dying and running away. For him, at his breakfast table, there was the booming of cannon, clearer and nearer now.

From Boston, after the British fleet had given up the city and sailed away, the big Virginian marched his army down to New York. At the time that had seemed like an obvious thing to do. It was almost like a victory, the way the English had been forced out of Boston. There was no fighting to speak of after he had taken command; but the British didn't know whether the thousands of New England farmers, sprawled around the town, were an army or not. Anyway, they didn't give two damns for Boston, and they sailed away and left it.

New York was something else. Placed like a gate at the mouth of the Hudson, it was the key to the whole colonial situation, and who controlled New York might control America. Or, at least, so the foxhunter had thought. Others thought differently; others thought that New York City might be a death trap, and they pointed to the maps and said, "See how it lies; what will you defend? Manhattan? It lies like a finger stretched out, with a broad river on either side of it. Hold the bay end, and the English sail their navy up the rivers and cut you off, neat as they please. Long Island? Another finger with water for the British to sail on. Staten Island? Even worse in the same way."

The big man shook his head. He had on his side the Congress, who wanted the city held. He considered himself their servant, for all his pride, and he liked to think of them as an august senate, such as had sat in ancient Rome. If they wanted the city held, it should be held, some way, somehow. And he had twenty thousand men. They were Yankees, for the most part; they were a slovenly, shambling rabble of militia, and on the march to New York they had sprawled aimlessly over miles of road. But still there were twenty thousand of them and they were an army.

And now Putnam had sent him a message for more men, all of it working out in the worst way, the worst possible way, half of his army in Brooklyn, trapped by the British who had sailed around Long Island, another part here in New York, waiting to be trapped; nothing was lacking but that the British should sail the rest of their fleet up the

East River and put an end to a comic-opera revolution that had appointed a foolish, prideful Virginia gentleman as its commander in chief.

2

THE BATTLE

His trouble was to know where they would strike or how they would strike or when they would strike. He wasn't a general, he wasn't even a soldier, he was a foxhunting plantation owner; if he tried to think out the whole complicated matter of military strategy in the defense of New York, the endless ramifications puzzled and bewildered him. His instinct was for a thousand small and concrete details which he could construct into one single fact, all of it shot through with the even thread of orderliness. Here there was no orderliness and no single fact.

The British might seize Long Island, so he put a part of his men on Brooklyn Heights, directly across the river from Manhattan. Or they might, on the contrary, seize New York itself; that meant a part of his army must remain in Manhattan. Another part to defend upper Manhattan, another for the Jerseys, another for the Highlands—and so on. An how many were sick? And how many deserted each day?

He no longer said, as before, that he had twenty thousand men.

He was all a bundle of hurts and pain as he left the room, his breakfast untouched. But he walked stiffly and certainly, and they said, "Look at him, he knows how things are going."

He stood in the street outside, and aides and officers crowded around him.

"Listen to the guns, sir!"

"Shall we be going across?"

"My regiment, sir. I have my regiment ready."

"No, mine, sir!"

Boys of eighteen and nineteen talking about regiments. He managed what was so hard for him, to smile.

He was not a revolutionist, so he would say to himself, over and over again, "My country, my country, my country." He would think of the river, flowing softly and gently by his acres, and he would think of the cold dirt in his hand, being crumpled farmer-wise, until grain by grain it slipped through his fingers; he would think of the house and the barn and the grass and the trees, and there would be many solid things for him to place his feet on. He needed solid things.

There was nothing solid about revolution. It was a shimmering unreality, and the only concrete form it took in his eyes was to produce thousands and thousands of slovenly, dirty, tobacco-chewing, nasal-voiced Yankee farmers.

So he said to himself, "My country, my country," shaking his head slowly like a bulldog who has put his teeth into something and will hold on vise-like until death severs the head from the body.

He knew now, this morning, August 27, 1776, that he had made a terrible, tragic mistake in trying to defend Brooklyn. His huge, grotesque body held a nature as soft as it was eager; and childlike was the trust he put in persons who knew more than he did. Their number was legion.

One of them was a General Charles Lee, a soldier and a darling of all the people who knew the Virginian was no soldier at all. Lee, a disgruntled, bitter soldier of fortune, hating a life that had given him nothing, leaped on the bandwagon of revolution; and logically he was the man to lead the army. But he was objectionable and ugly, whereas the foxhunter was a pleasant gentleman and magnificent in his bearing; Lee was penniless, and the foxhunter was, perhaps, the wealthiest man in all the colonies. For all that the war would be fought by a dirty rabble, money remained the crux of the situation, and people wept when they heard that the Virginia farmer had refused to take a penny for his services.

The foxhunter wrote to Lee, humble with a man so much wiser, and asked what the soldier would do about New York. Lee's answer was that he would build fortifications on Brooklyn Heights.

It was five days now since the British had ferried most of their German troops from Staten Island to Gravesend on Long Island. The Virginian had watched the action impotently, having no ship in his navy bigger than a rowboat; and then he made his answer, desperately, by sending six more of the dirty, tobacco-chewing regiments into the death's trap of Brooklyn.

Then, for five days, nothing happened, and the dull, sinking fear that he was to know for many days and weeks and months to come, lumped up in his breast. If he had been a real general, he would have taken advantage of some dark night and pulled all his troops back into Manhattan; if he had been a self-confident fool, he would have sent more and more regiments across the river and into the trap which the British had so neatly created. Being neither, he left his army divided, part in one place and part in another, hoping against hope for a miracle to save him from the looming disaster.

There was no miracle.

About three o'clock in the morning, on August 27, 1776, the British began their advance.

They had twenty thousand men on Long Island, a good part of them German mercenaries, altogether the best-officered, best-trained fighting force in the world at the time. There were less than ten thousand American colonials facing them on Brooklyn Heights. The ten thousand were a rabble of militia that had only one thought in common, the desire to go home as soon as possible.

General Nathanael Greene, whom the Virginian had placed in command, lay in bed with a raging fever. Greene was only thirty-four years old, a Quaker, a good man, solid and dependable, with brains in his head. He was young, but the whole army was young—boys who wanted to show the world what dreams they had. But Greene was sick, and in desperation the Virginian gave the command to Sullivan. Then his faith in Sullivan went out like a dying candle, and desperately—more desperately than ever now—he gave the command to Putnam. The generals bickered and fought, and their troops took up the quarrel.

The Virginian sent troops over, more and more of the slovenly, high-voiced Yankees, with their huge muzzle-loading firelocks and their baby-faced commanders. And all the while he was in a frenzy of apprehension that the British left on Staten Island might attack his depleted Manhattan garrison.

He still prayed to God that he might win the battle, the very first battle, the initial test of George Washington, commander in chief. He knew something of how the battle was going, of what was happening, but not a great deal.

He knew that a fatal mistake had been made; not his; his mistakes were plenty, but this was not one of his. From their redoubts on Brooklyn Heights, the Americans had fanned out to take places in a range of low hills that extended from the Narrows inland almost to the East River. There were three passes through these low hills, and two of the passes were fairly well defended, while the third was almost completely ignored. This neglect of the third pass was the fatal mistake.

It was two hours before daybreak on the twenty-seventh when the advance guard of the British army reached the inland pass, the Jamaica pass. The British expected a stiff battle, and came forward cautiously, but to their amazement they found the pass guarded only by five sleeping officers. Like school children playing at war and all wanting to be generals, this rebel army was laden with officers, sometimes as many in a regiment as there were private soldiers to do the fighting, their attitude being, "Dammit all and to hell—if you reckon yourself high and mighty enough for an officer, I do too, as good a man as you are."

They wore feathers in their caps, since having no uniforms there was nothing to distinguish one from another, and out of that love for cockades came the mocking tune of the British:

> *Yankee Doodle went to town, riding on a pony,*
> *Stuck a feather in his cap and called it macaroni—*

The five sleeping officers were awakened by bayonet pricks in their buttocks, and warned that if they made any outcry the steel points would be driven at their throats.

"I do allow," one said sleepily, and the others said nothing at all, only rubbing the sore spots on their buttocks and regretting that they had not followed an earlier impulse to put away their guns and go home.

"Rebels," a British officer said scornfully, the way he would say pigs or goats or cows.

"What command?" another asked.

"Huh?"

"Bless your sleepy souls, what command?"

"Milishy, mister," a seventeen-year-old grinned.

"Milishy," the others chimed in.

"But the regiment? The regiment?"

"Just milishy," they insisted.

"Oh, merciful God," the officer said softly, and then the five captives were taken away and the British column went on. Word was sent back that the left flank of the American army had been turned and was now wide open, and though the British command could hardly believe its senses, it didn't hesitate to take advantage of the gap. A frontal attack was launched at the right flank for diversion, during which time hundreds and hundreds of redcoat troops poured through the wonderful gap to take the Americans in the rear.

"And after that?" the big foxhunter asked grimly. He was not a man for regrets; when a thing was done, it was done.

"After that it was hell, just hell, just bloody, bloody hell."

He stood so calmly, so still, the Virginian, that those around him thought: "He's not human—or maybe he doesn't understand what happened."

He didn't know the full story of the disaster until he had crossed the river and got to Brooklyn himself. Afraid to leave Manhattan open for an even greater debacle, torn because his men were fighting a battle in Brooklyn and he was here, at last he crossed, and then the battle was almost over. His face remained as placid as a death mask when they told him what had happened to his two generals, Stirling and Sullivan.

They held the front where the German mercenaries advanced in frontal attack. That was after the cannonading which in its distant echoes had penetrated the Virginian's airless bedroom. The cannonading did little enough harm, but it frayed the nerve of the Yankee farmers, who had dozed uneasily over their guns all night.

Then came the German Jagers, marching knee-deep through the drifting mists of the morning, their green uniforms blending in with the trees and bushes, their drums playing, their bright bayonets dipping and sparkling.

"Hessians," the Yankees told each other. The farm-bred boys, eighteen and nineteen and twenty years old, stared with wide eyes and gripped their guns with wet palms. Along with their unreasoning hatred for the Germans was an aching fear. The big, ox-eyed, green-clad, guttural-voiced mercenaries were beyond their comprehension.

"Hessians," they told each other.

Still they would have made a stand, tried to make one, blowing off some of their unwieldy guns, holding for just a little while the ragged front of their line, except that suddenly, from behind them, sounded the drums of the redcoats. They looked around and saw that they were attacked from two directions. They tried to stand up before the Germans, and volleys from the redcoats slashed into their backs. They whimpered and moaned, and screamed that they were betrayed. They tried to retreat, and the columns in red drove them back into the arms of the Germans. They tried to swing their great, rusty twenty-five-pound firelocks in defense, and the razor-sharp bayonets of the Hessians slashed out their guts. They fell on the ground and wept for their mothers, and the ox-eyed German peasants rammed slivers of steel into their backs.

They had never fought in any battle before, except the few of them who made the stand at Bunker Hill. They had never killed or been killed. The leisurely wash of their lives had rolled gently around many box-like, white village churches in many New England towns; and for all the times they had sat in taverns and talked of freedom, they were paying now.

They ran every which way, and the Germans yelled and laughed and ran after them. They cowered back against trees, and their breath sighed and died as the bayonets cut through them and bent on the wood.

They hid in fields, and the Germans hunted them out and pulled them up and dragged them along, shouting, "Yonkee! Yonkee! Yonkee!"

The hell went on for hours. Between the wooded line they tried to hold and the American base fortifications was a slow creek running through a treacherous bog. The panic-stricken colonials floundered into this trap, threw away their guns, and sank deeper and deeper into the mud. And behind them, ever, came that guttural, mocking cry, "Yonkee! Yonkee! Yonkee!"

General Sullivan was in a cornfield, trying to hide. He crept between the tall stalks, and watched the Hessian boots trample past him. He lay very still, but not still enough. Three straw-haired Germans dragged him to his feet, and grinning, bore him off as their own, personal prize.

General Stirling ran, alone, not through fear, but alone with the enemy all around him, his men gone, his brigades scattered like chaff, the redcoats pot-shooting at him like men after ducks, never knowing their prize was a general, not a tobacco-chewing cockade brevet, but a real enough general who himself had once worn the red coat of Britain. He ran and ran until his feet were heavy as lead, until he blundered into a German patrol which grinningly made its second capture of an American general.

When the Virginian had crossed the river and come into the rear lines of the battle, his officers, colonels and majors and a general, came trailing to tell him how bad it was, how it couldn't be worse.

"We're done," they tried to make him understand. "All done, all finished, all done—"

He went up to the top of a hill, where he could watch the battle complete itself, and he knew that they were right, that everything was done, that nothing was left, that the impossible scheme had played itself out.

He stood there with the whole horrible picture spread before him. The bog lay at his feet. He could almost see the faces of the Hessians as they cut up and herded out of the fight the pleading Yankees. He saw a Maryland brigade drive into the redcoat flank in a vain effort to hold open an avenue of retreat. Grapeshot raked them and tore them to pieces. In the bog, the Yankees crawled like insects. The Hessians were making a holiday of it, and the wind carried to him, faintly, the guttural refrain of joy, "Yonkee! Yonkee!"

And someone was saying to him, "General, what shall we do now?"

"Now?"

He was thinking of how it was to be made commander in chief of a whole army.

"Now?" he repeated. "What is there to do?"

He walked along slowly, nodding his head, muttering, wondering, trying to recall all the long line of mistakes that had gone into the making of this. He tried to remember what he knew of war, of battles, of defeats, and his head ached, and his whole lank body was wet with sweat.

A Colonel Hart, mud-stained, asked him, "If they come on to attack us here—?"

"Then wait until they are close by," the foxhunter said

slowly, as if repeating a lesson he had learned in school. "Then just wait until they are close by before you fire."

But it was all over and all done, and he knew it; and nothing in the world could help him now, not advice to his frightened men, not waiting until the enemy was close by—but nothing at all now.

3

THE MARBLEHEAD FISHERMEN

They all admired him a great deal, as he walked up and down behind the lines, his steps measured, his long body severely erect, and his brow only slightly furrowed, like nothing ever seen in the way of a commander whose army had been sliced to pieces and whose hopes had been shattered. With his great height, he bulked high out of the confusion of dispatch runners, anguished colonels who had lost their regiments, heartbroken captains of nineteen and twenty, generals who had served their first and last command.

Morning had worn into midday, and midday into a hot, sulky afternoon, and now the murky sun was sinking behind the Palisades. The battle was not yet over, but only because the British had paused to rest from the wonderful sport of chasing and killing and capturing New Englanders. They had driven them into a cul-de-sac, ringed by strong masses of troops on three sides and water on the fourth; and feeling that the motley army was securely in his grasp, the British commander was in no hurry to close the issue and lose men who could not easily be replaced.

The retreat, which had become almost a rout, ran into the American entrenchments like slow flood waters over bottom lands; and all that long afternoon terrified and beaten men staggered out of the bog and woods. They were bewildered and frightened, each of them immersed in his own personal catastrophe, each of them certain that the whole thin dream of revolution was done with, that nothing remained except to save his own skin.

They streamed past the big farmer and clustered into

huddles of panic-stricken humanity. They avoided his eyes, but some of them glanced back at him after they had passed, fixing their gaze on his muddy boots.

Almost two thousand of them never came out of the bog and the woods.

It was not the first time the Virginian had lost. The whole warp and woof of his life was woven with losses and disappointments and unfulfilled dreams. Inside he suffered minutely over minute things; his humility was real because it evidenced itself not in a complex of inferiority, but in an understanding of inferiority. He, who placed courage above almost all virtues, knew his own cowardice; he, to whom love was as necessary as the air he breathed, had lost the only woman he ever loved; he, who wanted the affection of all men, had never had a real friend; his heart went out to every child he had ever seen, yet he never had children of his own; he worshiped learning because he knew his own ignorance and how painful and involved were the workings of his mind. His love and lust for life were matched only by the thin thread which connected him with life, and his long, frail body lingered constantly at the edge of darkness.

As night fell, he continued his tireless pacing, asking only one question of the broken men who came to him:

"How many have we lost?"

They didn't know; the forlorn battlefield of Brooklyn was still a scrambled jigsaw puzzle that would not be put together entirely for years and generations to come. Whole regiments had vanished. Generals and colonels and majors and dozens of lower ranks of officers had disappeared as completely as if the earth had swallowed them. Some said a thousand were lost; others said fifteen hundred; others said three thousand.

General Putnam came over to where Washington paced and said, "Whatever it is, we're hurt sore."

The commander in chief nodded his agreement, and Putnam marveled that a man could be composed of so little blood and so much rock and steel. Putnam thought it would be better if he would curse just a little at the wreckage strewn about them.

"It will be dark soon, and suppose they attack again, after it's dark—"

"They may," the foxhunter agreed.

"But my God almighty, sir!" Putnam said shrilly, "we're in no condition to resist another attack."

The foxhunter turned his cold grey eyes on the general, and Putnam wilted and swallowed and mumbled something or other.

"If they attack, we will fight again," the foxhunter said. "Yes."

"It's important for them to understand that we will fight again. The battle isn't over, general."

The Virginian resumed his walk, telling himself again and again that the battle was not over, but knowing, after he had fumbled sufficiently in his memory, that somehow for him, for George Washington, things were always the same, that dignity was not competence, that the ability to make foolish youngsters love a gangling farmer was not the virtue of a commander in chief. Now his army was cut to pieces, strewn about with their backs to the water; and in some ways it was much as if they had taken the theme from his life. From the horrible nightmare of Braddock's defeat up to now, everything that he had a hand in, that mattered, had been torn into shreds and strewn about. His big, clumsy hands laid waste wherever they fumbled, and like the bad music he made on his flute, it was always the same tune, played over and over without variation.

Still there must be something now; even when things came to an end, men struggled before they died. There must be something, but no one else would think. He had to walk back and forth, calmly for all the horror inside of him, and force his heavy wits to function, since there was no one else who had any wits about him at all.

They were all watching him. Through the gathering dusk he could see the hundreds of white faces turned toward him, and out of the intermittent drumming of cannon he could hear their whispering. He was General George Washington of Virginia, and you could tell by his walk that he had something up his sleeve.

To Knox and Putnam, standing over to one side, with their backs against a wickerwork bastion, the commander in chief loomed like a giant against the golden twilight sky. Knox, chief of American artillery—what there was of it—was a boy of twenty-six, bright-eyed, very fat, red-cheeked, loving four things passionately, books, his guns, his wife, and his commander in chief. The tall, skinny foxhunter was like a god in his eyes, calm, beyond fears and uncertainties, beyond all the lusts and hurts of human flesh. Before the war, Knox had been a bookseller, an ambitious bookseller who dreamed of some day becoming another Ben Franklin, a publisher who nurtured talented young writers and brought out endless editions of wonderful books. Now, as chief of artillery, he loved his black, stub-nosed guns as tenderly as he had regarded his first editions, and now his dreams were of a thousand pieces all belching in even volleys.

He lusted after guns, hoarded them, treasured them, counted them morning and night. His men made crude jokes about his sleeping with his guns, yet if he could be with them, he would sleep nowhere else. Now his pain was personal and singular; regardless of what happened, his guns would be forfeited to the enemy, the few precious cannon that had been trundled and dragged from every corner of the land. He felt bereft and naked, and as he stood next to Putnam, his whole attitude was hopeless dejection. For all that, the figure of the foxhunter, outlined against the sky, had power to elevate him, to take him out of himself for a moment.

"Look," he told the general. "Look at him."

Morosely, Putnam said words to the effect of his looking, since there was nothing else to do.

"How quiet he is," Knox marveled.

"Yeah, he's quiet enough, Harry."

"He'd be that way if the skies fell upon him."

Putnam resented Knox's turn of phrase, his endless bad quotations from bad books. "They did," Putnam growled.

When they began to pester him to lie down and sleep for a while, the big man realized that his inhuman mask of calm had accomplished something; it had taken them, at least for the moment, out of themselves, out of the individual pools of misery and defeat that each man had crawled into.

That it was for the moment, he realized full well. It needed only the light of morning to bring the renewed assault of the well-rested, victory-flushed British and Germans, and this time there would be no retreat for the defeated American rabble. They would be pushed back to the river and slaughtered like ducks in a game pond.

No one would ever know what it had cost him to maintain the mask of calm all afternoon and evening, while he wrestled with his problem. Forcing his mind to function, forcing himself to reason calmly and slowly, he had placed before himself a choice of three courses of action. Three there were, and no more than three, and hour after hour he searched each one for every last possibility it held.

The first, the most obvious, the easiest, was surrender; and something inside of him longed to give up the crazy, futile struggle, to get rid of the cowardly rabble he called his army, to lay down his sword in stately dignity and go back to his quiet home on the Potomac. Some would despise him and hate him; others would praise him; and some, like Patsy, would understand. But this, the obvious way, never fully reached his consciousness; it existed in the deep pit of doubts that tormented him; but he could not fully consider it because he could not fully admit to himself that he would even consider such a prospect. Death would be the same sort of peace, but he was not yet at a point where he would admit to himself that nothing remained but to die.

The second alternative was to fight. If he were to assemble the brigades and tell them that he had decided to hold his ground and fight the British to the last man, they would not cheer or smile or mutter proud words about dying for their country; they would only look at him blankly with their already-dead eyes, and then those among them who were boys—as most of them were—would begin to weep quietly as they remembered the folks at home in the neat little villages. The half-foreign element, those who had crept out of the ghettos and slums of Europe and were revolutionists body and soul, might cheer his decision, but they were only a fraction of the whole, as bad fighters as the rest, many of them speaking no English, most of them weak and sickly and undisciplined.

Some of the officers, men like Knox and Putnam and Carter and Dee, big, healthy young men who loved danger for its own sake, and feared nothing on earth, would follow him into hell. But a handful of officers cannot win a battle. He thought wistfully of those men as he numbered them off, envying their brute-like physical courage which was never troubled by doubts or fears or sickly pain.

To fight would not even be glorious, for the already-defeated Americans would break at the first British charge and run screaming from the merciless bayonets of the straw-haired Germans. To fight would achieve the same results as a surrender, except that a few hundred more Yankee boys would die, and another thousand would suffer with festering, gangrenous wounds. And if they fought, there would be none of the genteel terms of surrender; death he could bear, but not the gallows.

"And the revolution?" he asked himself. It was difficult to think of the revolution now, of anything abstract as opposed to the fact of the army that was his to save or see destroyed. If they stayed and fought, the revolution would not matter a great deal.

One alternative remained—retreat. Retreat would save his army, at least until the British had reorganized to attack the island of Manhattan. Retreat might give him a chance to rally his frightened men, and retreat would unite him with still-untouched brigades which he had left to defend the city. Of all the three courses, retreat was the only one which he could consider reasonably, and retreat was the only one which was utterly impossible.

For one thing, there was certainly no time to make preparations to evacuate an army which still numbered thousands of men. It was dark now, and the confusion of the stricken battlefield had been replaced by the confusion of the hopeless camp. The only thing that kept them at their barricades at all was the knowledge that the cold waters of the river lay at their backs, that there was no place to go. Whisper the word retreat, and the brigades would claw and fight to be the first at the water's edge.

For another thing, there were no boats. And if there were boats, who could row them and keep calm and steady under fire?

He saw the officers of his staff standing around him, and realized that he had been pacing back and forth in that way for hours.

"Sir, have something to eat," Knox pleaded.

"Yes, of course. Have you eaten, Harry?"

"Sir? Yes, I ate, sir."

"Stew?"

"But good, sir, very good, sir," the fat bookseller nodded. "And wine—I saved a bottle."

He managed to smile and nod; and given that signal of his inner peace, they crowded close to him and led him away. He saw how eager they were to be next to him, to brush his hand with one of theirs, to take comfort from

his big, handsome figure. They were only boys, and they
were frightened and heartsick, and he was so calm and assured that they were sure he held the solution for all their
woes in his tightly clenched fist.

The foxhunter was thankful for the darkness of his tent;
his throat had choked up and his eyes were foolish with
tears. He had never had children of his own, but now they
were like his own children, the young officers who had
crowded in, one of them kneeling and gently removing his
boots, another helping him out of his coat, another un-
buckling his sword, and all of them so gentle and understanding. It was almost a caress when their hands touched
him. He realized now that he had not deceived them, that
they knew as well as he that this was the end of their
fantastic adventure.

A captain of eighteen piped, "Easy, sir, lie down here, and
I'll puff out this pillow."

Carter folded his coat with loving care.

Knox said, with love and importance, "See, sir, the boots
are right here by the bed. Just drop your feet into them."

Putnam, older than the commander in chief, prescribed
a good night's sleep. "And then we all see matters differently," he said huskily.

"Sir, shall I drop the tent flaps?" the captain squeaked.

They tiptoed out, leaving him alone in the darkness. He lay
there for almost an hour, but he couldn't sleep. Instead, his
thoughts slid back through the weeks and months to the
time when he was riding north from Philadelphia to Boston
to take command of his army. The whole long, slow ride
was blurred by his fears and anticipations; from town to
town they had gone, reviewing company after company
of militia, the big farmer making so many speeches that he
acquired a formula: "—my sincere pleasure in being here
before you this day, this being a most glorious occasion."
All of which did not take away his wonder as to how they
would greet him, the Yankee New Englanders who had
fought at Bunker Hill, and who were waiting for him now
outside of Boston.

And finally he came before them, sitting on his horse in
buff and blue, such a long, handsome, aristocratic figure as
they had never seen before; and he saw what his army was,
the mass of Yankee rustics in homespun, thousands of
them slouching on their big firelocks, staring at him curi-

ously, flinging remarks at each other, spitting crudely, and
somberly chewing fat cuds of tobacco. And out in front were
the officers, boys mostly, some young men, and one or two
old men, but as Yankee as the rank and file, and much
more somberly cold and hostile in their judgment of him.
He was Virginia, and they were Massachusetts, Vermont,
New Hampshire, Maine, Rhode Island, and Connecticut, and
between the two worlds was an infinite limbo; he might go
into that limbo, they might too, but how could either get
across? He remembered thinking to himself at that time that
during his life he had met some hard men; cutthroats, rob-
bers, Indian fighters of the backwoods who for years did not
eat from a plate nor lay their heads on a feathered pillow,
privateer sailors who were no better than pirates, kilted
Scots clansmen of the Fincastle highlands; yet altogether
none so hard as these New Englanders who were hard in
their own Yankee way, hard and cold, with icy blue eyes, or
eyes black as bits of charcoal.

"They hate me," he had written to Martha after that first
review. "They all hate me and, I am sure, regard me as the
meanest sort of outlander; they, who hypocritically scorning
slaves, make of themselves worse slaves than tenant farmers, pecking and scratching at their bit of rocky, unhos-
pitable soil. . . ."

When he met with his officers in the first of what he
liked to call his councils of war, they stared coldly and
significantly at his lace cuffs, his silk stockings, and his
black pumps. And they disagreed with him wherever they
could unobtrusively, in their own sly Yankee fashion. He
felt their satisfaction when one of their cuts went home and
it seared him—to whom it meant so much to be loved and
admired by others.

Then how was it, he asked himself now, lying in his tent
after they had left him, that the change had come about? He
didn't know with any certainty, and almost fearful of introspection, he could not look inside of himself for an answer. He himself had not changed, but only gone on in
the line of his duty, doing the things he hoped and believed a commander in chief should do. He could not realize
that in going on alone, he had drawn them after him, gain-
ing in stature as he fell back on his belief in himself and the
path he followed.

Every bone in his body ached as he pulled on his boots,

got into his coat, and buckled on his sword. He went outside and walked over to one of the fires, so that he could
look at his watch. It was just half past three in the morning.

Walking slowly down the line of entrenchments he pre-
tended to inspect them. As he passed, the men on duty
snapped to what they considered military alertness. Some of
them grinned anxiously; others sulked. A few saluted.

He realized that the British lines could not be very far
away. The cannonading had stopped, and in the morning
stillness, he could hear the voices of the Hessians. He wondered what they were talking about. He had seen a good
many of the Germans, prisoners and deserters, and their ox-
like stolidity disturbed him more than it puzzled him. For
all his disgust at the arrogant independence of the New Englanders, it was better than the abject willingness of the Hessians to obey orders, anyone's orders. There was something
terrifying about the big, shuffling, straw-haired peasants.

The Virginian reached the end of the lines and turned
back. Already, a dirty-grey hint of morning had crept into
the sky, and now he walked more slowly, like a condemned
man who has used up the few hours of grace remaining to
him and holds back because his destination is implicit.
Somewhere a cock crowed, and somewhere else a dog began
to bark.

A boy came running, round-cheeked and cockaded as a
lieutenant, panting for breath as he saluted and stared at
the big man.

"Yes?"

"Yes, sir, General Washington. I was to tell you reinforcements are coming over from the city."

"General Mifflin?" the foxhunter asked calmly.

"Yes, sir, yes, sir." The big man's calm was like cold water
poured on the boy's excitement. "Yes, sir—sha'n't we give
those bloody lobsters the devil now?" The boy could hardly
keep from hopping up and down. "They'll attack at dawn,
won't they, sir, don't you think so, sir, begging your pardon—" His voice sighed out as he realized his temerity.
"General Putnam said you might come down to the
water—if you weren't sleeping, if you wish to, sir."

"We'll go in a little while," the Virginian said calmly.

"In a little while, sir?"

He nodded, noting the effect on the boy. It wouldn't hurt
for word to go around that Washington wasn't worried, so
little worried that he was hardly interested in the number

of men coming over from the city. It was better, at any rate, than to let them know that the reinforcements were coming to their death because the commander in chief hadn't the strength of mind to give up what he had already lost, but must drag more and more of his men into the hopeless trap.

For five minutes more he struggled between a desire to appear a hero in the boy's eyes and a longing to know what was happening on the river bank. Finally, he looked at his watch and said, "We'll go now, lieutenant."

The boy led the way proudly, shoulders thrown back, hoping that many of his friends would see him strolling with the commander in chief. As they walked, a faint, mist-like rain began to fall, and with the rain, a furious and buoyant hope sprang into the foxhunter's heart. In the rain, flints wouldn't spark and gunpowder would become a sodden, unexplosive mess. In the rush of hope, he felt his whole body trembling with excitement, yet he forced himself to walk calmly by the boy's side and to speak in even, unworried tones.

"What is your name, sir?" he asked.

"Tom Lackway, sir, begging your pardon."

"There's no need to beg my pardon. How old are you?"

"Seventeen, sir."

The big man raised his brows.

"Seventeen this April past," the boy explained hastily.

"I see. When did you receive your commission?"

"It's only a brevet cockade," the boy said anxiously, forgetting his "sir" for the first time. His hand roved to the feather he wore in his cap. "Yesterday," he said softly.

"Was your officer killed?"

"No—he run away," the boy said.

It was raining in earnest when the Virginian reached the riverfront, and the church spires and gabled roofs of New York were already dim in the mist. His cocked hat was drooping, and his uniform was entirely shapeless by now. He kept his face impassive, but his hand was trembling as he shook hands with Mifflin.

"Three regiments, sir," Mifflin said proudly. Mifflin was an ambitious man; at thirty he had been sent to the Congress. Now, at thirty-two, he was a general. Given a fair share of years, he was often dazzled when he thought of the heights to which he might rise. He was impatient, and a little jealous of a man he considered so very dull.

"I heard there was rough going yesterday."

The Virginian nodded. He felt Mifflin's contempt, saw in it one tiny piece of the contempt of all quick, intelligent men for a blunderer. He knew he hadn't the courage to tell Mifflin to turn around and send his men back to New York. So he stood there silently, watching the troops disembark.

There was a sense of order evident, the first bit of actual order he had seen since he came over to Brooklyn. The boats were sliding back and forth smoothly and expertly, and the men at the oars rowed as if they had done nothing but row all their lives. So fascinated was he by this expert performance that he allowed the imperturbable mask of his face to drop for a moment, long enough for Mifflin to note the expression and nod proudly.

"They know about boats," Mifflin said, nodding at the boatmen.

"They do know about boats," the foxhunter agreed mentally. He himself lost all sense of security where water was concerned; he could not think in the terms of a navy or even water barriers, that being one of the reasons why he had allowed himself to be drawn into the terrible cul-de-sac of Brooklyn. But even to him it was plainly evident that these men knew and enjoyed their work. They were leathery-skinned, long-faced Yankees, but they wore an air of confidence that the New England farmers did not possess. And there was uniformity in the blue jackets and stained oilskins most of them wore. Uniformity was one of the many things his army lacked; at least these men at the oars were of a kind.

"Who are they?" he asked.

"Glover's regiments, Marblehead fishermen. I didn't want my men blundering in the river all day—and these men know how to row. Maybe they can't fight, but they know about boats—they should; they've been fishermen all along."

"Fishermen," the foxhunter said softly. "How many are there?" The rain had increased, and now he laid his big palms against the drops, eagerly, almost with sensuous relief. The morning was growing on, and still there was no sign of a British attack.

"Six or seven hundred."

His mind fought with an idea. He didn't hear Mifflin ask

whether or not they would be better off taking shelter out of
the rain; his mind was plodding down a maze that might
lead out of ruin. But he told himself, doggedly: "I must do
it alone, alone."

For the first time in his life, he attempted the task of
crawling into the minds of little, frightened men. He must
plan a retreat, a retreat which the rain had given one
single, slim chance of success, yet he alone out of the whole
army must know that retreat was contemplated. If anyone
else knew, the terror of the defeated army would turn into
panic. He had wanted to lead an army, a proud, disciplined
army; instead he was leading a frightened rabble of children and fools. But he understood something of them now;
he no longer deluded himself.

"Sir?" Mifflin demanded.

For ten minutes the big man had stood motionless and
silent in the pouring rain. Putnam, old and tired, came
plodding down the slope to join them. Mifflin glanced at
him, past the big man, and shrugged his shoulders helplessly, as if to indicate that the Virginian had gone off the
loose end entirely.

"Sir?" Mifflin asked again.

Wherever the commander in chief stood, in his gaunt
height, a knot of officers gathered. Now they crouched in an
impatient circle, waiting for him to come out of the rain.

"I don't think they'll attack today," Putnam observed,
not sagacious, but sourly aware of sciatica and rheumatism.
"Why should they fight in the rain when they can sit in
their tents and wait for the weather to clear?"

Nobody wanted to suggest retreat, yet it was the prime
thought in the minds of each of them, a certainty that had
to come from the Virginian. They stared at him expectantly, and he braced himself.

"We won't retreat, gentlemen," he told them.

Now their faces said that he had gone insane.

"Gentlemen," he informed them quietly, "we are going
to bring over reinforcements and we are going to take our
sick and wounded back to New York. Today I want you to
gather every boat on this river, every barge or skiff or scow.
I want boats brought down from the North River and I
want every fishing craft out of the Sound you can lay hands
on—and I want them all brought here, to the Brooklyn
shore. I want you to get those boats. I want you, Colonel

Glover, to keep your fishermen here, on the riverfront—do you understand, on the riverfront?"

Then, weak, tired, but in a subtle way he had never known before, triumphant, he shouldered through them and walked back to the entrenchments. He was not a good hand at deceit; it was the least of his virtues; but the mere fact that he could cloak his intentions at all amazed him curiously.

4 ꆩ ꆩ ꆩ ꆩ ꆩ ꆩ ꆩ ꆩ ꆩ ꆩ ꆩ

THE RETREAT

Hours passed while he sat in his tent, looked at his watch now and then, and listened to the drizzle of rain on the canvas. There was nothing to do but think; at least twenty-four hours would have to pass before the boats began to arrive in any sort of quantity.

He realized that sooner or later he would have to divulge his plan to his officers. No one man, alone, could put into effect the retreat of an army of thousands. The duplicity would be too strained, too thinly drawn; and if one single factor went wrong, the whole structure would crash down like a house of cards.

Still, at this moment, there was nothing to do, and the very fact of his sitting quietly in his tent would reassure the army. The boys who were his officers could not match his patience; they hopped and squeaked, and every five minutes one of them would thrust his head into the tent. The commander sat at a little camp table, writing calmly, and the boy would whistle and go back to tell the others what he had seen.

"He looked up at me."

"Yes?"

"And didn't say a word, just looked at me."

"Annoyed?"

"No—I wouldn't say that he was annoyed."

"Smiling?"

"Maybe a wee bit amused."

"Christ, he's a cool one!"

And as the night wore on, the Virginian lay down on his bed, and rolled feverishly from side to side, pleading with himself for sleep. Doubts and fears paraded mockingly; all the British had to do was to sail their fleet up the East River and cut off the American retreat once and forever. Knox's six- and nine-pounder popguns could make no impression on their mighty ships of the line, while a single broadside from their carronades would blow the Marblehead men out of the water.

Then why didn't they? What held them back? What were they waiting for?

Why, why, why? he asked himself, drifting into an uneasy doze that brought memories walking like ghosts. He woke and looked at his watch, and saw that only a few minutes had passed.

In the wet, dismal dawn, he sat in his tent with Knox and Putnam and Mifflin. The tent drooped and leaked; there was an uneven rhythm between the drops inside and the drops outside, and the floor of the tent was a pancake of sucking mud. Putnam and Mifflin sat together on the sway-backed bed; the foxhunter sat at his rickety camp table, and Knox on a low ammunition box with a huge pewter pitcher of stale beer between his legs.

"What are you waiting for?" Mifflin demanded.

"Loggerhead," Knox said, drawing in his huge stomach and regarding the beer intently.

"Put in the rum and molasses."

"When the loggerhead comes," Knox said patiently.

"What the devil's the difference?"

"He's right, when the logger comes," Putnam nodded.

"It's the only way," Knox said. "Otherwise you spoil it."

"He's right," Putnam agreed. "You have to wait until the iron's hot."

"Damfool superstition," Mifflin muttered.

The Virginian shook his head wearily and tapped his long fingers on the table. "Gentlemen," he said quietly, "the flip can wait."

"Sorry, sir," Knox said. He poked a finger into the stale beer and licked absently.

"We're going to retreat," the Virginian said. His voice

was humble, almost pleading. There seemed to be no future and no end to the word retreat.

They stared at him bewilderedly. Knox was the first to look away; his round boyish face was puckered and frightened. He picked up a tin pan of molasses from the floor and let molasses run into the beer. It ran slowly and obstinately, and while Knox poured, a skinny, pock-marked runt of a boy poked into the tent, carrying a red-hot iron.

"Loggerhead, sir," the boy squeaked.

"Give it to me," Knox said.

"The rum!" Putnam reminded him gruffly.

Mifflin took up a bottle of rum and poured it into the pitcher of beer, and then Knox plunged in the red-hot poker. The whole mess sizzled and steamed, giving off a foul, leathery smell. The pock-marked boy watched, fascinated, until a glance from Putnam sent him scurrying away. Knox, meanwhile, had set the poker aside and was pouring the concoction into earthenware cups.

The commander drank from his mug slowly. No one had proposed a toast, no one wanted a toast. Mifflin, Knox and Putnam filled and refilled from the pewter pitcher with grim earnestness.

"It's filthy bad flip," Knox said.

And Mifflin muttered, "I can't understand that, sir, about retreat. I can't understand it, sir. I brought over my men and now you tell me retreat. I can't understand it, sir. Why shouldn't we fight them?"

"There's nothing else," the Virginian said. "The men won't fight—God knows if they ever will. And if the British sail up the river, that's the end of it. It's better to have an army that won't fight than no army at all."

"Sir, if you tell them to retreat," Knox said, "it'll be worse."

The big man nodded. How many times in the past twenty-four hours had he pictured thousands of panic-stricken men fighting madly to be the first into the boats! "You won't tell them," he said. "After dark, tonight, order certain regiments to be relieved, one by one. Each to think all the rest are holding the line. Maybe that way—"

"—sick and tired," Putnam was muttering. "Can't hardly move my hip."

"—most can be taken out of this. General Mifflin, I want you to man the redoubts with your men and hold them until I give word that you are to go."

"And get rid of me as he got rid of Stirling and Sullivan," Mifflin thought.

Almost tearfully, Knox asked, "But what about my guns, sir—what about my guns?"

"Spike them."

"All of them? Can't we take a few over, sir?"

The big man shook his head.

"All my beautiful guns," Knox whispered. He had downed too much flip, and he was almost maudlin now. "My beautiful guns," he sighed.

The rain went on. The commander threw a cloak over his shoulders and walked back and forth through the camp. The men were frightened and wet and miserable; they had no tents over here in Brooklyn, most of them, and they lay around in a sick sort of despair. They gave the commander in chief hardly a glance as he passed; they had made no effort to keep their muskets out of the rain, and there was hardly a piece in the camp in condition to fire.

Any sort of attack would have swept them away like overripe wheat; they had lost all semblance of an army; they lay where they were only because each and every one of them realized the hopelessness of retreat. Some of them, the sixteen- and seventeen-year-old boys for the most part, were still whimpering like hurt puppies over the shock of the rout. The Maryland and Virginia troops held themselves apart, still in some semblance of order; it was their private grudge that they had taken too great a share of the battering, and it needed only a tiny incident to send them at the throats of the New Englanders. The New Englanders, for their part, had discussed the miserable showing and defeat of the revolutionary army with Yankee thoroughness, and they were convinced now that the officers who led them had deliberately betrayed them. Given the chance, a good many of them would desert; and many were now planning how they would manage it, once they were out of this devilish Brooklyn trap. But others would go on, betrayed or not, because this was something they had started at Concord and Lexington and would finish because their need for freedom was more organic than logical. They had to be free; it was part of their blood and flesh, and any sort of servitude, real or imagined, was like a raw cancer inside of them.

Every movement of the foxhunter's tall, straight body was

an affront to them. They cursed him for what they knew
him to be, a stupid, heartless Virginia foxhunter.

Their common sense told them that he, the wealthiest
man in America, could have no real interest in the war.
His hardness and bitter temper were constant subjects of
discussion among them. Even that outlandish name of his
was an affront to them. Washington—who in all hell had
ever heard of such a name?

His feet hurt. Through all the pains of a sickly body that
had been denied sleep for sixty hours, the pain of his feet
was most persistent. And as the dreary afternoon closed,
with the British still patiently waiting in their tents for the
rain to stop, he decided that he could not walk another step.
He called for his horse, mounted, and rode down to the
riverfront; as he rode he dozed constantly, and he had to
pull himself awake again and again with a definite effort of
will.

Now that all preparations had been completed, he was
certain that the retreat would not come off successfully. It
was inconceivable that the British, who were only a few
hundred yards away, should allow this beaten wreck of an
army to withdraw in safety. He saw ruin and disgrace and
the gallow's noose, and tired as he was his thoughts took
on the drift of a fantastic nightmare. He wondered vaguely
what force made him do one thing after another; he had
never thought a great deal about forces.

At the riverfront, he was amazed by the number of boats
the Marblehead men had gathered. They were only now beginning to approach the Brooklyn shore, but the river up
toward Hell's Gate was alive with bobbing craft of every description. They came out of the murk of fog and rain in an
endless stream, driven by the wind and the laughing, rain-
soaked fishermen, and the same fog and rain hid their
approach from the British fleet, stationed out on the bay.
And the Marblehead men were enjoying their task; sick to
death of endless marching and drilling, they had turned at
last to a job that suited them, and they alone of all the
army worked well and quickly and efficiently. Their colonel, Glover, was a Salem man himself; he had raised the
regiment of fishermen; he knew his men, what they were
capable of, and how to get the last ounce of work out of
them.

As the boats came in, Glover was having them moored

and beached, stripping them of all gear except that absolutely necessary to a ferry, and assigning a crew of men to each boat. The larger boats, sailing gigs and a few cutters, were kept separate, so that they could have room for a circular tack. As dusk fell, the massed boats made a solid rank on the riverfront.

Knox came crunching down to where the commander sat on his horse. The boy's pudgy face was twisted with despair.

"About those guns, sir," he said.

"Yes?"

"Where are we going to find more guns when we spike those?"

The big man shrugged.

"An army fights with guns," Knox insisted doggedly.

"And with men—and we have neither."

They looked at one another, the bookseller who had once dreamed of being a successful publisher and the foxhunter who had once dreamed of having many peaceful years—with the woman he loved and children of his own.

"I'll start to spike as soon as it's dark," Knox said.

"Quietly as you can."

"You can't spike a gun quietly, sir," Knox said morosely. "I'll do my best."

"And when it's done, send your men down here to be taken across the river."

At about seven o'clock, Glover came over to report that his boats were almost all in, as many as could be expected, and that he was ready to start ferrying when the word was given. A dozen officers had come down and clustered around the commander in chief, making him realize again that the only force capable of stirring the broken army lay in his thin, weary body. He looked at the officers with bloodshot eyes, staring at face after face, wondering vaguely that these children should be colonels and majors and generals, and then singling out one, said, "Bring down your regiment and put them in the boats."

"Retreat, sir?"

"No, you fool—I'm relieving your regiment, sending them over to the city for rest and dry clothes. The rest of you go back to your posts."

He almost laughed aloud, it was such a silly, childish deception. He walked his horse down to the boats, that he

might be on hand to supervise the embarkation, and there
in the flickering light of a lantern held by one of the fishermen, he began to doze again.

"Sir?"

He looked up sleepily.

"You looked somehow sickly," the fisherman grinned.

"Get to your post!"

"Yes, sir—"

"Get to your post! By God, Glover, keep your men in
hand!" They were the only ones left he could discipline;
the rest were beyond discipline.

He sat there, trembling with fatigue, biting his lips to drive
away sleep until the blood ran down inside his mouth.

He was astonished to discover how well the scheme
worked. Its very simplicity was the factor that made it successful. Each regiment, believing that it alone was the lucky
one, believing that it alone was to be relieved, crept down
to the riverfront in the deepest silence. Their fear was not
that the British should hear them; as an enemy and a factor
to be considered, the British had vanished entirely from their
minds: their fear was that their less fortunate comrades
should hear them and destroy this, their last chance for life
and liberty.

After the first regiment had left the Brooklyn shore for the
dim lights of Manhattan, the Virginian's weariness vanished.
There was still a chance, and it appeared to be a good
chance. His thought-process was meticulous, but all his
grown life he had sat at card tables, and the heady lust for
a stake placed on a good deal was deep in his blood. He
drove his horse back and forth, being everywhere at once,
shepherding the men into the boats as he would a herd of
sheep. As with many sickly men, he had an almost inex-
haustible store of nervous energy; later he would pay the
price, but now he was a furious, challenging man on a
horse.

He spared no one. The boys who called themselves generals wilted under the lash of his tongue. The Marblehead
fishermen, who were already laboring superhumanly, were
not laboring well enough. He dragged the patient Glover over
hot coals, and when the Salem man dared meekly to protest, he roared, "I'll have no back talk, sir! God damn you,
do your duty!"

He had been born in a saddle and weaned like a colt, the foxhunter; as he rode now, the horse was of his flesh and slave to his flesh.

The night wore on and still the regiments came and still he herded them into the boats. He had lost count, and when he asked his aides they knew no more than he about how how many were left holding the lines. But they were exuberant, heady with the success of the maneuver.

"Let me go see, sir," one of them, Scammel by name, begged.

"Yes. But leave Mifflin."

"What?" Scammel had reared his horse.

"I said leave Mifflin and bring the others. Mifflin goes last."

"Yes, sir." Scammel dashed away.

"I don't think he understood you, sir," Glover observed.

But another regiment was creeping down from the heights, and the Virginian rode off to direct them to the boats. Nothing would go wrong now.

The orders he had given Scammel, which Scammel did not understand, yet hastened to carry out, fearing to face the commander with his confusion, set off a chain that threatened to blow all his plans sky-high. Scammel dashed up to Mifflin and told him that the commander in chief desired him, Mifflin, to march all his troops down to the boat landing to be embarked for New York.

"My troops or them?" Mifflin demanded, pointing to the thinned, nervous ranks of New Englanders, as contrasted with his own fairly well-disciplined regiments.

"Your own troops, I think," Scammel said.

"You're sure?"

"That's what he told me."

"And them?" pointing to the New Englanders.

Scammel shook his head, and Mifflin shrugged, giving orders for his men to abandon their places in the entrenchments and fall into line. The New Englanders watched openmouthed, trying to comprehend the fact that while Mifflin's fresh troops marched away, they were to be left for a sacrifice, they who had fought so well and shed so much of their blood in the battle of Brooklyn. For just so long as it took them to comprehend the fact, they stood there and watched, and then the spell broke and they bolted. And every brigade within sight or hearing joined in the flight.

The wave of men was like a flood rolling down to the

boat landing. They gave themselves to panic and fought and clawed. They climbed over each other's heads; they crawled between feet; they punched and ripped and tore; they wept in terror and pushed their comrades into the black waters of the river. They cursed the Marblehead fishermen hysterically, and the fishermen fought back with clubbed oars.

And in the center of it, roaring like an enraged beast, was the commander in chief. He was everywhere at once, furious and terrible—and quelling them; it was like cold water poured on hot flames, and out of the wretched dizzle came a single moment of deep silence.

"Get to your ranks!"

They gave way before him and cowered; many of them sank to the ground and wept into their trembling hands. And the big man rode through them, looking neither to left nor to right.

When he found Mifflin, he had himself almost under control once more, enough to keep from flinging himself on the general with all the terrible fury he was capable of, enough to sit rigid and demand, "Why did you withdraw, Mifflin?"

"I had your orders."

"God damn you, no! You had no orders!"

"By God, I did!" Mifflin raged. "Didn't you send Scammel to me? Didn't you order me to fall back?" His eyes ran with tears of rage and he slapped his hands helplessly against his thighs. "Didn't you send Scammel to me, didn't you?"

The foxhunter climbed down from his horse, walked over to Mifflin, and took the man by the shoulders.

"Didn't you send Scammel to me?" Mifflin sobbed.

The Virginian was restored to sanity now; he was able to recall the question in Scammel's eyes that the boy had not dared to ask.

"What did Scammel tell you?" he asked Mifflin.

"To come down here!"

The Virginian shook his head. "Forgive me."

"Sir?"

"I'm sorry, General Mifflin, believe me. It wasn't Scammel's fault nor yours. I don't know what I'm saying sometimes."

"What are your orders, sir?" Mifflin asked hoarsely, feeling then, at that moment, that he would have died for the tall foxhunter, and gladly.

"Go back to your post and hold it until I send for you."
"I'll hold it until hell breaks loose," Mifflin whispered.

It was close on morning, and the fog had lifted. The Virginian sat in a boat with Knox and a schoolboy captain of artillery whose name was Alexander Hamilton.

"Push off, sir?" the Marblehead man at the tiller asked.

"Just a moment."

The oars wavered and dropped to the water. The captain of artillery pointed to the slope where Hessians were already scrambling through the mud.

"Better go now, sir," Knox said morosely, still mourning the loss of his guns.

"We'll go," the big man nodded.

The tillerman fended off and the oars scooped at the water. As the boat glided out into the river, the Hessians formed up and let loose a volley.

The commander in chief hardly moved; he was dozing already, and in a moment more he would be asleep. He didn't want to think now; he still had his army, for what it was worth, and there would be time for thought later.

Part Two

--⊰{ MANHATTAN ISLAND }⊱--

5 🇺🇸 🇺🇸 🇺🇸 🇺🇸 🇺🇸 🇺🇸 🇺🇸 🇺🇸 🇺🇸 🇺🇸 🇺🇸

THE ARMY OF LIBERTY

On August 29, the good burghers of New York City had
gone to sleep with the comforting knowledge that the patriot army was somewhere else. And these good men, solid
men who knew the price of things and minded their own
business, asked only one thing of the patriot army—that it
be somewhere else.

When they woke up, on August 30th, they discovered to
their horror and dismay that the army of liberty had returned. Not in the best order, it is true; there was no beating of drums and playing of fifes; there were no Yankee
farmers in close rank, trying to march as if they were soldiers; there were no gay cockades and arrogant boasts; instead there was a bedraggled, crawling thing that occupied
the city in silence and misery.

When the burghers came out in the morning to open their
shops and swing back their shutters, they saw the soldiers
of liberty moving through the streets, wet, glassy-eyed, and
beaten.

The commander in chief slept in a deep cavern of darkness that was only faintly punctuated by pinprick musket flashes; he slept not restlessly, but log-like, chained down by weariness; and afterwards everything from the moment he stepped into the boat to leave Brooklyn was masked by that same fog of weariness. He hardly remembered how he dozed on the seat with the muskets roaring behind him, nor did he recall his stammering insistence that he had left something behind him. He had no memory of taking off his clothes, of sipping at a glass of wine someone held out to him—and of falling asleep while he sipped, of giving orders in a faint, dream-like whisper.

In his sleep, the battle became more vivid and more terrible, and once he woke with the grating cry of "Yonkee, Yonkee" ringing in his ears. But after that he slipped back into a deep and restful slumber.

He slept through the morning and afternoon, and as evening came on, he still slept. His officers, for all their desire to know his plans, did not have the heart to wake him. Younger men than he, their stretch of wakefulness had been neither so long nor so painful, and now they were up and gathering in little knots around the house where he slept.

Their talk was all of the battle and the incredible escape from Brooklyn; none of them seemed to realize the full import of the loss they had sustained—a full fifth of their effectives on the Brooklyn shore. Their youth gave them a heady, insane confidence; out of their farms and their shops, they had come to this magnificent adventure, and when the adventure threatened to end abruptly, they had escaped, and therefore one thing followed absolutely:

They would always escape.

The army of liberty slept too. They had crawled into whatever dark corners they could find. Above Canal Street, there were dozens of old Dutch barns, and each of these barns was crammed full of patriots, snoring and complaining, shaking with fever and trembling with fear. Some of the Yankees lay in the gutters, and others slept curled against doors of houses that were closed to them. Two lieutenants and four privates lay on a wet tent fly, spread in the mud of Bowery Lane. A church was filled with moaning wounded, but there were neither doctors nor nurses to attend to them. A boy lay dead on Pearl Street with his face in the mud, but the worthy burghers regarded him as they might a

dead cat or a dead dog. The Jewish Synagogue on Mill Street
was packed so full of sick and wounded that there was no
room left for the old men to pray; they stood outside and
listened to the cries of the tortured creatures that had once
been their sons and grandsons. In Fraunces Tavern a half
company of Delaware Swedes had finished all the rum on
hand, broken most of the furniture, and gone to sleep on
the floor. On Bowling Green, fourteen Poles, all that was left
of a brigade, had built a fire of driftwood and sat around
it, not for the warming of their bodies but of their poor,
lonely souls. They knew not one single word of English;
they sang their mournful Slavic songs and remembered the
days when they had fled like beasts through the desolate
Pripet Marshes; and they told each other that it was always the same when men looked around for a way to
make themselves free. Two men, a Virginian and a Rhode
Island Yankee, had fought like devils in the bushes north
of Old Slip, and the Virginian left the Yankee with his throat
cut and his blood running out.

They slept through the morning and most of the afternoon, but toward evening they began to awake and their
courage returned to some degree. They came out of their
dark holes and sought for something to quench their thirst.
They stormed the taverns, and with a mug or two of flip
under their belts they became heroes. There was not a man
among them who had not killed his share and more than
his share of the cowardly British, and what they had done
to the Hessians was something for their grandchildren to
hear. They cursed the Virginia squire who had misman-
aged everything, and they said what a damned fortunate
thing it was he had men he could depend on. As more
and more red-hot loggers came out of the fire, as more and
more flip flowed into their bellies, their boasting turned
into a desire for action, and bands of Yankees set out to
find some of the God-damned Virginians, and bands of
Maryland men set out to revenge the deaths of their comrades by breaking some Rhode Island heads. Arm in arm,
Pennsylvanians roamed the streets, filled with sullen hatred
for everyone, and Down Easters swore they would make
New York a hell spot for any filthy tidewater aristocrats they
could find.

Pitched battles raged, and cobblestones and clubbed
muskets left broken heads behind. A jeweler who had the
reputation of being a Tory, but who had stayed on in New

York protesting his love for the patriots, had his shop broken into, and a whole brigade of Connecticut men strutted with watches and pins.

Two boys came out of the jeweler's house and went after the Connecticut men. Their names were Aaron Burr and Alexander Hamilton; Hamilton, a wraith of a lad with violet, girl-like eyes, lit into the Connecticut brigade like a fury out of hell. There were other splashes in the whirlpool; Knox beat in the heads of two drunken Virginians who had torn the clothes off a Dutch girl, and old Israel Putnam went through street after street, driving Yankees out of the mud with his bare sword, while he tongue-lashed them in a way that could be heard blocks off. Other officers followed his example, and as night fell on New York, the town became a bedlam of cursing, pleading officers, drunken soldiers, weeping boys, and bitterly complaining citizens.

The bickering was endless and childish—over muskets, knapsacks, handkerchiefs, loaves of bread. In the mad scramble out of Brooklyn, everyone had grabbed what he could, and everyone claimed everyone else's possessions. Now, with brigades scattered through the narrow streets, with drunkards lost, forgetful even of the name of their regiments, weeping for comrades they had seen killed when they ran away, with hundreds of deserters racing like mad for the wooded hills of Harlem Heights, the situation was well-nigh hopeless.

Yet the baby-faced officers persevered, and presently as the night wore on, some sort of order came into being. And later, once more, the army of liberty slept.

Billy brought in six bottles of Madeira. "Instead of flip," the foxhunter said diffidently, smiling a little in the first feeble attempt at a joke that his young men had heard in many days. He was very fond of Madeira, and now that he had slept and rested and changed his clothes and combed his hair, nothing else would do.

The dozen or so officers who sat crowded close to the round table made up a sort of council of war. The Virginian had summoned them to talk about the retreat, the future, and the revolution: Knox and Putnam and Mercer and Mifflin and Spencer and Clinton—and others, generals, major generals, colonels, and the boy Hamilton who could write so well, sitting to one side with his open notebook on his knee,

his own nineteen years slightly in awe of these men in their
late twenties and early thirties.

When they first gathered at the table, the commander in
chief had not yet appeared. He sat over a little table in his
bedroom, painfully composing a message to the army which
had been so miraculously restored to him. When he wrote it
was with difficulty and even with shame, for he spelled
badly, and in a time of magnificent penmen, his penman-
ship was not of the best. He had a love of words that
verged upon humble supplication, yet all his life words had
eluded him. He could not transpose emotion into letters; if
the world fell on him, he could only report that there was
a disturbance, and if his heart was breaking, it made him
ashamed and self-conscious to say that he was somewhat
uneasy.

It was difficult enough to compose what he believed,
but now for an hour he had written and scratched out a
mockery of the truth, finishing with something he hardly
dared to read through.

"They'll laugh," he told himself. He made up his mind that
if they laughed, he would not trust himself to words, but
just stare at them with great composure and an even glance.

Before he left his bedroom, he examined himself carefully in the mirror. He set his face in a very calm and knowing expression, thinking with some satisfaction that they
would say to each other afterward:

"He's got ice in his veins, not a bit disturbed. It may be
bluff, but more likely he knows about things. That whole
mess of Brooklyn doesn't disturb him."

He straightened his coat and smoothed out the wrinkles in
his fawn-colored breeches. Billy had sewn two bits of lace
under his cuffs, and now he let the lace droop onto his
wrists in the lazy manner he managed so well. Instead of
boots, he wore white silk stockings and black pumps—with a
calculated purpose: so they might say that he was more
prepared to dance than to fight, and certainly not disturbed. He looked at his watch, saw that he had kept them
waiting for more than a half hour, and then he made his
deliberate entrance, his six feet two and a half inches stiff
as a ramrod.

When the wine had been poured, he proposed the first
toast. "To the Continental Congress," he said calmly, won-

dering grimly how long it would be so, how many days or weeks at the most before the toast would again be to "His Gracious Majesty, the King." And the boys around the table reflected his thoughts, drinking soberly, thoughtfully.

The second toast he made to "America." His men looked at him curiously and uncertainly. It was facetious of him, or clever, or foolish; he was a Virginian. They were Yankees, most of them, and they could never forget that he was a Virginian. And the word America had a strange foreign sound in their ears.

"To America, gentlemen," he had said.

The third toast was for the gallant men who had died, shot through or pinned in the back by a sliver of steel or trampled underfoot. Looking at their faces he realized that they were thinking more of the men who had run away than of those who had died. "Let it be that way"—he said to himself—"only judge not."

The fourth toast was for the future, for the success of their arms, and now he saw them looking at him as if he had mentioned something foul, not to be spoken of.

The fifth toast was for them, his officers, and as he proposed it he saw the red flushes mantle their faces, and he felt choked and lonely in their esteem.

Billy brought more of the Madeira.

The sixth toast was for him, for "His Excellency, George Washington, Commander in Chief of the Continental Forces."

"Thank you, gentlemen," he said quietly, almost miserably, hating himself for the manner in which he had prepared and developed this whole scene, calculating every reaction in the headstrong boys who followed him.

He sat for the most part in silence, letting them talk as they wished. In his own mind, he knew what he desired to do and knew how impossible it was. What he wanted was retreat, constant retreat, long, hard marches that would never allow his men to stay for a moment in one place, never allow them to think, never allow them to desert. The business in Brooklyn had given him some insight on one terribly important fact: that it was his army that counted. By the grace of God, he still had his army, and nothing else mattered. He would take his army and go away—burn New York to the ground and give the British only a heap of ashes for winter quarters when they took New York—go on for months if necessary, go on across the great green bulk of the Alleghenies, but keep his army intact and together.

Yet he knew it was impossible. Congress had made him commander in chief to fight battles, and to fight battles they had given him an army of Yankee children.

"We're safe enough," Knox was saying. "We're on an island. An island's like a good fort; you can hold it forever."

"And we're like to be there forever."

"I say to hell with all that and burn the town, and get out and leave them the ashes."

"Burn it?"

"Burn it! That's what I say. Burn it!"

"I live here, sir!"

Scorn and hate and bickering destroyed the radiant warmth of the toasts, and chairs were pushed back; and then military tactics thrust into a well of personalities.

"Gentlemen," the big man said.

Then they sat in silence for a while, their commander telling them that he had wanted to burn New York, but that Congress forbade it and that he would hear no further talk on the merit or lack of merit in any Congressional policy.

"Retreat, sir?"

He shook his head. "We'll try to hold some of the city," he said.

They looked at him perplexedly. Was this another of his tricks? He had been damned clever at Brooklyn.

"We must make sure of Kingsbridge," he said, allowing just a faint note of hopelessness to creep into his voice. Kingsbridge was a way off the island at its northernmost tip, a wooden bridge crossing Spuyten Duyvil.

Old Putnam was afraid and he shook his head; he felt ancient and foolish in that circle of hotheaded boys.

Mifflin, a little drunk, regarding the foxhunter more highly than ever after the incident at Brooklyn and the Virginian's selfless apology, said, "Whatever comes, we can hold Fort Washington—we can hold it until hell freezes over!" And then there was a moment of silence, for the fort was his own, the first place named after him, to give him dignity and dignity to the Congress that had elected him, the first place in all the broad miles of America called Washington. Yet it was almost never called that in his presence; instead they spoke of "the fort" or "that hill north of the Heights."

"We can hold Fort Washington," Knox said shyly, stressing the name. And the others nodded.

He felt that he could not bear much more of this; his life had been with his kind, Virginians and aristocrats, not Yankee boys; he had never been loved. Respected, admired, but not loved. Still there was a heady sort of joy in knowing that they would follow him anywhere, to hell if necessary, but anywhere he chose to lead. It was something he had not done deliberately; they had hated him at first, but for their hatred he returned a measure of justice. The rest, that he might appear fearless, honorable, wonderful to look at, something to regard with admiration, did not occur to him; their love of him left him puzzled and deeply moved, the more so since he had no complete understanding of their reasons.

"We will do what we can," he said helplessly.

"We must not fight them here," old Israel pleaded.

"What we can do and must do—"

"We should abandon the town!"

"No!"

Spencer, drunk on six glasses of Madeira, cried, "By God, hold the city and blow the filthy swine to hell!"

"You're drunk, sir," old Israel said evenly.

"Sober enough to see you in hell, you damned old lady!"

"Spencer, hold your tongue!" the Virginian said icily.

After that, the long silence was a dumb admission by each and every one of them.

"You will form your brigades," said the commander in chief. "You will get them out of the streets and take away whatever they have stolen. Common thieves will receive thirty lashes, and for desertion a hundred, and for rape five hundred. I want that understood. I want them paraded. For those of your men who threw away their muskets, find something, if not muskets at least a pike or a pitchfork or a knife. I have written out an order for the men—to encourage their spirits and to give them some feeling of devotion. I will read it to you now, and then I will have my secretary make copies for you to read to your brigades tomorrow. Here is the order as I have written it:

"Now, our whole Army is collected together, without water intervening, while the Enemy can receive little assistance from their ships; their Army is and must be divided into many bodies, and fatigued with keeping up a communication with their ships; whereas ours is connected and can act together; they must effect a landing, under so many disadvantages, that if officers and soldiers are vigilant, and alert, to prevent surprise, and add spirit when they approach, there is no doubt of our success.

"The General hopes the several officers, both superior and inferior, will now exert themselves, and gloriously determine to conquer, or die— From the justice of our cause— the situation of the harbor, and the bravery of her sons, America can only expect success. Now is the time for every man to exert himself, and to make our country glorious, or it will become contemptible."

He had finished speaking, and it was out, and he stared straight ahead, waiting for them to laugh. No one laughed. He looked slowly at Knox, whose eyes were filled with tears.

Meanwhile, one of a thousand deserters had been caught by the patrol at Kingsbridge. The man, a Vermonter, fought and struggled, and finally collapsed in impotent rage when he saw escape was hopeless. Curiosity impelled the soldiers of the patrol to open the huge bag he was carrying. It contained a ham, a lady's silk dress, and assorted products of six or seven other New York shops. All that they understood, and even admired his very capable looting. But the presence of an eight-pound cannonball stumped them.

"What's this?" they demanded.

"A ball, ye damn fools."

"What for? Why are you stealing ammunition?"

"Lor', ye damn fools, I'm bringing a bumper for my maw to ground out mustard with."

6

ONE TERRIBLE SUNDAY MORNING

Riding from the little cluster of houses that was called New York, a country village on the southern tip of Manhattan Island, up to his headquarters in Harlem, in the cool Saturday afternoon of September 14th, the Virginia squire reviewed the events of the past two weeks.

All in all, he had not done badly; and he reflected with some satisfaction that the defeated rabble which had fled so miserably from Brooklyn Heights had once again some semblance of an army. Two weeks ago, immediately after their return to New York, he had almost lost hope; men were deserting, not singly, nor even in groups of ten and twenty, but in whole brigades. All discipline had been forgotten, and the army had terrified New York, rioting through the streets, brawling, looting, raping and killing. Pitched battles had occurred between the Virginia and North Carolina brigades and the New Englanders, and the whole army appeared to be in a state of rapid dissolution.

Only by the grace of God had the British refrained from some attempt to make a bridgehead on Manhattan, and now he dared to hope that they had held back too long. He had regrouped his forces into three divisions, one under the command of old Putnam, assigned to hold the city itself, another under Heath to hold the northern bottleneck of Kingsbridge, and the third under Spencer to hold the body of Manhattan in-between. He was uncertain of Spencer, whom he did not completely trust and whom he considered a fool; but the only other major general available, Nathanael Greene —whom he trusted and liked—was just recovering from the fever which had laid him low before the Brooklyn affair. Spencer would do until Greene returned, and now, in the bright coolness of the autumn afternoon, the Virginian felt wonderfully exhilarated and not at all disposed toward worry.

There had been times during the past two weeks when he had been so sick with despair that all the strength had gone out of his body, when he had lain on his bed, in hopelessness, for hours on end. As when, for instance, the Congress had lost courage entirely, flinching from the thousand and more men lost on Brooklyn Heights, and had sent Dr. Franklin and Mr. John Adams to talk with General Howe about surrender. He, their servant, could not protest; he was a soldier taking orders; but heartbroken, he had pleaded with those around him, those he knew and had come to love as he had never loved men—Knox, Putnam, Mifflin: "Why, why, why? Why surrender?"

"No," they told him. "It won't turn out that way; there won't be any talk of surrender."

"They let me fight the battles," he said miserably, "and then they send Adams and Franklin to talk about surrender. It doesn't matter that men have died for liberty."

"It matters, sir," they tried to convince him.

"Franklin's an old man; he's got no guts."

"He won't give up."

"And Adams put me here. Is he afraid now?" And then he said, "They're all afraid, that's the long and short of it. They're afraid and they want to give up. God help us, that's all, they want to give up."

Afterwards, when the discussions had produced nothing more than a flow of keen wit from Dr. Franklin, the Virginian tried to understand why he had been so shaken by the thought that the revolution might peter out after the disgraceful rout of Brooklyn. He was slow and awkward at introspection, which he regarded as something slightly sordid, yet he probed himself enough to realize that there were other reasons than the desire to prove himself a leader of some quality instead of a fool. What those other reasons were, he didn't quite know; certainly there was no real bond between himself and the rabble of Yankees, backwoods Southerners, and foreign revolutionaries he led; yet there was a drive and a force, and an ache in his heart for something unseen yet tremendously powerful and forthright.

But today, he had dismissed the painful and rather nasty business of introspection; he had dismissed fears and worries and doubts and had given himself to the good feeling of a wind in his face and a hard dirt road under his horse's hoofs. Riding through the lovely woods of mid-Manhattan, with meandering brooks, silver-faced ponds, and stone-hedged fields on either side of him, he thought that never in his life, even on the shores of his beloved Potomac, had he seen country so placidly beautiful. He was a farmer and countryman, out of many generations of farmers and countrymen, and he reacted to things instinctively and gratefully, to a flight of birds dark against the rosy sky that rimmed the black Palisades, to the waving surface of bright and golden wheat in the neat Dutch fields, to the exquisite scarlet of the early turning red maples, to a windmill looping against the cold green sky of the east, to little pink lizards swarming over the dust of the road, to the baying of hounds in the spirit of an evening chase, to a tiny red-cheeked boy teetering on top of a split rail fence —to fading sun, and wind and scudding clouds.

It was a moment when life was inordinately good, good beyond measure to this thin man whose love of life was sensuous and grateful.

Along with him, there rode a troop of about a dozen light horse, one of the few cavalry units in his army, fat Colonel Knox, grinning and happy to be near the man he worshiped, young Burr, sent along by Putnam to accompany the commander in chief back to his headquarters on Harlem Heights, and a Lieutenant Grayson and a Captain Hardy. The light horse had not been light horse for very long, and they found it difficult to keep in order, two abreast and two abreast; instead they bunched up and strung out as the procession wound along, and the officers were in such good spirits that they hadn't the heart to criticize.

The men began to sing, chanting their everlasting ditty about Yankee Doodle and the pony he rode to London Town. The verses were endless, most of them smutty, but the Virginia squire screwed up his face not at the content but at what he considered a wretched melody. His own taste was for Mozart and Bach, and now he had a nostalgic memory of the hours he had spent with his flute, painfully picking out the difficult counterpoint. He was like a child about his music, loving it, quick with eagerness when a new piece came over from London, sitting alone behind a locked door and making the air sigh with wordless outpourings, yet ashamed of the fact that in this as in everything else, he was mediocre.

They rode on northward, turning east from the Bloomingdale Road which wound along the river bank, cutting across the fragrant meadows, threading through the wall of trees that humped like a backbone north and south over the whole island, stopping at a farm to drink from a mossy wooden bucket, and then turning north again under the high ridge of Morningside Heights into the gathering twilight. From there it was only a few miles to the house which he had selected for his new headquarters.

This house, a graceful, white Georgian structure, which was almost painfully reminiscent of Mount Vernon, had belonged to Captain Roger Morris, and was one of many magnificent homes scattered among the Dutch farmlands of the island. Captain Morris had prudently gone to England to await the ignoble end of the miserable rebellion, and his wife was with some Tory friends in Yonkers, spending long evenings discussing the Yankee scum. In their absence, the Virginian had taken over their house, ostensibly because it was more or less centrally located, about three miles south of Kingsbridge and nine miles north of the city; actually, because sitting as it did, on a grassy lawn over the Harlem River, it was another Mount Vernon.

He arrived there late that night, past midnight, and remarked cheerfully to his secretary, Robert Harrison, who had waited up for him, that he was glad the next day was Sunday and that he could look forward to a day of rest.

There was little enough rest. He had hardly started to undress before a panting messenger burst into the Morris house and demanded to see the commander in chief.

"He's gone to bed," the Virginian heard Harrison say.

"Well, I reckon he'd better git up."

"Mind your tongue, damn you!"

The Virginian came onto the stairs and said, "That will be enough, Harrison. I'll talk to the man."

The messenger could hardly help from grinning at the skinny naked torso sticking up out of the tight breeches.

"Well, what is it?"

"About four, five thousand British air crossing over onto that island from the Long Island way."

"What island?"

"Montresor's," the messenger drawled.

"Who sent you?"

"Spencer."

"General, damn you!"

"General," the messenger grinned.

Stifling his rage, telling himself that he would remember that face and teach the fellow a thing or two when there was time, the big man dashed upstairs and flung on his coat. Without any explanation, he ran out of the house, leaped on his horse, and galloped through the darkness, giving the beast its head. In less than an hour, he saw the fires of Spencer's camp.

"It's all right," Spencer drawled lazily, raising his brows at the naked flesh that showed under the commander's coat. "I'm digging a trench alongside the river. They're on the island, but they won't come over here tonight or tomorrow with what I've got waiting for them. It's all right."

The big man rode back to the Morris house slowly. His

elation had passed away; his bones and muscles ached, as they did in the Virginia lowlands when a storm was brewing.

They were Connecticut troops selected to hold the bank, he was told afterwards, and that same Saturday evening Spencer had sent them marching down the bank of the East River to make breastworks against a British landing. It was a poor choice, not because the Connecticut men were in any way inferior to the New York or Pennsylvania men, but because the Connecticut brigades had been less carefully watched, and thus out of six thousand, some four thousand had succeeded in deserting. The two thousand left were disgruntled and bitter, and their feelings were not elevated any by their being forced to march mile after mile through the blackest of nights on a twisting little path that followed the bank of the East River.

The leader of the Connecticut troops, a Major Gray, was disgruntled too; he was close on to forty, and he was thoroughly disgusted with being a major in an army where there were generals in their twenties and thirties.

When the troops reached the portion of the bank they were supposed to defend, a section about four miles north of the lower tip of Manhattan, the order was given to halt, remove knapsacks, and man the entrenchments. The entrenchments, as they were, consisted of a hastily dug ditch, about a foot deep; and word was passed to deepen the trench and construct an actual breastwork of the excavated dirt and of logs and branches lying about in the woods behind them.

No one made any real effort to follow these orders. The troops were tired and angry, and confident enough that nothing would happen to be content with a ditch a foot deep. They sprawled out, some of them in the ditch, some of them on the ground in front of it and behind it. Most of them slept, but there was enough responsibility among the officers to cause them to post sentinels and make some effort to keep a watch.

Not that they could see anything; the night was as black as ink, and even the still waters of the East River, a few feet in front of them, were hidden in the darkness. But it was reassuring to hear the voices sounding back and forth:

"All is well!"

"All is well!"

For about an hour the silence was unbroken, except by the lonely calling of the sentries, and then there began many strange, muffled noises, creakings, strainings, splashings. The noises started, stopped, and started again, and the sleeping Yankees began to stir restlessly.

Presently, to the mournful call of the sentries, there sounded what was almost an echo out of the black river:

"Not so well!"

The sentries stopped dead still in their slow pacing.

"Hello,"

"Hello," came back the ironic echo.

"There be someone out in that river," a sentry said prosaically.

There was giggling and gurgling among the straining and creaking.

"All is well," the sentry said uncertainly.

"Not well—not at all!" came back from the black river.

The captains and lieutenants held a council, and then some of them crept silently to the water's edge; but there was nothing to see, absolutely nothing.

"A boatload of British," a captain reported to the major.

"Yes, I guess so."

"Shall we give them a volley, sir,"

"What for? You can't see them."

"That's so," the lieutenant nodded slowly, and then added, almost triumphantly, "They can't see us."

"Oh, damn it, go to sleep," the major said.

The captain went back to sleep, but the sentries, once they discovered that there was nothing ghostly about the voices coming from the river, managed to make the night more interesting by injecting a little Yankee humor. The repartee went on through the long, slow hours.

The grey of dawn unfolded the darkness without haste and through the lifting mists the Connecticut men saw what they had thought to be a boatload of British—four mighty ships of the line, anchored prow to stern with broadsides facing them, guns rolled out, and gunners standing by. And beneath the guns, along the whole line of the ships, were boats full of British marines.

The Yankees stared, rubbed their eyes, and stared again. They began to talk in anxious excitement, and the officers ran up and down the lines, waking up those men who still slept.

But no one fired. Minutes passed; the sun broke through the mist and cast an enchanting halo about the tall spars of the battleships, and still no one fired. It was all too unbelievable, too unreal, too fantastic; it was a strange, terrifying, colorful picture, the tall ships with their hundreds of open gun ports, the gun crews standing by with ramrods and powder sacks, the ship's officers, poised on poop and quarterdeck, coolly watching the American lines, the marines crowded into the boats, but metallic and disciplined none the less, their red coats bright as fire and their bayonets nicking at the sky.

And still the Americans stared in horror and astonishment. Then, on the British decks, pipes began to twitter, sounding like foolish sparrows in the clean, still morning. The oars in the longboats and barges dipped down, and the wide flotilla of marines began to move toward the shore.

Major Gray gave a hoarse command, and there was the snickering sound of hammers scraping on firelocks; but no one heard an American musket fire. For at that moment, one of the British officers let his hand drop, and an inferno of fire and hell and roundshot and grapeshot was let loose on the world. The four ships became roaring furnaces of destruction as the combined broadsides, enough to blow any vessel in the world out of the water, were discharged into the American lines.

The Connecticut men never saw the ships of the line again. A solid wall of smoke had formed in the river, a rolling, ghastly pall broken only by ribbons of light as the gunners reloaded and discharged fresh broadsides. They tried to aim their muskets, and found the weapons ripped from their hands by an almost solid blast of grape. They tried to rise up, and the grape struck them down and tore them to pieces. They tried to call to their friends and saw that their friends were lying headless and dead.

Yet they stood it and died, not breaking until they realized that the boats of the marines were nosing out of the smoke, saw the redcoats leap into the water, form, and march for the shore with machine-like precision, wet bayonets like lace in the smoke. Then they broke; then the boys and young men of Connecticut leaped from their trenches and fled inland. And even now the grape pursued them, lashing over the heads of the redcoated marines.

They ran inland for perhaps a hundred yards, throwing away their guns as they fled, before they found some re-

lief from the dread panic that had overtaken them. They
left the smoke and grape behind them and saw green fields
splashed with the morning sunlight. And over the fields they
saw a column of men marching in close order, men they
knew were their own—for who else would be on the mainland
of New York?—men they ran to with sobbing cries of welcome.

And then the Yankees stopped; the marching men
were in green. And someone shouted, "Hessians!"

They tried to flee; they cast about desperately; behind
them were the marines, in front the Germans.

The big guns of the battleships had ceased fire. There
was a new stillness, broken by a derisive shout:

"Yonkee! Yonkee! Yonkee!"

They plunged away wildly, but not wildly enough; and
in their ears, punctuating their own screams and mocking
their pain, came that horrible roar:

"Yonkee! Yonkee! Yonkee!"

New York, the town itself, clustered tightly on the south-
ernmost tip of Manhattan Island. It was still more a village
than a city, though it had spread above the old wall that
the Dutch settlers had built as a stockade against the Indians. Already, at that time, people had begun to call that
lane Wall Street. The town itself was full of crooked little
avenues, fronted mostly by red-brick, step-roofed Dutch
houses, although of late the building style was almost entirely Georgian, as in most of the mid-Atlantic colonies. It
was a bright, cheerful little town, and it had as its pros-
perous hinterland the wooded hills and green meadows of
Manhattan Island.

In accordance with Washington's plan, Old Israel Putnam
had taken command of the city itself, garrisoning it with
five thousand men. These were, for the most part, New Jersey
and Pennsylvania militia, men who had stood up to battle
just a little better than the New England Yankees and were
therefore very contemptuous of the Massachusetts and Connecticut and Rhode Island troops. Aside from that it was
good policy to keep the mid-country men apart from the
Yankees, for they could hardly meet each other without a
pitched battle occurring.

The five thousand militia were camped on the outskirts
of the city, the greatest part of them on its northern edge
and on both lower riverfronts, Putnam had noticed the

movement of British vessels in the bay on Saturday afternoon, and during that black night, certain sounds coming from both rivers made him suspect that at least one or two of the big ships of the line were being kedged up the rivers. But young Burr, riding back from Harlem, assured the old man that Spencer had dug entrenchments all along the East River front, and that patrols were covering the whole Manhattan shore of the Hudson. So Putnam went to sleep, more or less uneasily, and slept until he was awakened by the thundering British broadsides.

He struggled into his clothes, ran outside, and found that his Pennsylvania and New Jersey militia were already in a turmoil. The guns had turned them out of their camps like rabbits out of a bramble patch, and they were crowding nervously through the narrow streets and grassy lanes of the town.

Aaron Burr, haggard after an almost sleepless night, had already heard the worst. He hung over his lathered horse in front of Putnam's headquarters and told the old man what he knew.

"They've landed!"

"British?"

"Hessians, too—on both sides of the island."

"How many?"

"I don't know," Burr cried hoarsely. "How can I know how many! Thousands, I guess."

Old Putnam shook his head; one hand he held on his tinny sword trembled violently. "They couldn't have landed," he insisted.

"Thousands, I tell you."

"If they landed, we're caught like rats in a trap—"

The boy nodded, his slim body arched with excitement.

"Retreat—"

"Right away, there's no time to lose—don't you see, on both sides of the island."

"Yes, yes," Putnam faltered.

"Right away, I tell you."

"If we could join the general," Putnam said vaguely.

"But they're between us," Burr pleaded. "On both sides of the island, don't you understand! And then if they come together, where will we go—into the river?"

The old man kept nodding.

Afterwards, for long years, Burr had a silent, bitter scorn

of those who said glibly, "Retreat is easy." He knew that it was easy to advance, but a man is dying when he retreats, and it's not easy to die.

It was not easy that day. The hot morning sun baked all movement out of the autumn winds, and the tall golden wheat in the Manhattan fields stood stiff and motionless. In the city, the burghers opened their windows and doors and saw the Continental militia streaming north through the narrow lanes. Word of what had happened spread like fire, and only for a few minutes was there anything orderly or self-possessed about the Pennsylvania and New Jersey men. Then they pressed forward, and soon they were running, and soon they broke out of the city, and then almost all of the five thousand men were swarming north in a wild panic.

They ran and outdistanced their officers. They crowded the little lanes and they spread like quail across the fields. They broke through bushes and blundered in woods. The whole breadth of the island was filled with frightened men racing frantically for freedom before the British closed their trap.

Some, as they ran, held their muskets with blind instinct; others threw their muskets away; others fired insanely at their own comrades. Some fell and died, stabbed by their own bayonets, and officers died, shot through by men they tried to command.

Most of them, as they ran, verged to the west, where the Bloomingdale Road made a dusty path to Kingsbridge; others swerved eastward and presently, half dead of weariness, stumbling, crawling, falling, came in with the hacked remnants of Spencer's New Englanders. There, on the eastern shore, it became a horrible, tragic melee, Yankees, Pennsylvanians and Jersey men staggering along blindly, croaking with parched tongues, and trying like terrified children to shield themselves from the glittering bayonets of the Hessians. And the Hessians stabbed ponderously and intently, dry themselves as they croaked, "Yonkee, Yonkee," driving the boys and children onto the metallic, redcoated ranks of the Royal Marines.

Henry Knox, in the city with Putnam, had arranged what few cannon remained to him, with gentle and loving care. Some he set with their noses sniffing at the bay, others flanking them, others back a bit on an elevated platform with their snouts down, ready to spit grape and

cannister, and others barking gallantly at the mouths of the
East River and the Hudson. For all that, it was a futile gesture; he had no guns capable of more than stinging the
great ships of the line; his little popguns, six- and eight-
pounders, would make a noise and a flash, but would
hardly be heard above the killing roar of a British broadside. His other guns, his wonderful, precious monsters that
could hurl a forty-pound mass of metal, had been spiked in
the mud of Brooklyn.

The result of that loss was an almost insane desire on
his part to hoard what guns remained. The boy, whom other
boys called colonel, was a born collector; once he had collected minerals, then leaves, then insects, then books, and
now guns. He knew every gun in his batteries. He had
walked hundreds of miles through frozen forests to bring
some of the guns from the Canadian border. He had fished
guns out of the water and lowered others from mountains.
He had polished them with his own hands and designed his
own carriages for them. He had no desire to kill; he had long
ago decided that he was on the right side; then he stopped
thinking about it and thought only of how many cannon
he could gather. His deadly earnestness, his devotion to
the Virginia foxhunter, who was the opposite of him in almost every particular, and his utter unselfishness, made him
seem a good deal older than his twenty-six years. And his
massive, slightly ridiculous body and almost pathetic lack of
cleverness made his men love him.

On this Sunday morning, when the British broadsides
rocked the island into wakefulness, when the headlong flight
to the north began, Knox turned the other way and went to
his guns. He went without haste, stolidly and gloomily, without giving orders for anyone to follow. He had no plan, no
thought except that he wanted to be with his guns, that he
didn't want to run any more.

His gunners, who were stationed near the batteries, made
no secret of their desire to run away. They started to go,
and only stopped when they saw their colonel standing
moodily beside one of his cannon, for all the world like a
boy suddenly made an orphan and waiting with the terrible knowledge that there is nothing to wait for. They
paused and stared at him, and then some of them went
back and then the others. And then a Captain Miller said
simply, "The army is running away, colonel."

"Yes—" Knox came out of his trance slowly.

"There's nothing we can do here."

"The guns are here," Knox said, and his thought was that when he left these guns, there would be nothing else, absolutely nothing else.

"Sir, it's no use staying here," the captain argued.

"You don't have to stay here," Knox shrugged.

"But my God, colonel," the captain said vehemently, "what good will it do to stay here and let the British have us along with the guns?"

"You don't have to stay here," Knox repeated.

"But my God, colonel, just because those other bastards ran away—"

"Yes, they ran away." Knox spoke the last two words slowly, savagely.

The artillerymen shifted around, but no one made any move to go, the men scuffing their feet and staring at the ground, and one boy of fifteen sobbing unashamed. From the north came the shrill sound of the fleeing army and over and above it the dull boom of the British broadsides.

For a few minutes no one said anything, and then a Plymouth boy, seventeen years old, a lieutenant in rank, piped cheerfully, "Lor', colonel, if we're all a-going to die, this is a mighty poor place. There's a pretty little hill some miles to north of here where we could ring the guns and make a fight. Shade trees, too," he added eagerly.

"It's almighty hot here," someone else offered.

The men began to chuckle, half in fright, half in excitement at the wonderful venture they were proposing when all the rest of the army had run away.

"What hill?" Knox demanded.

"Bunker's, they call it."

Knox saw the smiles on the faces. It was a good sign; the one half-victory that raggle-taggle army had won had been on another Bunker Hill. He came alive, gave directions for loading the ammunition carts, and sent some of the men away to see whether they could find a horse or two. Three ancient nags resulted from the search, and they were harnessed to three of the eight-pounders. The men themselves dragged what others of the guns they could manage and the ammunition carts. In a little while, the motley procession was under way, creaking slowly through the littered streets of the town, where countless knapsacks, rusty bayonets and ancient muskets marked the trail of the American army.

The townspeople, who were already making ready to welcome the British, whose attitude toward the Continentals was good riddance to bad rubbish, lined the streets to grin at the slow-moving batteries. Children ran along, screaming, "Get a horse! Get a horse!" And dozens of brightly painted ladies, whose living had gone with the army, screamed and cursed and spat at the gunners and pelted them with all the filth that lay in the gutters. Looking neither to left nor to right, Knox labored at the wheels of one of the guns, the sweat pouring from his forehead.

When the sweat-soaked procession finally got to Bunker's Hill, they found it already occupied. General Silliman, a heavy, plodding, sullen man, had kept most of his regiment together and steered them off onto the hill. There they lay over their muskets, half afraid, half defiant, and almost murderously bitter now that their first panic had left them.

"What are you going to do?" Knox asked, unable to believe his eyes.

"Let those bastards come. We'll know what to do," Silliman growled.

Knox nodded. He didn't know Silliman very well and had never felt drawn toward the man, but now they were together, two of them with one thought. Knox was coming out of his black mood and passing into a state of mingled fear and exultation. Putnam's army had melted away, and from their little sun-drenched hill they could see nothing but a tiny brook and a placid white farmhouse. Knox knew it was the end; the revolution had melted in a scummy pool of panic and rout; the harlots of New York would laugh and blaspheme for months perhaps, but in time even they would forget. He, at least, would not hang from a gibbet nor rot in jail nor spend his years in some lonely backwoods town, lying about glories that had never been. He would die here, giving his life for a cause he had believed in and had the courage to fight for.

"Batteries two and five up on the hill!" he cried. 'Ring and load with solid shot! Batteries one, three and four, flank action with cannister and grape!"

A ragged, tremulous cheer floated up from Silliman's men, and they came running to help drag the guns up the slope. Silliman nodded and nodded wordlessly, grasping Knox's hand. Then, in the next few minutes, all was action and excitement in which even fear and hopelessness were forgotten—so much so that almost no one noticed the rider who was spurring his lathered horse down the road toward them.

It was Burr, more haggard, more tired than ever, so dry he could only croak until one of the artillerymen held up a canteen for him to drink from. Then, after he had spat out a mouthful of sand and swallowed twice, he demanded angrily of Silliman, "My God, general, what's all this?"

"You can see that. We haven't run away."

"Oh, Jesus Christ, I know! But do you know that in one hour from now, the British will have cut you off—completely?"

Silliman tightened his mouth and shook his head.

"Oh, Christ, oh, Jesus Christ," Burr cried, "is that it, is it suicide, is it all you can think of to kill a regiment that had guts enough not to run away? Will that give us our liberty? Will that make the revolution?"

"We've run enough."

"You've run enough! You've run enough! You sit there on your ass and tell me you've run enough!"

"God damn it, major, I'll not have you talk like that!"

"I'll talk as I damn please!"

"God damn it, no! I won't take that from any twenty-year-old fool!"

"You'll take it!" Burr almost screamed. "You'll take it because twenty or not, I'm man enough to—"

"Burr!" Knox roared.

The boy subsided and lay on his horse's neck trembling and pouring sweat. "All right, Harry," he said in a hoarse whisper. "I'm sorry. I'm right, too. I'm sorry."

"Colonel Knox," the artilleryman said evenly.

"All right, Colonel Knox—only for the love of God, Harry, come with me and don't stand up for these crazy heroics."

"Is it heroics to want to stand instead of running away —instead of running away always? Did you see what happened in the city today?"

"I saw it."

"And now you want us to run away."

"I want you to live, that's all—to live."

"For what?" Knox demanded. "What's left?"

"The revolution, and that's more than death! Death's no good! That doesn't help! I swear to God, Harry, believe me!"

"I won't leave my guns."

Burr turned to the men, his white face a mask of desperation, his voice shrill and penetrating, "Do you hear

me? Do you want to die? Is that all you want, you dirty
Pennsylvania bastards? There's an army at Kingsbridge
that's going to fight, maybe for twenty years, maybe forever, but all you dirty Pennsylvania bastards want is to die!"

A roar of anger answered him, and the boy, tired as he
was, judged their temper perfectly. "Follow me!" he
screamed, and spurred his horse to the north, not even looking back to see how they spilled down the hill and ran
after him. Even Silliman went, at the tail end, cursing Burr
at the top of his lungs.

The artillerymen were left. They had stayed with Knox,
and now they stood without moving, looking at him, serving
him and placing in his hands the decision of life or death.
He couldn't speak. Sobbing, he started north, and with their
heads and arms hanging limply, they followed him.

They didn't look back to where all the bright guns stood
more lonely than any living men.

Only the dead did not hear that crashing broadside from
the four British ships of the line.

On that Sunday morning, the commander in chief had
awakened before dawn, after a night of deep slumber.
Billy, who slept outside the room, who could hear in his
sleep when his master rolled from side to side, helped him
to dress in the candlelight, wagging his black head and
chuckling happily.

"A good night," Billy said.

"Yes, better than most."

"Getting better than it was after you left Missis Patsy."

"A little better," the Virginian smiled. He was in high
spirits this morning.

"Going to set the skillet on," Billy said, running down the
stairs. "Going to set the skillet on," he sang, "and get the
water boiling."

The Virginian's breakfast, as always, was cakes and honey
and tea. He ate with a good appetite, noticed that Harrison
had not yet awakened, and decided that he would go out
for an early inspection of the troops holding the line in
Harlem. Billy had anticipated his thought, and when the big
man came out of the Morris house, the Negro was standing
there with the horse saddled and ready. Washington
mounted, waved, and set off down the road at a smart
canter.

The first grey of dawn had dispersed the inky blackness

when he rode past the tired sentries into Mifflin's camp, Mifflin, with a few regiments, formed the most northerly outpost of Spencer's division, holding a thinly manned line across the waist of Manhattan. Now, early as it was, the general stood dressed, grinning happily as he recognized the tall form of his commander in chief. He waved an arm and opened his mouth to speak when the four broadsides rumbled in the distance.

The Virginian stiffened, bent, and then spurred his horse through the awakening camp. Mifflin ran for a horse, but before he could mount the Virginian was out of sight.

Washington rode four miles, lashing his beast heartlessly, before he saw the first and fleetest of the panic-stricken army. By then the mists had lifted and the sun had put a golden glaze on the meadows and wheatfields and orchards. He had driven his horse recklessly, leaving the road, clearing a wall with a bound, a brook, a fence; he rode full into them, saw them as far as he was able to see, hundreds and hundreds of men, men crawling, running, hiding, staggering.

He pulled in his horse and tried to talk to them; he rode slowly across their front, but there was no recognition in their blank eyes. They ran on. One fired at him.

He yelled at them, "Halt!"

They swarmed past him.

"Do you hear me?" he called.

He pleaded, "Halt!"

"You know who I am! I'm your commander! I'm your general!"

"Halt!" he shrieked.

"Get behind the stone walls!"

"Use your guns!"

They swarmed on, like rabbits driven by long-eared dogs.

"By God, halt!"

He spurred his horse again. He rode among them, lashing until the quirt was torn from his hand. He drew his pistols, but the guns missed fire, soaked as they were with sweat. He flung the pistols at them. He drew his sword. He rode among them, cutting, slashing, screaming at the top of his lungs, pleading, begging, slashing again—but they ran on.

He rushed across the fields like a demon. His voice screamed and raged until it cracked.

And then he no longer urged his horse, but sat there without moving while they fled past him. The sword dropped from his loose fingers and fell into the wet, jewel-like grass, lying all a-sparkle in the bright dew-drops. His spine, braced like a ramrod, had lost its support; he sagged in his saddle like a long bag of disjointed bones.

He saw the column of British coming, marching smartly, only a few hundred yards away, the marines like red ribbons fluttering where there was no wind. Yet he didn't move; it seemed to him that he was suspended in a void; he felt that he was dead, and wondered vaguely why he could still see and hear and feel.

The British were only a hundred yards away now.

He saw Mifflin next to him and heard Mifflin's voice as from a great distance.

"Come away, sir, please, please," Mifflin was begging.

There were others around him. Why did they want him to come away when he was already dead?

"Please, sir, please."

He saw how Mifflin's face was contorted.

"Please, sir."

Then he gave Mifflin the reins and allowed his horse to be led away. It didn't matter that the British were firing at him. Nothing mattered.

7

THE GRACIOUS MRS. MURRAY

The British army had been trained to fight; it had been drilled and drilled and drilled until it had emerged as the finest fighting machine in the world; it would march into hell and high water with impassive calm. The British general who boasted that he could lead his army onto the sands of the channel beaches and order it to march across to France, and have it march until the last man's head had disappeared under the water, was not exaggerating; he was stating a fact; in the same way he could lead his army to the edge of a cliff and have it march over rank by rank, and there would have been neither hesitation nor annoyance among the redcoated soldiers.

But there was nothing in the training of British troops that told them what to do when the army they were supposed to fight ran away. A retreating army was one thing; then they were supposed to pursue in close order with the purpose of breaking morale and sowing disorder. But this was not even a retreating army.

By the time General Howe had landed a substantial amount of his troops in New York City, there was not a hale Continental to be seen, only the sick and wounded, packed into the churches and synagogues. The weather was very hot, and the portly Howe was very uncomfortable; among the many things American which he disliked intensely, the weather stood well in front. One could never be sure of the seasons; summer became winter and autumn became summer, and a mild spring day could occur in January as well as any other time of the year. The weather was as beastly, as stupid, as inconsistent as the Americans themselves.

With the thermometer at ninety-two in the shade, with the redcoat columns standing packed in the narrow streets, General Howe had to sit in his damp saddle and receive the congratulations of a committee of earnest, grateful, and well-to-do citizens. Phineas Thatcher, the grain merchant, voiced their gratitude.

"I have no desire, Your Excellency," he said, "to dwell upon our miseries, upon what we have suffered from this rascally band of thieves and cutthroats."

"Ha—quite true," Howe nodded impatiently.

"Nor to put forward our patience as loyal subjects of His Most Gracious Majesty—"

"Quite true."

"But to welcome you as our liberator—"

"Of course, of course," Howe agreed, wondering whether this would go on forever.

"Our protector—"

They were finally under way and out of town, the long column crawling over the road like a gorgeous scarlet snake, the drums and fifes playing, the regimental banners held proudly, the artillery rumbling and grunting like a counterpoint to the steady thud, thud, thud of marching feet. At the head of the column rode General Howe and his aides, all on white horses, making as pretty a sight as the peaceful country lanes of Manhattan had ever seen. And all around them, in the meadows, on the road, were evidences of the

Americans' headlong flight—knapsacks, muskets, belts, hats, power horns, bags of shot, old bayonets.

"They must have been in a frightful hurry," one of the aides observed.

"Beastly hot to hurry," Howe sighed. "Provincial energy, even in retreat, is most amazing."

"They won't go far."

"Why," Howe complained, "do provincials talk so much? We could have been on our way an hour ago if not for all that talk, talk, talk."

They rode on; the heat increased; their beautifully pressed, colorful uniforms became limp and wet. Presently, they met the first of the Hessians, who had landed further up the island, from the East River. Laughing and shouting, the Hessians herded along groups of American prisoners, clusters of dirty, frightened boys who could hardly walk for weariness. They were very proud of their achievement, the Hessians, but the redcoats marched by looking straight ahead, not even deigning to notice them.

"War is dine commander?" Howe demanded of some of them.

They shook their heads and went on with their prisoners.

"Stubborn beasts!"

"Dine commander?" Howe insisted, wondering why they could not understand their own tongue.

"Bad business, breaking order like that," one of his aides observed.

"The devil take them," Howe said. He was hot and tired and bored, and he had nothing more to look forward to than a wearisome day of collecting American prisoners. He had expected a battle, certainly stubborn resistance in attempting the most difficult operation in military practice, the establishing of a bridgehead against an entrenched enemy, and instead there was nothing less than a complete melting away of Washington's army. He had a good deal of respect, almost admiration for the tall, stubborn foxhunter, and as a Whig, many of his sympathies were with the revolutionists, at least abstractly.

He felt no hate, only an impatient desire to meet the Yankees in battle and administer a sound and sportsmanlike drubbing, something that would end the war as, he considered, all wars should be ended, in a mood for the gentlemen on both sides to sit down at a table and exchange toasts. But this—this utter panic, this foul cowardice—turned his stomach; the revolution was over; the ideals were blasted and had gone the way of all other ideals; and it was so very hot.

He was glad that he would be sailing back to England soon.

An officer of the light infantry, who had been landed from boats a few miles north of here, came riding to meet the column, saluted, and gave Howe more details of the flight.

"We can have them all before night," the officer said eagerly.

"How many would you say?" Howe asked, not with too much interest.

"Ten thousand, perhaps, here on the island."

"A good catch," Howe sighed, taking off his hat and wiping his brow.

"If you'll only hurry, sir!"

"There's time enough."

"Yes, sir, of course, sir—but it's my opinion that a few thousand of them are directly across the island, west of here. We could cut them off, you know, like snaring rabbits."

"Yes, certainly—you know, I'd give my soul for a drink. I don't like the idea of these Jagers breaking ranks; find someone who can talk their beastly doggerel."

"Yes, sir. They've been taking prisoners, got almost five hundred."

"They shouldn't break ranks. Whose house is that, over there?" He pointed to a pleasant Georgian house, set back about two hundred yards from the road, with a shady veranda and a rolling green lawn. Two colored servants were occupied in taking down wooden shutters that had evidently been put in place when the dawn bombardment began; and on the veranda three ladies sat and fanned themselves.

"I don't know, sir. I suppose they broke ranks to pursue the enemy."

"It's bad for discipline. Do you suppose they'd offer us a drink?"

He didn't wait for an answer, but started his horse off for the house, waving for his staff to follow him and calling back for the files to stand fast. Still arguing his case, the light-infantry officer followed, the whole colorful party moving at a smart trot to where the ladies sat.

The ladies rose, more excited than alarmed; General Howe swept off his hat and smiled so gallantly that in a moment they were smiling too. They were all three of them younger than thirty, and they all had that innocuous charm that Howe considered the most wonderful thing about the American colonies. One was blonde and blue-eyed, with hair like combed flax; the other two were dark; they were all quite pretty.

"I most earnestly command your pardon," Howe said, "but I and my men are dying of thirst, and seeing this haven of shade and restfulness, like an oasis in a desert—"

They were laughing as Howe dismounted, bowed, and presented himself. "William Howe, humbly at your service."

"Your Excellency!" they cried, and dropped in very graceful curtsies.

"Please, the honor belongs to your humble servant," Howe insisted, and went on to present Colonel Bently, Colonel Jameson, Major Lass, Captain Loring, Captain Atterbee, Lieutenant Greystone, and Lieutenant Bart. They were all most honored.

The ladies, who had certainly never seen such a magnificent display of uniform and color and polite bearing before, introduced each other as Mrs. Murray, Mrs. Van Cleehut, and Miss Penrose. Miss Penrose was the blonde, and she stilled even the captain of light infantry's desire to be somewhere else. They chattered and curtsied until General Howe gently reminded them of his thirst.

"Oh, what savages you must think us!" Mrs. Murray cried. She clapped her hands, called one of the servants, and told him to bring some iced punch and some claret. "You must forgive us," she explained to General Howe. "I know you would prefer port, but unfortunately port is so hard to come by here in the provinces."

"And claret will be ambrosia," Howe said.

"It's so cool inside," Mrs. Murray smiled. "If my humble house could—"

"Your humble house is a haven of refuge," Howe interrupted gallantly.

It was after lunch had been served and the whist tables were being set up, that Miss Penrose remarked how perfectly miserable the poor men out in the road must be. The endless column of British troops seemed from this distance like a raw red ribbon flung on the sun-soaked mead-

ows. None of the men had moved from their places, and it
seemed that they would stand there in their ruddy glory
for all eternity.

Colonel Jameson rubbed his mustache, peered out of the
window, and declared, "Not at all, not at all, my dear.
Soldiering, you know, not a picnic, not at all a picnic." The
colonel had been so attentive that the young subalterns
could hardly do more than gaze at Miss Penrose from a distance.

"Why must war be?" Miss Penrose demanded passionately.
"I couldn't sleep a wink after dawn with those horrible guns
firing all the time, and then all morning those wretched
men came running past, until Mrs. Murray put up the shutters and said there was nothing else to do but sit quietly
and hope the house would not be burned over our heads."

"War, you know," the colonel shrugged. "Nasty business
for ladies."

"James wanted to fight," Miss Penrose told them incredulously, not explaining who James was. "But mother
packed him off to England. James always had a temper."

"Nasty business for ladies," the colonel said again, wagging his head and including all the others in his apology.

Mrs. Murray was calling Colonel Jameson to make up another four at whist. Miss Penrose didn't play whist, and immediately all the subalterns decided that they were very
poor hands at cards.

By tea time, Howe had finished his third bottle of claret,
and was ready to swear to God that never in his life had
he spent an afternoon with more devilishly charming company.

"But we are rebels, you know," Mrs. Murray protested.

"Oh, come now, my dear Mrs. Murray!"

"Rebels, bosh! There are no more rebels," Colonel Bently
said comfortably.

On the subject of rebels, Mrs. Van Cleehut said that her
husband was in Philadelphia and would stay there until the
last of these wretched persons had left New York. "Really,
they're quite horrible," she smiled. "You should have seen
two of them this morning, all over dirt and filth, trying to
hide in the carriage house."

"Jackson made short work of them," Mrs. Murray explained.

Miss Penrose said, "It would be different if they had uniforms. You would think, wouldn't you, that those persons
and their Congress would have uniforms, if they're going to

have an army, I mean, anyway some sort of uniform," glancing admiringly out of the window to where the redcoat files still stood in the sun.

"They're so miserably poor," Mrs. Murray smiled. "None of the better people will have any part of them."

"I hear the Schuylers and Pintards and Beekmans are with the rebels."

"Some—oh, yes, the best blood has dark spots. The Roosevelts and Bensons and Hoffmans have gone off with that rabble, too. But they'll learn. They'll come back dragging their fine feathers in the dust."

"To the end of the war," Howe said, raising his glass and starting on his fourth bottle of claret.

"You do think so?"

"By all means. Nothing left but to take prisoners."

"It's been so disturbing."

"Nasty business for ladies," Colonel Jameson agreed.

"And prices have gone up impossibly," Mrs. Murray added.

At dinner time, General Howe protested, "No, no—you've been too charming and too gracious, Mrs. Murray, but we are uninvited guests."

"But you can't know how secure we've felt since you're here," Miss Penrose insisted.

"One is fighting a war," General Howe said. "Not a very pleasant business, but a man's duty."

"But you said yourself that the war was over this morning," Mrs. Murray pointed out.

Jackson brought the general his fifth bottle of claret.

The afternoon passed and evening came, and a breeze rustled through the fields and trees of Manhattan. Candles were lit in the Murray house, and a tinkle of dishes and the sound of laughter came through the open door.

Meanwhile the last fleeing American had passed on north and found refuge behind the lines at Harlem.

8

VIEW HALLOO

Old Putnam, nudging Mifflin, said, "Speak to him."

"What?"

"Speak to him."

"What? What should I say to him?"

"I don't know, speak to him. My God, don't you see, somebody has to speak to him?"

"What?"

"Anything. Tell him to come out of the rain."

"Just that?" Mifflin said stupidly, and added, "Would you tell him to come out of the rain?"

"I can't speak to him," Putnam said, thinking of how he had run away with an army running after him.

The rain had come with darkness after that terribly hot and sultry September day. It came strong and keen and cold and lashing, but it meant respite; for British guns could not fire at Americans who had thrown away their guns. It gave the beaten Yankees a chance to crawl through the American lines at Harlem and to lie shivering, without tents, even without clothes in the drenching downpour.

This American line, manned by Mifflin's brigades, by Massachusetts men, Marblehead fishermen, Boston militia, Middlesex farmers, still held firm; perhaps only by virtue of the fact that the British and Hessians had not yet pushed that far north on Manhattan Island.

The entrenchments had been built on the northern slope of a deep and narrow valley that cuts the island two-thirds of the way from its southern tip. Deep and narrow at Claremont on the Hudson, broadening out as it approached the East River, it was called at that time the Hollow Way. It was a good position, even for a shattered army, for to make an attack, the British would have to come pouring down one slope, cross the bottom of the valley, and climb the other slope. All the afternoon and evening of

September 15th, frightened Connecticut, New Jersey and Pennsylvania militiamen had staggered into the Hollow Way and found security behind the Massachusetts entrenchments. Beaten and spiritless, they sprawled on the ground and listened to the mocking jeers of the New Englanders, who, not having been attacked nor encircled, could boast of their courage, forgetting what their courage was two weeks ago on Brooklyn Heights.

The midlanders had no heart to reply. They lay almost without movement, watching dumbly the officers' efforts to collect a brigade here and a brigade there, hardly moving when the cold rain began.

Walking through the shattered troops, the Virginian looked neither to left nor to right. But after he had passed, the men nodded at him and asked each other whether they had seen his eyes. Connecticut men gained importance by detailing his actions of the morning and describing how he had gone completely insane, lashing at them with his sword.

"Took Jones' pinky off," one of them said.

Another displayed a welt behind his ear. "Got me there with his stock."

"He's addled," another decided. "Gone and walked away and addled. Lookee at his eyes."

In a muted voice, a Hartford boy told how the commander in chief had sat on his horse and waited for the British to kill him.

Knox and Putnam and Mifflin and Knowlton and Burr stood together under a tree and watched the Virginian pace back and forth in the pouring rain. It was past midnight already, and he had been walking like that, back and forth and back and forth, for almost four hours. His pace never changed and he walked always in the same line, and under his boots the ground was mashed into spongy mud. His blue coat was limp and shapeless and one of the cocks of his hat had come loose and hung over his ear, pouring a steady stream of water down onto his shoulder. His long arms hung limply by his sides and sometimes the grotesquely huge hands clenched and unclenched.

Knox, who could not stand much more of it, added his voice to Putnam's, begging Mifflin to go over and speak to him. And Putnam reiterated, almost pitifully, "Tell him to come out of the rain."

"All right," Mifflin nodded, and walked over to his commander in chief and said, "Please, sir—"

The tall man stopped in his walk, peered at Mifflin inquiringly, and then began to walk once more.

"Please, sir, come out of the rain."

"What?"

"I said, come out of the rain, please, sir. Please. You're soaking wet."

"Wet? What are you trying to tell me, Mifflin?"

"You're wet, sir—you're soaking wet. You'll catch a death of cold."

"I'll thank you to mind your own damned affairs, Mifflin," the Virginian said quietly.

"Please, sir, say what you want to, it's no good in the world to stay here and catch a death of cold."

"I'll thank you, Mifflin, to go to hell and be damned."

"Please, General Washington—"

Now Knox had joined Mifflin, Putnam just a little distance behind him. Washington stopped pacing and demanded, "What is this, gentlemen? Have you no duties, no brigades—?"

"Please, General Washington, come out of the rain," Knox said, and then his voice broke and he turned away, and they all stood there helplessly around the tall man.

And then the foxhunter said softly, "We'll go to my headquarters, gentlemen. We're none of us dry, are we?"

Knox and Mifflin took him up to his room. While Billy was out, heating a loggerhead for a mug of flip, they undressed him. He was meek and sleepy, and he made no protest when they helped him into bed and covered him with blankets. Knox supported his head and shoulders while he drank the flip, and a moment later he was sleeping as soundly and peacefully as a child.

When they came out of his room and Billy looked at them inquiringly, they nodded and said, "He's sleeping," gently and considerately, as if the colored man were a father and entitled to know.

"He ain't sick?" Billy asked.

"No—" Mifflin shook his head. "Not sick, I don't think." Mifflin didn't know what more to say; there were no words for what had happened in the tall, weary body. And Knox, not trusting himself to speak, sat down in front of the fire and stared at the curling flames. And in the licking, curling tongues of fire, Knox found neither peace nor hope; waked out of a dream, his dogged, unimaginative self could not find another to replace it. So many things were gone: for the tall foxhunter, honor, since he was a Virginia aristocrat; but for Knox, a great deal more than honor, a round, comfortable wife, a warm home, many books, many hopes, a nation, a republic, a screaming vision that had banged on his eardrums until he was ready to lay down his life and fortune for his country, his miserable, dirty little backwoods country.

"Flip, gentlemen," Billy said, taking another loggerhead out of the fire and filling the kitchen where they sat with the good, homey smell of burnt sugar.

"Will you drink?" Mifflin asked Knox.

Then the two of them, sitting on either side of the hearth, drank mug after mug of the boiling hot rum with deadly and silent earnestness.

They were good and drunk when they went out on the porch, a while later, hard drunk, mad and bitter and black, lost from joy and all the good things of drinking, lost even from lust and savagery, from dirty ditties and bad humor, holding onto each other and walking slowly across the broad veranda of the Morris house. The rain had stopped; there was the ghost of a moon, and in the misty night a sentry paced back and forth over the sloping lawn. And Knox, glancing over his shoulder at the magnificent portico, thinking of the Tory owner, mouthed a foul imprecation.

Mifflin nodded in savage agreement.

The commander in chief was up a little before dawn, as was his custom, and he appeared rested and composed after the few hours' sleep he had had. He had dressed quietly and quickly, and now he sat at the breakfast table eating pancakes and honey and listening to Adjutant-General Reed, who was full to the neck with information gathered by a patrol sent to investigate the British movements. About Reed, a delicate, almost languorous young man of thirty-five, there was a certain feminine timidity—accented by his cameolike features and his large, violet eyes. He was possessed of a sensitivity that kept him in the background when other men suffered, as if he were afraid to test his own capacity for being hurt, and sometimes the Virginian felt that Reed feared him.

Thus, the day before, knowing that there was nothing he could do, Reed had done nothing, only watch the gathering ruin through half-closed eyes and cringe inside of himself and bite his full, round lips. Then, very early in the morning, when men stunned into absolute impotence the day before could think of nothing and therefore did nothing, he selected the most reliable body of men he could find and sent them out to discover just where the British were and what they intended to do.

This patrol was led by a man called Thomas Knowlton, a Yankee who had not been convinced at Brooklyn Heights that all Yankees were cowards. There he had been with a regiment of Connecticut troops, and not running away himself, he was amazed to find that a number of other men had stayed by him and duplicated his feat of not running away. One in particular, a Coventry schoolteacher called Nathan Hale, when questioned by Knowlton as to why he had stood absolutely motionless and uncovered in a rain of British grape, had answered, "Because there was no place to go—" and then added thoughtfully, "They don't know about a revolution. It's not a diversion. It's either the beginning or the end."

Knowlton was not certain that that made sense. He was a professional soldier more than a revolutionist; he had picked this side of the fight because he was a Yankee, because his one pride, after being clean-shaven, was to be his own master, and because the only time during his adult life he had been moved to tears was on seeing an old farmer, who had lost everything, go to work for someone else, losing his soul as his old feet moved him toward a means of existence. Knowlton's inclination toward freedom was not logical; he reacted like a vixen in a trap, who bites off her own leg to go back to her pups and her death. The only thing he thought of particularly was that if he got together a group of men who would not run away every time a gun was fired, they would be worth something. Spencer reluctantly gave him permission, and Knowlton formed a little patrol of sharpshooters with the twenty-one-year-old Hale and seventeen-year-old Morton and nineteen-year-old Lake as his captains. Nobody in the patrol was over thirty and most were under twenty, but even the children shared in one trait, that at Brooklyn, for some obscure reason, they had not run away.

This was the patrol which Reed had sent out to look

around and see where the British were. And now, sitting across the breakfast table from his commander, he pleaded his cause earnestly.

"Don't you see, sir," he said, "the redcoats know we are beaten, if you'll forgive me, but they know it, they know it!"

The big man looked at his handsome adjutant stonily. "I don't have to be reminded of that, Mr. Reed," he said.

"But that's the point, sir, that they know it! If we hit at them now, they go reeling back."

The big man shook his head listlessly, and in answer to his unspoken words, Reed cried, "But that was yesterday, sir! What good is yesterday?"

"It serves to remind us," the Virginian muttered.

"But we can fight!"

"No, Mr. Reed, we can't fight. We can't even run away—decently."

The adjutant spread his hands and admitted his defeat. "I'm sorry, sir. I was wrong; I concede it," he said. "But what about the patrol?"

"They will come back," the big man said dully. "They have legs to run with, so they will come back."

They rode down from the Morris house to the lines at the Hollow Way, where they met Mifflin, who glanced at Reed significantly. A little behind the Virginian, Reed spread his hands and shook his head helplessly.

For the tall farmer, today had ceased to exist. There were only memories and a compulsion that kept his body moving and performing certain necessary things. He was living in all that had come before this nightmare of senseless defeat; the years of his life had buckled together, and twenty years ago seemed like yesterday; the present was a long, heartbreaking pause, and there was no tomorrow. And out of his memories, jumbled and formless, came all sorts of things, good and bad, a time when a pointer puppy, loving with the infinite, unselfish love of a beast, had looked into his eyes as it became sick and died, leaving him with a grief so strangely full that it was not too different from what he had felt when his wife's daughter, Patsy, his own, beloved, darling Patsy, had died, setting her poor, sick mind at rest. Grief was not all bad; it could have a kinship with love. And he could remember now going to a neighbor's house where there were sixteen children, sixteen laughing, handsome healthy brats, frolicking around him and mixing grief with a love he could not bear, he who had never had a child of his own, forcing him to lock himself into one of the outbuildings and sit with his face in his hands, grieving not for sixteen children that could never be his, but for a nameless pointer puppy and a half-insane stepchild.

But this, all of this that had been yesterday and for three weeks before that, was not grief and not fear, but despair so numbing that it broke his pride.

Because it was better to move than to stay still, he had walked his horse through the front line of his entrenchments, through the spread of dirty New Englanders and midlanders and over the bottom of the Hollow Way. Reed and Mifflin followed him, afraid in their hearts of what he might do left alone and riding in the direction of the British. It was a bright, clean morning, cool and comfortable after the heavy rain of the night before, with the song of birds in the air, the crowing of cocks and the baying of hounds. A sharp wind blew across the Hudson from the Palisades and wound down the valley, tossing dry leaves and causing trees to sway gleefully.

They had started up the slope that led to Morningside Heights, when they heard the splutter of musket fire, sounding from what might have been a mile's distance. The big man stopped his horse and listened without any show of interest, but Reed spurred up and cried, "That's Knowlton's patrol, sir. They've made some contact, and now they can draw them on."

The big man didn't move. The sound, which once would have vitalized him with energy, left him undisturbed and uninterested, listening without hearing to Reed's proposals to draw the British into a trap, to reinforce the patrol Knowlton led. Reed talked and talked, while the musket fire continued, and then his voice died away and he looked at Mifflin's grim face for some sort of sympathy. Then the two of them sat on their horses in silence.

It was after the firing stopped that Reed said, "They'll be coming back now. But they made a fight of it, sir. You'll not deny that they made a fight of it. You could tell their shots from the volley fire."

Still the Virginian didn't move.

The first of Knowlton's men appeared through the brush and woods. They were not running, but walking backwards with measured steps, their pieces in their hands, without panic or haste or disorder. Some were wounded, limping along with their arms over comrades' shoulders, and others were carried. Knowlton himself appeared, huge, bear-like, grinning and waving at Reed until he noticed the commander in chief. The little patrol gathered itself together and began to move at a run to where the three generals sat.

And at that moment, a view-halloo came winging down from the heights.

It was the last, bitterest thrust. It cut into the Virginia foxhunter, because he knew it was meant for him; it sang merrily over the bright air, canting from a half-dozen trumpets:

> A hunting we will go,
> A hunting we will go,
> We'll catch a fox and put him in a box,
> And then we'll let him go.

For him, for the foxhunter, there was no need to see what was transpiring behind the screen of woods in the fields and meadows of Morningside Heights. The gentlemen, the bloods and snobs and macaronies, were having a game, a game inspired by their own delicate, rapier-like British sense of humor, a game measured to hit precisely what it was aimed at, a foxhunting backwoodsman, a provincial who in his own way had dared to consider himself something of a gentleman.

He would understand it, if no one else in the army did; he would know how precisely a snob can destroy a human being by refusing to admit the simple fact of his existence; he would know how they had destroyed his wretched mockery of revolution by turning it into a foxhunt, by gaily finishing it in a sporting fashion. He could picture them so clearly, riding along in the fine morning with their dragoons behind them, sniggering and prodding the winded trumpeters to keep sounding the view-halloo, knowing that he would hear it somewhere, somehow, calling to each other:

"Yoicks! Yoicks!"

He had leaped off his horse and had his big hand tangled in the jacket of the startled Knowlton. "Tell me, you Yankee bastard," he roared, "are you afraid?"

"By God, no, sir!"

"Not of me, not of them?"

"I'm not afraid of anything on God's green earth," Knowlton said coolly.

"Then tell me, could you lead a party down that valley to the left of here and scale the eastern side of the heights—and come in behind those—foxhunters?"

"I could try it," Knowlton grinned.

"Then try it, God damn you! Reed, go with him! Take a regiment, no, not Yankees—take Weedon's Virginia men and Major Leitch! And remember, behind them, not a foxhunt, a beartrap!"

Reed waited to hear no more; he was off, spurring his horse back to the lines to pick up the Virginians, while Knowlton mustered out his wounded. Meanwhile, the view-halloo had twisted down toward the Hudson.

The foxhunter turned on Mifflin and pointed toward where the gorge opened on the river. "I want a frontal attack in that direction," he said curtly.

"A frontal attack?" Mifflin asked stupidly.

"General, do I have to repeat a thing twenty times to get it into your head? I want a diversion; I want a few hundred of your filthy Yankees, if you can find that many to hold their guns and shoot them off, to advance on the southern slope. For at least a half hour; after that they can run away!"

Mifflin nodded and swung away; his emotions were a tangle of rage and joy.

Knowlton led his Connecticut men and Leitch his Virginians up the glacial outcroppings that frosted the eastern edge of Morningside Heights. They climbed silently and quickly, their heavy muskets slung over their shoulders where they had slings, or else thrust through holes torn in their shirts. So intent were they upon breasting the cliff that for the moment the Virginians and Yankees forgot their deep and mutual hatred. Knowlton was completely happy, understanding only vaguely the change that the taunting bugles had wrought in the foxhunter, but realizing nevertheless that the Virginian had passed through a moment of hell, realizing too that in their brief verbal exchange they had come as close to each other as men may who approach as strangers, exchange blows, and come off blood brothers.

Knowlton's was not a deep nor an intricate nature. He was neither an intellectual nor a revolutionary, but a man who loved action and excitement and the comradeship that went with a camp. He had wanted to get into the fight that had been brewing for so many years, and as a result he was here; and it satisfied him somewhat to believe that he was on the right side. He hadn't thought it out in detail, and he was content to take the word of men who could spin a feeling into a reasoned argument. He was fighting on the side of freedom because to him freedom was bald and simple; it was the opposite of being put in jail, chained down and bound around.

He and Reed had not begun their climb far enough south of the Hollow Way; instead of coming in behind the British, they topped the cliff and blundered square into the flank of a column of green-clad Hessians, cautiously feeling their way toward the American lines.

A German officer happened to be looking at the cliff-edge when Major Leitch placed both palms on a rock and cautiously drew himself up to ground level.

"Was ist das?" the German cried.

Leitch roared like a trapped bull. Knowlton vaulted up beside him, and the Virginia and Connecticut men followed, cutting hands and faces on the rocks in their mad haste to reach the top.

The cry, "Yonkee, Yonkee!" was running down the line of Jagers. An officer spurred up on his horse and yelled:

"An die Gewehre!"

Precise as dolls hung on strings, the Germans halted, presented arms, and revolved into a wide formation. Still roaring, Leitch raised his pistol, aimed at the officer who had first seen him, and shot the Hessian through the heart.

"Legt an!" the man on horseback cried.

The line of muskets drooped, like wet wheat in a strong wind.

"Feuer!"

The blaze of musketry crashed into the faces of the Americans. Three bullets, two in the belly and one in the hip, stilled Major Leitch's roaring; he rolled on his face and groaned and bled out his life. Knowlton, waving at his men, shouting, trying by the motions of the long arms to pull them over the cliff, received a round musket ball full in the temple. Reed caught him as he fell.

"Legt an!" the order came again.

Still the Americans fought at the rocky ledge.

"Feuer!"

There was no breasting that storm of shot. With insane stubbornness, the Americans clung to the ledge, but they could not climb over onto the heights. They laid their muskets on the rock and discharged them, and then, clinging to the cliff surface like goats, tried to reload. It was entirely hopeless.

Reed backed down, supporting the great weight of the dying Knowlton, and with the aid of two of his Connecticut Rangers laid him down on a sheltered ledge of rock. In all the noise of the skirmish, Reed had to bend very low to hear what Knowlton was trying to say. It was something about the foxhunter, and pointing to the ledge, Knowlton said, "Tell him—because I was wounded, I had to stop here. Tell him I wasn't afraid—"

Mifflin ordered Lieutenant-Colonel Crary to take about two hundred Massachusetts Yankees and create a diversion. When the men were told off, Mifflin strode across their loose line and said to them, "You don't have to fight, there's no guts in you for that. But for one hour you're going to stand up on that hill across the valley, and so help me God, I'll kill the first man who runs away."

They stared at him sullenly and made no answer; their homespun shirts blew loosely in the wind.

"March!" Mifflin said.

They started off across the valley bottom, walking first, then beginning to run. The foxhunter, spurring down on Mifflin, demanded to know why they were running.

"I don't know, sir," Mifflin said uneasily.

They pressed into the woods, and until they reached the top, Mifflin could see their shirts, spots of white in the green. They passed over the top, and a moment later a crackle of musket fire broke out.

"There is your diversion, sir," Mifflin said.

The big man waited for them to come back; he waited for them to come pouring down the slope as fast as their legs would carry them. He looked over his shoulder, and saw that all along the line of entrenchments thousands of the dirty, beaten Yankees were standing up and listening to the musketry.

The firing went on, and Mifflin said softly and incredulously, "Oh, my God, they're holding."

The Virginian stared at the slope that should have been full of fleeing men, but was strangely empty.

"They're holding, sir," Mifflin repeated.

"Damn you, Mifflin, don't you think I have ears and eyes! Get out of here! Take a regiment and reinforce them!"

Himself, he drove up the slope. Mifflin was calling after him to return, not to go into it alone, but he plunged his horse on through the trees, onto the heights until he came to where a thin, stubborn line of New Englanders crouched behind a stone wall. They had already beaten off a charge of dragoons, and now they mutely faced a smart column of light infantry that was marching down on them, still about four hundred yards away.

He pulled in his horse just behind them and stared at the Yankees as though they were men from another world. In the meadow beyond the wall, two dragoons lay in the deep grass, and the rancid smell of gunpowder still lingered on the air. The Yankees turned to look at him, but only a few officers saluted; they didn't cheer at the sight of the commander. And he, on his part, gave no orders and said nothing.

The light infantry came nearer, their regimental battle flags waving, their drums playing briskly. They were only a hundred yards away and still no shot had been fired, when Mifflin came hurrying up with the regiment. With him was Greene, still deathly pale from his long sickness, but with burning eyes.

"Putnam's coming up with another five hundred, sir," he called.

There was a crashing sound further back, and glancing over his shoulder the big man saw Knox and young Hamilton, straddling a two-horse team that dragged one of their light field pieces. And in front of him, the Yankees, seeing the reinforcements come running toward them, scrambled over the stone wall and charged the British infantry. There was no order, no formation, no method, only hundreds of yelling, screaming New Englanders swarming down on the British, firing, clubbing their muskets, clawing at the bayonets with their bare hands, laughing, sobbing and dying—and forcing the British back.

The Virginian followed them into it; he yelled the way they yelled; he sobbed and laughed; he knew this was no fight according to military standards and he didn't care; he cared only that he led men willing to fight. He roared at Mifflin to hurry Putnam and the five hundred. He sent an aide flying to Knox to see if he could wheel his cannon out to their flank and rake the British. And a moment later he sent another aide racing after Mifflin with orders to bring up not only Putnam's five hundred, but five hundred more deployed in a wide skirmish line to protect his raving mad Massachusetts men from encirclement.

Meanwhile, the single column of British light infantry, who had expected no opposition whatever, whose intention had been only to feel out the Continental line, found itself vastly outnumbered and reeling back before what seemed to be a screaming mob of lunatics. It gave back and back, and the Yankees, seeing for the first time British regulars giving them ground in the open field, went completely berserk. They forgot that guns were made to be fired, using them instead as clubs, using their hands and feet and rocks, rushing, smashing with their heads and shoulders, kicking, clawing. Yet the British held their close order, unable to reload yet presenting always the glittering points of their bayonets.

They had retreated almost a mile before the Yankees, when the Hessians, having put a finish to Reed's disastrous attempt to flank them and attack in the rear, swung westward and struck the American flank. At the same moment, a battery of artillery opened on the other flank with grape; and two columns of redcoats, drawn by the firing, came up at double-quick to support the light infantry.

The Yankees gave back, their whole front torn and mangled, but they didn't run away. They walked backwards, clubbing, striking, cursing, carrying their wounded, clinging to each inch of ground until they were again at the lip of the Hollow Way; and then screamed in derision as the British refused to follow them down into the valley and chance a frontal attack on the American lines.

They had been beaten, but they hadn't run; they had held onto their guns and kept their faces to the enemy; and they were as proud as the foxhunter who sat on his horse again as straight as a ramrod, his heart choking so that he couldn't say a word to the grinning boys pressed around him.

Part Three

---◦⊰{ WESTCHESTER }⊱◦---

9 🏴🏴🏴🏴🏴🏴🏴🏴🏴🏴🏴

LET FREEDOM RING

Within a few hours after the British occupied the city, New York had cast off whatever faint affection it had at one time held for the revolutionists. A stranger might have remarked that there was something like a contest raging among the good citizens as to who had despised the rebels most. Certainly the wealthier citizens vied desperately in the sending out of dinner invitations to the officers of the various British regiments. It was a great and desired honor to net a general, a good deal to net a colonel or a major, and young captains and subalterns were by no means to be sneezed at. And in their feelings, the good families of New York were quite sincere; from the beginning they had known precisely on what side their bread was buttered.

That went for the aristocracy and the wealthy; the middle classes breathed a sigh of relief and felt that now they could unlock their shops and take down their shutters. For them, the occupation meant stability; it meant that they could resume business as usual, not on promises to pay and worthless paper money, but for good, solid, shining gold. It meant that in the thousands of British troops and sailors, they would have valuable customers, and it meant that perhaps, in the Port of New York at least, overseas trade would be resumed under the protection of British guns.

In fact, hardly anyone at all felt anything but joy or relief in the fact of the British occupation. New York was overflowing with a worthless scum that had trickled into the city from all the surrounding countryside, men who had never done an honest day's work in their lives, who had attached themselves to the revolutionists until it appeared that the Yankees might have to fight, and women who plied the oldest trade. Of these last, there was truly an amazing number in the city, literally thousands, ranging in age from girls in their teens to toothless old crones, and ranging in appearance from beauty to ghastliness. Where they had come from, no one knew; it seemed incredible that the thin fringe of settlement could have supplied so many ladies of shady repute. When the Yankees had occupied the city, these ladies were an unabashed raggle-taggle worthy of the New England rabble; but now that the British were here, they blossomed out in an amazing display of finery. They strutted all over the narrow, twisting streets, displaying their features and silks and whispering their prices into the ears of any and every redcoat, German, or Highlander they met. And the good burghers tolerated them and were even glad of their presence, for they were a sort of a certification against rape of decent women, the citizens saying, "Who will pick the forbidden fruit when apples grow everywhere?"

In the weeks following the British landing, the city took on a holiday appearance; there were dinners and balls and more dinners and parties and dances and receptions. Not only among the ladies who sold their charms, but among the so-called honest citizens the female outnumbered the male. Men of substance had taken themselves to Canada and England, many of them leaving their families behind, and the younger bloods, hating the revolutionary upstarts as only one American could hate another, had hied themselves to Westchester to join the forces of a certain Robert Rogers. This Robert Rogers was a cold, calculating, and strangely cruel soldier of fortune, who had already, some years before, made a name of blood and brutality with his Rogers' Rangers.

Robert Rogers had made a reputation out of his complete

contempt for the human species. For him no cause had any more to recommend than its strength, and his belief that might makes right was not intellectual but purely physical. Loving nobody, not even himself, he despised the rabble who had taken it upon themselves to remake their small part of the world. His life had been like the path of a burning ball, leaving a wake of death and misery, but after many years of defeats and misfortunes he was at last coming into his own as the leader of the young Tories of New York and Westchester. As yet, he had no more than a nuisance value, hanging on the fringe of the American army, cutting out sentries, catching deserters and facetiously lynching them, developing and refining the delicate arts he had learned from the Indians and from the Corsairs of North Africa with whom he had had a good deal of experience.

New York City had given both ways. Young men, the sons of tradesmen and workers, had alienated their fathers and broken their mothers' hearts by dealing with a flimsy, foolish underground organization called The Sons of Liberty. When it came to action instead of words, many of them had joined an artillery company led by a West Indian boy named Alexander Hamilton. Now they too were gone, and they and the bloods had been replaced by the British and an infiltration of worthless, illiterate tramps.

Among the few in New York who did not welcome the British were the Jews—who saw their hopes and dreams flee with the tattered Yankees. Instinctively, they had cast their whole fortune with the revolution. Every Jew able to bear arms had joined the insurgent army; their emotional impulse had caused them to speak out violently, and once they had crossed the bridge, they had destroyed it behind them. They had left no way back; they had filled their synagogues with wounded and their parlors with plots, and they had given their cash with the impulse of a gambler who plays one card to win or lose all. Now their youth had gone away with the Yankees, except for those who lay in their cellars moaning with gangrenous wounds.

This was not a new situation for them; it echoed and re-echoed back through all the long, dusty hall of history. The women sat in their houses, behind locked doors and barred shutters, weeping quietly, shedding the only tears that were shed in New York for the defeated and the dishonored, and the old men gathered in the synagogue to pray that this, the last retreat of the exiled, might still retain some hope for a promised land. Only one, a consumptive Polish-Jewish immigrant called Haym Salomon, a frail, thin man, too weak to bear arms and therefore left behind, bared his teeth as he addressed a group of desperate plotters in the cellar of his house, coughed blood, and swore to God that this was only the beginning.

In this New York, in the early evening of September 20, 1776, a young man wandered from street to street, his progress quite aimless. His suit of plain brown homespun was patched at elbow, knee, and seat, and his old round hat had the flat brim that was then much in favor with up-country folk. He was very young, only twenty-one, and his clear blue eyes and red cheeks made him appear even younger. He had the ambling, slightly hesitant gait that country people so often assume when they are in an unfamiliar city, and his whole attitude was that of an innocuous sight-seer.

When he saw a redcoat, he gawked and grinned, and once he picked up a rusty Yankee bayonet and tested its blunt edge with a curious finger. His steps took him everywhere and nowhere, from the East River slips to the old fishing shacks along the Hudson, and from the uptown Dutch windmills to the smooth sward of Bowling Green. On Bowling Green, the British had ranged a battery of sixteen-pound carronades, and in these the young man took an almost childish interest. He edged closer and closer, until he was able to touch their cold surface with his hand.

"'Ere, now," the sentry said. "None of that."

"They're wonderful big guns," the young man remarked.

"Well, I seen plenty bigger. Now, get along, get along!"

He was found loitering next to a rambling warehouse that the British had converted into a military storeroom, and he was soundly cursed and sent on his way.

Uptown, a few blocks north of Wall Street, he was stopped by a patrol and questioned as to who he was and what business he had in the streets of New York after dark.

"I came down out of the Jerseys," he told the sergeant blandly. "I was looking to join up with Major Rogers."

"And what dirty ragback in New York ain't looking to join up with Major Rogers?"

The boy shrugged.

"Now get off the streets and mind your business, or you'll do your joining in gaol," the sergeant warned him.

After that, he stayed in the darker alleys and bolted like a rabbit when he saw the lantern of a patrol coming. He was very tired, having slept only a few hours in the past three days, but he didn't care to go to any of the inns or public houses; there was just a faint chance that someone might recognize him. As the evening wore on and his weariness increased, he thought of going to a Jew's house, throwing himself on the mercy of the owner, and begging a bed and shelter. But the first house he chose was empty and desolate, with a redcoat sentry in front of the door, and then he felt that approaching another would be like thrusting his hand into a hornets' nest.

Again and again during that evening he had been stopped by ladies of the street, to all of whom he gave the same answer, "I have no money." But now, halted by one and mumbling the same words, he found his arm caught and held.

"Don't go away," she said.

Just that slight pressure on his arm made him feel like an animal in a trap and showed him on what thin threads his nerves were strung. He wrenched away, turning to look at her as he did, seeing a dark-eyed, slim girl, heavily and vulgarly painted, wearing a torn lacy gown and a green hat with a bedraggled feather drooping over her shoulder.

"What are you afraid of?" she grinned.

"Nothing. I haven't any money."

"I didn't ask you for money." She was looking at his handsome boyish face with frank admiration. She faced him and the world with cocky defiance, her arms akimbo, her little chin tilted up. "You're a Yankee, ain't you?" she demanded.

"No—"

"Well, what are you afraid of? I ain't a bloody lobster." He started to walk away, but she skipped after him and took his arm again. "What are you afraid of? I know you're a Yankee. I seen you before when the army was here."

He turned slowly and looked at her with such dumb desperation that she recoiled in fright. He took hold of her wrist and held it so tightly that she gave quick little animal gasps of pain. And then he saw her eyes go wider as she looked past his shoulder.

"Oh, let go! There's a patrol."

He glanced quickly, saw the bubble of light, and bolted. He heard her running after him, and when he came to the end of the street found his way blocked again by another swaying lantern. Caught between the two, his senses bat-

tered at the blank walls of the dark little alley, his body
fought for knowledge, and his feet munched the ground
hopelessly, until wakening to her grasp on his hand he followed her into a crevice, a hole solid with darkness, through
a door and into darkness beyond, standing close to her after
the door had closed and listening to her panting breath.

"There, now," she whispered. "You're strong—my whole
hand hurts."

He giggled nervously in the darkness. The pressure of
her warm body against his thigh and chest upset him, and
now that he couldn't see her, only smell the strong per-
fumes she had poured onto her hair and clothes, he could
feel gratitude for her refuge and offer his thanks to something other than the painted tart who had accosted him on
the street.

"I got flints. You want a light?" she asked him.

"No."

The reply was too quick and too definite; he felt her body
stiffen, and for the first time in his young manhood he
sensed the unseen, indefinable effusion of hurt. He faltered,
found his pride and background, and remembered what she
was; he remembered sermons in a white clapboard church
where sinful women were described simply and certainly,
the devil behind them and hell in front of them; and he
repeated, "I haven't any money." And then he was glad he
couldn't see her face.

She took his hand and led him across the room and told
him to sit down. The hard, straw-filled bolster whispered
under her weight, but she was not near him now. He sat
awkwardly and stiffly, his back straight and his hands
clasped, but weariness was returning and the mere fact of a
bed made him long for sleep.

"What's your name?" she asked him.

"Nathan Hale."

"Are you a rebel?"

"Yes." There was no more need for concealment; somewhere, his Yankee shell had been broken.

"You run away from the army?" she asked him.

"No."

"I could have let them lobsters get you," she complained
plaintively, for the moment her voice emerging from the
darkness a little girl's voice. "All you Yankees care about is
money—all you tell me is that you got no money. I don't
care."

"I want to thank you for taking me in here," he said carefully and precisely. He felt large and strong and important, and more a man than he ever had before in his twenty-one years. But she didn't answer him, and after a moment or two, he realized that she was crying, the noise in the dark like the purring of a lonely cat. He sat uneasily for a while and then fumbled clumsily for her, touching a warm arm and then a soft breast, drawing back, excited and tired, fighting his own silent struggle with sin. He had to force himself to speak, and his lips were dry as he asked her name.

"Helen," she said.

"Well, don't cry," he told her.

"I'm not crying. You can stay here until they go away, if you want to."

He nodded, forgetting that in the darkness his every action was hidden from her, and then sat still, half-dozing until he felt her hand touch his sleeve.

"How old are you?" she asked.

"Twenty-one."

"I'm eighteen," she said. "Are you married?"

"No."

"You got a girl you bundle with?" she inquired simply.

Again the darkness prevented her from seeing the reaction on his face. The straw rustled as she moved closer to him, and her fingers tightened on the homespun, feeling for the flesh of his arm.

"Where you from?" she wanted to know.

"Coventry, Connecticut." He was half asleep, his hardly overcome passion making his weariness lascivious and as sweetly heady as wine, and as he spoke his lips barely moved, his voice a whisper.

"Lie down," she said, pushing him back, and he allowed himself to yield, drawing his feet up on the rustling straw. She sat beside him and stroked his round cheeks, while he lay in delicious comfort, mechanically answering her questions as he drifted into sleep, once protesting that he would dirty her bed with his mud-stained clothes.

"That's nothing," she laughed, and he let her take off his shoes. "I never been to Connecticut," she said. "Is it pretty,"

"I hardly remember," he whispered.

"You a farmer?" she wanted to know.

"Schoolteacher."

"Never! No!" A note of deep and sincere reverence crept into her voice. "Real? For sure?"

"For sure. I went to Yale College," he added, not wondering, in his drowsiness, why he should want to impress this little harlot with that.

"Never!" And then she confessed, "I can't read."

He giggled sleepily.

"I can't even read," she repeated, in a tone that one would confess to God an inability to create worlds and fling them out into space.

In the cellar of his house, in candlelight that gave him the appearance of a shrunken-limbed imp, the consumptive little Jew, Haym Salomon, plotted and pleaded and coughed into a cambric handkerchief. With him were a Scotch riverman, a fat Dutch shopkeeper, a wounded Pole who spoke almost no English, and the aging but fiery-eyed beadle of the synagogue. It was a terrible and desperate thing that Salomon was nerving himself and the others to do, and they had been arguing about it since early in the afternoon; now, only a few hours before midnight, they were worn out but still had arrived at no conclusion.

They sat in silence and stared at each other out of red-rimmed eyes. They knew that soon, very soon, they would have to come to a decision, one way or another; but in this pause they were able to form the first vivid and complete picture of what their plans meant. Here was a city, New York, the key to America, the finest harbor, the best anchorage; here was food and shelter and comfort, and here was the enemy. Here was the snug nest, unapproachable by land, but capable of being defended almost forever by Britain's powerful navy; here was a poisoned thorn stuck into the side of America that would make the land twist with agony whatever else happened.

There was one way out, a way that Washington had foreseen long since, but which Congress had forbidden, a way that every practical military observer in the colonies had known was the only way. An ulcerous sore which cannot be healed must be gouged out; New York must be destroyed, burned, left a heap of smoking cinders that would give comfort neither to the Tory partisans nor to the British and German invaders. If innocent people must suffer, then that was simply the price one had to pay for revolution. Revolution was not a game; it was a one-way road with inferno raging behind the men who traveled it.

"And you can't look back," Salomon broke the silence.

The Dutch shopkeeper shook his head stubbornly. "Destruction does not make a solution," he said with his thick accent.

"You can't look back," Salomon insisted.

It was a little after midnight that Nathan Hale awoke, groped through his first sensation of blindness in the pitch-black room, rolled over on the straw, and remembered how he had come to the place. His recollection of the girl, immersed as it was in darkness, was fuzzy. He could not re-create through the pitch. Fumbling, moving his stocking feet across the floor, he found his shoes, put them on, and stumbled toward where he thought the door to be, possessed by an urgent need to be out of the place and into the fresh air.

Not until he had opened the door and allowed the silvery starlight to stream in, was he able to make out anything of the place where he had slept, the windowless cube of the room, the bed, a chair, and a blob in one corner which let him know in a rush of shame and misery that the girl had not shared his bed, but had given him in his god-like elevation the place of comfort and honor. He did not have the courage to go back and wake her; instead he stumbled down the street, his Yankee shell of sufficiency and right shattered in many places. He walked on and on, the short sleep serving only to accentuate the aches in his tired body, and he had come at least six or seven blocks from the harlot's house before he realized that New York City was beginning to burn.

At first the licking tendrils of flame were so unreal that their impact was meaningless, and not until the streets were full of hurrying, shouting citizens did he realize the full significance of the fire. Then he too ran along with the others, propelled by the instinctive knowledge that where the press was thickest and where the excitement was greatest his most certain safety lay. Not alone that; he was boy enough to love the fury of a fire and be caught up in all the futile, senseless gestures of the volunteer fireman; and this, with the colorful army uniforms, the screeching harlots, the booming alarm cannons and the wildly yelling citizens, was more colorful than any of the tiny blazes that had brought rare moments of action to Coventry. In common with all Americans in that time of small towns and primitive fire-fighting methods, he was convinced of the omnipotence of any fair-sized blaze, and only opposed it because that was the one emotional outlet of a person attending the catastrophe.

By now the old Dutch houses were going up like the tinderboxes they were, and the crackle of flames and the sound of falling rafters and walls was like the noise from a battlefield. Night was turned into day, and to Hale the brightly illuminated streets, packed with night-shirted citizens and British redcoats trying desperately to clear a path for the hand-pumps, were wonderfully reminiscent of those vague pictures he had garnered from his study of ancient history; and he thought to himself, in a sudden thrill of elation, that this was as surely the end of an era as the burning of Rome while Nero fiddled. In that moment of incendiary glory and crazy excitement, he forgot the punishing and bitter defeats of his comrades and thought only of how puny and helpless the British were while their conquered city burned.

At that moment, some miles to the north, Robert Harrison had dragged the Virginian from a sound slumber to a window that faced the glowing southern sky. For a while, the two men stood there, still not fully awake, speculating upon what might have caused that wonderful, unearthly glow. Harrison decided, as calmly as he could, "I would say, sir, from all indications, that New York is on fire. Certainly nothing within our own lines could make a glow of such proportions." And then he cast a quick, keen, sidewise glance at the Virginian, to see whether the expression on the long face might denote joy or elation or disappointment. But the commander's features were incredibly placid, and all he said was, "Please see that my horse is saddled, Mr. Harrison."

As he rode south, the big man noticed that the glow was increasing, until by the time he approached Harlem the southern sky was filled with a sunburst of glory and fire. At first he had considered that perhaps a single large house was on fire or that one of the enemy ships in the river had been set alight, but now he realized that nothing less than a whole city in flames could brighten the sky in such a fashion. Thrilled and elated as he was by this almost miraculous accomplishment of all he had dreamed of doing and—held helpless by a timid Congress—been unable to do, he nevertheless determined to make no gesture nor action until he had accurate information about what had happened.

In a clearing on a hill to the north of the Hollow Way, he dismounted, and there one by one the members of his staff joined him. Knox, Putnam, Mifflin, Spencer, Silliman, Greene, Reed, Smallwood, and perhaps a dozen others. They stood in a close, silent group, the most verbose of them speechless in the presence of this awful and wonderful destruction. A few of them were religious men, most were freethinkers, and some were atheists, but the least believing of them felt the awe and solemnness of the occasion.

For hours they stood and watched, until the star-speckled sky haloing the fire, turned into grey mist, and the bright morning sun transformed strange terror into mere actuality.

When Nathan Hale remembered the painted little tart, who had given him shelter in a hard-pressed moment, it was too late; and when he tried desperately to find the miserable alley where she possessed a windowless cubbyhole, a bed and chair that made a home, he found himself confronted everywhere by a wall of raging fire. He ran and stumbled and bruised himself and thrust through crowds and shouldered redcoats aside; but always the laughing flames were ahead of him.

He came away, finally, hating the city and all it contained, telling himself, "I'll go back now. I've been here long enough, and I know all that I'll ever know. They wouldn't want me to stay here any longer."

He walked north, away from the fire and the crowds, but he was very tired, and when he saw a shed with some hay in it, he burrowed into the hay and fell asleep; he fell asleep easily and quickly, out of pure exhaustion.

In the morning, when he awoke, the fire still burned, closer to him than before, not so impressive in daylight, but more ominous in its crackling insistence. He cleared the hay from his hair and clothes, endured some scathing remarks from the owner of the shed, who saw him emerge, drank some water from a trough where he doused his head and face, rubbing off the soot, and continued his progress north.

Now he no longer saw the excited, half-crazy crowds of the night before; people were calmer and more deadly; the damage had been done, and they were searching for some sort of vengeance. The flames could not be stopped, but there were still rebels and rebels could be made to suffer. Once he saw a screaming wretch dragged by at the end of a noose, again he saw a bearded old Jew lying dead in the street.

As he came to the outskirts of the city, he went more cautiously, but it took him only a little while to realize that redcoat patrols were on every road and path. Again and again, he attempted to make his way north out of New York, and again and again he had to double back on his own tracks; he was beginning to feel like a trapped beast, nervous, sweating, his eyes red and tearful from the smoke. Once he had to run for it, leaping stone walls and finding refuge for the moment in a chicken house among the cackling hens. He left there and crawled along a fence, burrowed through a briar patch and found a moment's peace in a bit of woods. He found a little brook, lay down on his stomach, and drank until he could hold no more. He went cautiously through an apple orchard, edging from tree to tree, until he came to the fringe of a broad meadow. The highroad ran about a quarter mile to his left, and on it he could see the crimson blob of a patrol. To the north were woods and shelter, shelter that might continue all the distance to the Hollow Way. Stooping low, he began to run across the meadow.

He was almost across it when the patrol sighted him and let go with their clumsy muskets. He twisted away and saw redcoats at the edge of the woods; he ran to the right and then saw the green of Hessians cutting off escape in that direction.

He doubled back and saw four dragoons driving their horses straight at him.

His coat torn, a long gash across one pink cheek, his full lips trembling just a little, he stood in General Howe's headquarters and faced Major Rudly Clare and stared at Major Clare's blinking, somewhat bored lashes. Major Clare sat behind a table on which were spread pieces of paper scribbled over with notes and bits of rude map-making. In a tone as bored as his glance, Major Clare said, "You don't deny having written these?"

"No, sir. They were found on me."

"You write an excellent hand."

There was a shade of wistful pride in the boy's voice as he said, "I'm a graduate of Yale College, bachelor of arts, sir."

"Really? I'm an admirer of your provincial centers of learning. What's your name?"

"Captain Nathan Hale."

"Never mind the title. What regiment?"

"Colonel Knowlton's Connecticut Rangers, sir."

"Rangers—oh, my aunt, what a bloody variety of services you beggars have! And where is your regiment now?"

"I couldn't say, sir."

"You couldn't say!" The major's voice betrayed a shade of impatience. "Damn it all, boy, you're a spy—don't you understand?"

The boy nodded, his bright blue eyes creasing with sudden realization.

"Damn it all," the major said, "these papers—civilian clothes, at the fire—"

"We have no uniforms," the boy said helplessly. "We none of us have uniforms."

The major fingered the papers for a moment or so, and then said to the sergeant standing beside him, "Take him out to Cunningham and have him hanged in the morning."

The sky was so blue the next morning, and the wind was blowing and the birds singing, and the grass green and crunchy, and the maple leaves turning their wonderful nutty crimson. And in the crowd that had gathered to watch the hanging, there was hardly anyone who didn't remark on the perfect weather, for in the fall the weather in New York can be like the weather nowhere else in the world, with the strong wind traveling from over the Palisades, making little whitecaps on the Hudson, with all the scent and smell of a million miles westward sighing down on the queen of cities.

When he came out, to the rumble of muffled drums, he had only one prayer, one single prayer to God to give him the strength not to be afraid, not to be a part of all the fear he remembered, the fear that had sent them running from Brooklyn, running from New York, the fear that had robbed them of dignity and glory and beauty, the fear that let little girls sell themselves and become tarts, the fear that made free men speaking his own tongue sail across three thousand miles of sea to take away his and his comrades' dreams, the fear that built stony shells of retreat for all his kind. So he clenched his hands, bottled his heartsickness inside of him, and walked across the greensward.

He looked like a child, with his red cheeks, his blue eyes, and his sandy hair, and he was woefully, pathetically

brave, trying to smile, trying not to think of the little bit
he had lived, the one woman who had offered herself to
him and been refused, his mother and his father and all the
gawking faces of the Coventry rustics when he had walked
away to war, trying not to realize that this was the last part
of fresh air, blue sky, green grass.

And then, in the end, the whole thing broke down, and
he knew only that he wanted to live, to go back to the
warm embrace of the others, the poor, ragged devils who
were making a terrible and wonderful and mysterious thing
called revolution.

But they didn't know, the good citizens of New York who
stood and watched a red-cheeked boy with a tremulous
smile on his face, standing and waiting to be hanged.

10 🏴 🏴 🏴 🏴 🏴 🏴 🏴 🏴 🏴 🏴

HOW THE FISHERMEN
WERE NOT AFRAID

Like a flaming meteor out of the south, General Charles Lee
descended upon the beaten army that crouched on the lip of
the Hollow Way. For days and weeks, his coming had been
anticipated; the New Englanders nodded wisely and agreed
with the Southerners upon this point, that as a soldier and
a leader, Mr. Lee had everything the Virginia foxhunter
lacked. They pointed to the manner in which he had re-
pulsed a British attack on Charlestown; they read aloud his
military prognostications; they wrote his strategy in the sand;
they exalted his courage; they praised his cunning. The
most miserable, loutish, craven Yankee in the revolutionary
rabble protested stoutly that he would have been the best
soldier in the world if only General Lee had been there to
lead him. Already they had pushed every bit of blame,
every single mistake onto the bony shoulders of the foxhunter; now they speculated upon how differently everything would have gone had only General Lee been in the
saddle.

And in great measure, the foxhunter agreed with them,
for deep in his own heart he knew only too well that as a
military man Charles Lee was everything that he, George

Washington, was not. His reverence for Lee was deep and sincere and unselfish, the same reverence he had held, a long time ago, for his wonderful brother, Lawrence Washington—for Lawrence had been all that he was not and all that he held so dear—graceful, charming, courtly, a leader of men and a fantastic adventurer; and that was the reverence the Virginia squire had for all the world's great and brilliant men, who moved ahead without doubts and fears. Constantly, in those trying days, he had written to Lee, telling him of this and that, hanging on to his replies as pearls of wisdom. And every letter from Lee only served to convince him of his own unworthiness and Lee's superiority.

And now, at last, Lee was coming here to Harlem.

It didn't matter that some of those who would follow the Virginian into hell did not share his opinion of Charles Lee, that Knox fairly bubbled with dislike of Lee, that Putnam sneered openly, that Greene said he would trust Lee with anything that was nailed down but with nothing that was not, that Reed mentioned certain other factors at Charlestown as having more to do with the repulse of the British than General Lee. They could not shake Washington's faith, the more so since he realized that their own regard for him was shaped by anything but military factors.

When Charles Lee strode into the encampment on Harlem Heights, those of the army of liberty who had never before seen him were more than a little astonished at his appearance and at the dozen dogs that yapped at his heels. They were all of them dog masters, owners of one dog, even two dogs, and some few the possessors of hunt packs; but for a general on campaign to be followed by a howling dozen—that was too much. You could hardly hear the man speak for the uproar which his dogs made when anyone approached him.

His appearance, too, was very unusual; he was tall and fantastically skinny, not in the way of Washington, with big, fleshless bones that could hide themselves under a uniform coat, but thin as a reed, narrow and long, narrow sloping shoulders, no hips, tendril hands, a long nose, a small mouth, and almost no chin at all. He spoke in a high-pitched voice, blinking his eyes rapidly and affecting the English "Beau Nash" drawl. Another British affectation was his habit of seeing only what he wanted to see, whether the object was a hundred yards away or right under his nose.

. For all his unusual, almost out-of-the-world appearance, Lee was a good soldier, a far more experienced soldier than anyone else in the American army. He was that strange thing, a man born into battle; and in all his forty-five years he had never known any other life than that of the army. He was a soldier in the same fashion that one man is a painter and another a butcher. He did not and never had fought for a cause or a reason or an impulse, nor to inflict wrong, nor to right a wrong. He fought because soldiering was his trade, and while he didn't always sell himself to the highest bidder, having an eye to glory and advancement, he certainly never let ideological purposes influence him.

He liked to boast that he held a commission in the British army at the age of eleven, and possibly it was true. He was the English-born son of an officer, and he had no memories that were not of army life. He had fought in almost every corner of the globe, in America during the French War, in Portugal, in Poland, anywhere and everywhere there was a market for a sword or a gun. When he turned to America once more and was offered a position second only to the commander in chief, he demanded a thirty-thousand-dollar guarantee before he would accept. His price was high, but trained soldiers who were also English gentlemen did not grow on every tree; and therefore his bid was accepted—with the feeling among most people that at thirty thousand dollars here was a better bargain than the fox-hunter, who came without price and even with the understanding that there would be no payment.

Admire him they did, in the way the midland bumpkins and the nasal-voiced New England rustics admired anyone who came from the old country, not as an immigrant, but as a free soldier of fortune; but like him even they could not. God knew, they boasted enough. They had to cry out loud to reassure themselves, spread thin as they were on the edge of nowhere; but their boasting was nothing compared to the drawling value Charles Lee put on himself. His price was thirty thousand dollars, and he made sure that no one would undervalue him.

He approved of the Morris house, where the foxhunter had had his headquarters these past weeks; he filled his pocket with fat black cigars from the humidor and lashed the placid Billy with contempt, his attitude toward Negroes learned and overlearned during his Southern stay. He kicked the turf of the lawn—which the Virginian treasured and preserved in its soft green beauty—and let his howling dogs into the lovely Chippendale parlor. At the table, in the cool, chaste dining room, he fed his dogs along with himself, and told jokes so filthy that they offended even the ears of his fellow officers, men bred and raised on very strong meat, as stories and songs went. And the Virginian bore it all tolerantly, even gladly.

Lee had not been at headquarters more than two hours before he demanded a council of war, telling Washington exactly which men, in his opinion, should attend. The officers came without eagerness, filing into the shadowy dining room of the Morris house, taken aback by Lee's sprawling presence in the commander's seat at the head of the table. When the Madeira was poured, Lee proposed the toasts; when the discussion was opened, Lee took it and held it.

Sitting almost motionless during the discussion, which waxed high and then waned, heated and then slowed, calmer, bitter in the memories it evoked, Washington retreated deeper and deeper into the shadows thrown by the candles, not moving, but effacing himself none the less.

Lee's first words were a comment on the insanity of their position. He put into corrosive expression what most of them had been thinking for months, that without a powerful navy the defense of New York was utterly hopeless. Viciously and barely, he drew a picture of what would have happened to the miserable little army had the British only followed a course that any sane commander would plot. He was certain on that score; for him, war was a science; and his contempt for the British and their methods was as obvious as his confidence in his own. But that very fact turned the officers present against him.

"Damn it all!" he cried. "We must get out! There's no other way to it. It's a filthy, bloody trap, and if those marvelously stupid lobsters only had the sense to put a ship up the river and turn its guns into Kingsbridge, we'd be here until hell froze over."

They knew he was right, and for that reason they snarled at him.

"We held them for weeks," Putnam growled.

"Why don't they take the Hollow Way if it's that simple?" Reed wanted to know.

And Greene pointed out, "There's no way in the world to take Fort Washington. Ten men and a battery could hold it until your hell freezes over."

"Oh, you bloody fools!" Lee drawled. "Ten soldiers could drive your New England stench out of it in an hour."

They wrangled; they almost came to blows, shaking the frail table; they spoke of duels and challenges; they called each other names: and through it all the big man sat without speaking, without voicing any opinion. Lee didn't know them; they were not like any soldiers he had ever seen, not even like the gentry of the South; they were bumpkins, rustics, shopkeepers; they were boys, and he had not seen them, unafraid, lead other boys who were terribly, woefully afraid. To it all, he had one answer: "You bloody damned fools."

In the end they leaned back exhausted, and the Virginian's decision, gentle after the row, came out of the shadows. "General Lee is right," he said quietly. "We can't fight—here of all places. Perhaps we can't fight anywhere. We are going to leave New York and retreat. Perhaps we will try to hold the fort that bears my name and perhaps we will not; I don't know yet. But our way, our only way, I tell you, gentlemen, is to retreat until we have made ourselves into an army. We have one advantage—that we don't overestimate ourselves. Do you know, gentlemen, that when I went away from my home I thought it would be for a little while? It will not be a little while, gentlemen, but a long time. We will retreat, if we have to, over the mountains where there is a forest twice as large as Europe. But someday, gentlemen, we will become an army, the sort of an army General Lee has had experience with, and then we will turn around—and then we will not run away."

For a long time the Virginian repeated those words to himself. "We will not run away, we will not run away, we will become an army, we will become an army."

He tried to make an army. Awkwardly, he plodded through what measures he could conceive of, trying to mend this and fix that, lecturing, advising, scolding, pleading. At some of his efforts, Lee nodded benevolently, but for the most part the thin Englishman drifted through the camp like a guest of honor, telling endless tales of his experiences on the battlefields of Europe, the moral of all being that no cleverness was like the cleverness of General Charles Lee.

And the Yankees loved it; they loved his cleverness; they loved his obvious hints about who would be the commander in chief in time to come; they loved his many small failings, as contrasted with the virtues of the Virginian.

When men deserted by the tens and twenties and fifties, Lee could afford to shrug his shoulders at this strange army, but when some of them were brought back and the commander in chief grimly ordered them to be whipped until the blood ran from their backs, the Yankees told each other that the Virginian was a stone-hearted tyrant. The day, every day, was one steady plague of mutiny, desertion, thievery, and complaint.

Yet hard on the council of war, the commander's veneration for Lee found confirmation; for the British at last did precisely what Lee had predicted they would do sooner or later. They sent a force through the East River into the Sound, in a flanking attack on Westchester, an attack planned to cut off the American army and end its existence.

The flanking movement should have worked. Under cover of night and fog, British boats crept up the East River searching for an outjutting bit of land called Pell's Point. But the fog further confused their none too accurate geography, and they landed instead at Throgg's Neck, also an outjutting of the Westchester coast, but almost an island, since it was connected with the mainland by a wooden causeway.

A fourteen-year-old Dutch boy, Peter Rauch, was digging clams on the beach when he heard the British voices. His wits were keen, keen enough to send him running barefooted for a whole mile through the night to the camp of a red-faced Irish colonel by the name of Hand, who disliked the British but had a deep and generous hatred of Tories, and who had dragged his regiment into Westchester in the hope of meeting the dashing Rogers and some of his green-clad rangers.

Peter Rauch burst through the sprawling men and descended upon Hand with a torrent of Dutch, waving his arms wildly, nor did he calm down until the Irishman had picked him up by his belt and shaken him, puppy-like, in the air.

"Now what is it in English?" Hand demanded.

"Der lobsters!"

"Where?"

"In der wasser, in der boats, I tink mabe dey come up from der town, like how you say, dis," and he made violent rowing motions with his hands.

"Rowing?"

"Ya."

"How many?"

"I chust hear dem, I don see dem."

"Where will they be landing, boy, do you know?"

"I tink, der way dey go, dey go in der neck."

"Can you lead us there, boy?"

"Ya, ya, ya," gleefully avenging his ancestors, who had lost New Amsterdam.

And an hour later Hand's men were ripping up the causeway and yelling their peculiar Pennsylvania derision at the British.

The big man studied his map, one long finger laid on Throgg's Neck, and tried to understand and anticipate what the British would do next. He was caught, yet in a way the British were also caught, though only a torn-up causeway and a few muskets kept them back; it was a question of whether he could get his army out of New York before the British returned to their boats and landed somewhere else on the Westchester shore.

He thought not. He was under no delusions concerning his army, and he had learnt by now that there was a most definite difference between retreating and running away. He had seen his army run away once, and the memory was bitter; all that had saved them then from dissolving like a cloud of gas was the fact that they were on an island and that most of them could not swim. Now the very thought of what might happen, if he were to pick up his army and race from Manhattan with part of the British behind him and another part threatening to cut off his front, made his blood run cold. No, his army must move slowly, deliberately, gently; it must move in a close mass, so that the men could crowd together and feel each other's warmth, and it must have the knowledge of a solid rear guard behind it.

The rear guard was less of a problem than the British force on Throgg's Neck; the Delaware and Maryland troops had held once before, and they might hold again, but there were so few of them. And Throgg's Neck—

He put his finger back on the map and forced himself to plan and contrive; he said to himself, hopelessly, "If there were only five hundred more who would stand and fight."

Riding through Westchester, along the Sound shore, he and most of his staff had agreed that Pell's Point would be the most likely place for a British landing attempt, and to that consensus of opinion, Lee had added his own. For the moment, the British were frustrated on Throgg's Neck, but what would happen when they slipped away and found the next spur of land, without a torn-up causeway to hold them back?

As he sat there, thinking, planning, contriving, there came to his mind's eye the picture of several hundred men in blue peajackets and stocking fishermen's hats; he was back in the desolate cul-de-sac of Brooklyn, watching the rolling, un-hurried gait of the Marblehead men. They were Yan-kees, nasal-voiced, shell-encrusted, boastful, yet in a way different, lashed by a thousand days of wind and salt sleet, quietly aware of death and not seeing too much difference between lead bullets and an icy-cold sea. He had seen them with oars in their hands, and now he wondered how they would be with muskets.

He sent for Colonel Glover. The man was his own age, tightly knit, light-eyed, with the very slight, grudging smile that his kind would permit themselves for a Southern out-lander.

"Can your men fight?" the Virginian asked.

"Maybe they can."

The Virginian indicated Pell's Point on the map. "I think the British will land there," he said. "I don't want them ashore until the army is out of the island."

"Uh-huh."

"Can you do it?"

"We can try," Glover said.

"It may be twenty-four hours, it may be forty-eight, but I want them held until all danger of encirclement is past."

"Uh-huh," Glover nodded.

And then they shook hands, Washington's smile as thin and grudging as Glover's own.

The fishermen took up their position that night, grumbling, swearing, dragging by main strength—for they had no horses—the three tiny field pieces allotted to them, stum-bling through brush and fields and briars, and finding finally a stone wall which suited them. Near as they were to the Sound, they were nevertheless sullen over the fact that they had had to abandon the fleet of small boats which they gathered for the retreat from Brooklyn. Vaguely, they felt that this was a war which should be fought as much on the sea as on the land, and they had the small boatman's contempt for the mighty British ships of the line. They knew that their light Salem fishing smacks could dance merrily around the lumbering giants, and they asked no more than a chance to set the invading fleet ablaze with fire boats and then go home. Instead, here they were crawling through the poison-ivy patches of Westchester, tearing their faces, hands, and clothes in the endless briar tangles, and going God alone knew where.

When they had settled down behind the stone wall and primed their muskets, Glover lit his pipe and called up his officers for instructions. Of the sixteen men who gathered around him, nine had been captains of their own boats, three had been country schoolteachers who went out for cod when classes were off, one had been a parson, one had been a shoemaker, one had been a carpenter, and the last was Hiram Threemercy Ploughman, one of the most skillful and famous figurehead carvers on all the Gloucester coast. They were hard, sharp men with long faces and long noses and salt in their blood, and they were in the war because freedom for them was not an ideal but an obsession.

"Them"—Glover said, puffing at his pipe and nodding at the grey haze of dawn that was showing over the sound— "will be coming from yonder."

They waited.

"We'll be a-setting here," Glover continued.

They nodded sagely.

"We'll keep a-setting here," Glover said.

The parson said, booming in the darkness, "Lord God of Hosts, Mighty Jehovah, kindle thy wrath against the iniquitous, strike down them that would profane Thy Holy Name and give might to the virtuous and the God-fearing, and damn the Church of England!"

"Amen," said the others.

They loaded the cannon heavily in their own peculiar way, not with shot, but with the sweepings of a blacksmith's shop, rusty nails, bits of wire, old iron bolts, broken horseshoes, pieces of glass, and finely minced pewter pots and pans. They had no ideals nor illusions about war, and there was in them a cold streak of Puritan ruthlessness. They were not riflemen, and their huge, wide-bore muskets, some of them bell-mouthed ancient matchlocks, came in for the same treatment of rusty nails and old wire. Not being riflemen, but being Yankees and efficient, they turned their muskets into shotguns and then sat and waited.

With the dawn, the British came marching down to sweep them away.

The fishermen waited calmly. The sun poked up out of the Sound, and dawn was a pink burst of glory, bloodspotted by the red coats of the British. They had tried Throgg's Neck and found the causeway torn up, but here there was land for their feet and nothing had ever stopped the redcoat columns where there was land for their feet. They marched in with their fifes playing and their drums beating, with their shakoes swaying and their glittering bayonets slicing the morning air. And when they were thirty yards away, the fishermen let go with the sweepings of a blacksmith shop.

They were fishermen; they had seen cod squirming and bleeding when the hooks were pulled out, but they had never seen a whole field of men like a slippery deck of cod; they were hard, as their fathers and grandfathers had been hard, but they were not hard enough for this, not hard enough to keep the blood in their faces and not hard enough to keep from retching.

Still, they reloaded.

The British came again, straight and precise, as if the whole field had not already been harrowed with death, and again the sweepings of a blacksmith shop tore out their life.

They came again and again.

They came hard on the run, pressing through the field of death to the stone wall, and the fishermen dropped their muskets, seizing the long, hooked poles that were tools of their trade, and using them as pikes.

All morning the British attacked in a senseless spectacle of bravery that was as stupid as it was glorious, and all morning the rusty nails of the coldly efficient Marblehead fishermen hurled them back.

At noon, Howe withdrew what was left of the redcoat light infantry and threw the green-clad Hessians into the battle; and they came on with their harsh battle cry of "Yonkee!" They had none of the cool precision that took the cockney boys of London into that blazing hell; they came on dogged and furious, and they died the same way. They raged up to the stone wall and they were thrown back. They spotted the field with their green coats and their bulky knapsacks and their unwieldy shakoes.

All through the afternoon the attacks went on, and all afternoon the fishermen beat back the sweating, gasping Germans. Three or four of the fishermen had died and a dozen more were wounded, but in the field in front of them lay more than five hundred British and Hessians. Even the faltering mentality of General Howe, never penetrated by fear of anything on God's earth, could not stand any more of this. He drew off his men, and gentle evening hid the horror of Pell's Point.

While the Marblehead fishermen lay behind the stone wall at Pell's Point, the commander laboriously began to evacuate his army from Harlem, to begin what he felt would be a retreat of many long years. Up to now, he had been the commander in chief of an army that proposed to fight the enemy and destroy it; but only by the grace of God, by the virtue of falling rain, by the calm stamina of six or seven hundred Yankee fishermen, had this enemy been kept from completely destroying his own army. Defeat had become so constant a factor that victory was not even to be thought of; only ways and means of retreating in good order were to be considered. And out of all this there was coming to the tall Virginia farmer a strange and curious knowledge: that wars and freedom of men are not won on a battlefield.

He did not have complete understanding of this new awareness yet; but the change in him was indicated by the acquisition of an almost godly patience. Mount Vernon, in its sunny glory, seemed very far away, indistinct, part of a dream; and though he still looked forward to his return there, it was something neither immediate nor calculable. Mount Vernon was no longer the solid, eternal fact of house, barns, smokehouse, storehouse, winehouse, orchards, fields, lawns, shadetrees: all that—and it was his life, for he was no man to exist inwardly, but only in the radiant warmth of good, solid fact—had been laid on the table, and Mount Vernon, which had been his, was no longer his, only a promise.

His patience was incredible; he had made for himself a simple credo, "My friends I will trust and my enemies I will endeavor to destroy." He no longer blamed and scolded and raged, and when things were done wrong, as most things were, he gave the impression in a most matter-of-fact way that on such a basis even the best armies in the world operated. Over the whole comic-opera war he presided in such simple dignity that even Charles Lee was moved to a certain respect.

"If only he wasn't such a fool," Lee thought.

But when the young hotheads, Knox, Mifflin, Mercer, McDougall and the others, came raging to the Virginian with news that Lee had said this and Lee had said that, he closed his ears and sent them on their way with the plain statement, "General Lee is a good and loyal soldier, gentlemen. That is all I ask of any of my staff."

A month ago, a year ago, the things Lee and certain others said about him would have turned him mad with anger; but he was not the same man that he had been a month ago and a year ago.

The Yankees trailed north. Brigade after brigade, some with arms, more who had thrown away their arms, they trudged north, through the narrow bottleneck of Manhattan, over Kingsbridge and into Westchester, escaping from the trap while Howe hurled his wonderful troops at the Marblehead fishermen. From the Hollow Way, which had been the Continental defense line, to White Plains, where the Virginian had been accumulating supplies for the expected retreat, was a distance of eighteen miles, less than a day's march for a trained corps, but more than a day's march for this broken, defeated army.

The Virginian had hoped and planned to establish another camp and make a stand at White Plains, but now he realized that such a policy would serve to play directly into the hands of the British. They only needed to surround his army to end the war, and sooner or later they would realize that and act accordingly. Therefore he changed his plans; already he had word that Glover and his fishermen were momentarily holding the British in check. With the main army out of Manhattan, he would place a rear guard at White Plains, while the stores were removed. After that, he would retreat—

But Greene, hating Lee as bitterly as he did, persuaded the commander not to give up New York entirely, but to leave a garrison of three thousand men at Fort Washington, which Greene and Knox believed could be held forever.

Lee's opinion was: "That, sir, is the final price of insanity."

Licking itself like a great wounded lion, the British army moved inland and north. In the darkness, the Yankee fishermen had slipped away, having shot out all the rusty horror they used to load their guns, yet not before they had inflicted, considering time, and the number of men involved, one of the most awful defeats the British army ever suffered in all its military history. Yet what they had done was in the way of a sideshow, a brief effort to delay a landing attempt, an action that passed almost unnoticed in the dark pall of defeat.

11

HOW OTHERS WERE AFRAID

Once the army of liberty was out of Manhattan, across Kingsbridge and sprawling through the low hills of southern Westchester, the Virginian felt a great relief. He had accomplished one thing that again and again in his dreams had promised to be the worst of debacles, the removal of his army from Manhattan Island. But the relief was short-lived, for the water-barrier that had kept his men from wholesale desertion was now removed, and in the promise of sudden dissolution, he began to lose the sense of reality. On his horse, he felt himself a big, awkward farmer, holding aloft two huge hands that were filled with powdery sand, sand which he could not hold, which sifted away, which dissolved, which puffed away on savage bursts of wind, which resolved into laconic and merciless communications:

"Sir, I'm sorry to say fourteen of my men deserted."

"It was no fault of mine, Your Excellency, the Vermont rifle regiment has gone home."

"We caught six deserters, but over a hundred escaped."

"The Carolina Republic's own Loyal and Devoted Artillery Company has slipped away with two six pounders."

"The Gadby Rangers are gone, sir. I don't know when they left camp."

"Captain Atterson walked off with all his men."

"Lieutenant Jones and six of his men."

L

"Colonel Arlen—"

"Sixty-two of the Green Borderers."

"Eleven of the Pennsylvania Rifles."

"Captain Bixbe—"

"Seven of my regiment, sir, with two ho'heds, all our powder, and what am I to do for munitions?"

"Twelve of the Third New York."

It filled his ears and hammered into his head, a dreadful, relentless repetition, a dogged reiteration. Ten men, six men, nine men, a hundred men, two hundred men—and if it continued, very soon his hands would be empty. He pleaded with his staff, "Keep the men close and post sentries at night."

But one of the boys said, "Sir, even the sentries run away."

So he rushed north, hoping that mere impetus would keep his army together.

The densely wooded hills of Westchester were in many ways a no man's land. Major Robert Rogers and his rangers had instituted a sort of guerrilla warfare, which heretofore had been devoted mainly to burning the homes of revolutionist sympathizers and inflicting other minor deviltries upon them—desultory rape and banditry, some lynching, and a good deal of riding on a rail, the second being viler and more terrible than the first, since it consisted of seating a man on the sharp edge of a plank, with a fifty-pound weight hanging from either foot, and keeping him there until he fainted away or died, or screamed and wept and pleaded for mercy. The revolutionist party, though greatly outnumbered in Westchester, had come to a position which in any case makes very good revolutionary material—they had no more to lose. They retreated into the tangled forests of the Pocantico Hills and the dense marshes and lonely lakes of the Mahopac region, and from there they sallied forth in raids and counter-deviltries. They burned and raped and stole on their own, until the whole pretty woodland country had earned itself a nation-wide reputation for lawlessness and disorder.

To travel alone through Westchester, whether to White Plains, Tarrytown, or Dobbs Ferry—or to any of the lovely old Dutch villages that clustered along the Hudson bank and in the valleys and on the shore of the Sound, was worth a man's life, whether he was Tory or revolutionist. Already the fields had gone to seed, fruit trees were untended, and lonely houses were either black ruins or armed and barred like fortresses. Perhaps no other section in all the colonies had felt so intensely the bitter and unrelenting hatred of civil war.

And into this region, now, came a new diversion, two armies of about thirteen thousand men each, one a mass of beaten, frightened Continentals, pouring up out of Manhattan Island, the other an orderly and wonderfully trained fighting machine of British and Germans, come up by boat to the region near New Rochelle and driving north and west on a sharp angle, calculated to cut off and trap the Americans. It was a slow race, in which the British were held back by their fear of pitfalls and ambushes and by their ignorance of Westchester geography, an ignorance which had induced the Admiralty in London to issue an order for the English fleet of mighty three-deck ships of the line to sail up the Bronx River and harry the Americans along its length. Thus Howe made all sorts of elaborate preparations to force a crossing of the Bronx River, only to shake his head in bewilderment when he discovered it was the tiniest and prettiest of woodland brooks, never deeper than a few feet and never wider than a few yards. The Americans were restrained by their very inability to march as an army.

And around both armies like a pack of famished wolves lurked the irregulars. They shot down deserters, cut off stragglers, and knifed sentries. They fought their own horrible war while the two masses of men jockeyed for position.

Position, to the Virginian, was an eternal hope. Dreaming at night, or dreaming awake in the daytime, he won battles, simply because his tactics were correct, even inspired, and his men were not afraid. And that made him say to himself, "Next time, if I do it right, if I plan everything the way a soldier would, it will be different. I will win."

To him, it was so plausible and obvious. He himself was not afraid; all the fear that had been his was gone in the knowledge that there was no way back, that from here on he could travel only in one direction; and he could not see why with his men it should be otherwise. Even experience was blotted out by that pleading hope. Thus when he found himself at White Plains, in a position that might be held even against the forces of hell, he said to Charles Lee, "If we could stop them here, general, we might change everything." Yet it was more a hope than a statement. His army was building entrenchments on a line from the meandering little Bronx River to a swampy lake. There were hillocks and there was a general rise of ground in their direction, and Lee recognized the entire thing as a tactical picture out of some old and formal military manual. For a moment he was caught with sympathy for this blundering, foolish farmer, who could never be either a leader or a soldier, and who, bound as he was by his slow mind, could only see the part and never the whole of anything.

But Lee still burned over the affront that had been placed upon him by disregarding his advice and leaving a garrison at Fort Washington. He was brutally noncommittal.

"We might drive them back to the Sound," the foxhunter dreamed.

"Or they might go around us and have us in a bloody trap," Lee said.

"No, they won't do that," the foxhunter murmured, and of this he was quite certain. He knew the contempt the British felt for him and his army—a contempt which would make the English scornful of surrounding what they could defeat in battle.

Afterwards, what came to be known as the Battle of White Plains, remained as a confused, bad memory in his mind, of no great importance in itself, but as the beginning of his greatest debacle—of that black horror that stayed with him as an uneasy ghost and rose to torture him in dreams.

In itself, the battle was not so different from his others; some of his men fought, but most of them ran away, the difference being that this time it was not Yankees who ran as if the devil himself was behind them, but Delaware and Maryland brigades, men of his own southland and men he had put some trust in. Yet they ran just as hard as Yankees, just as fast, and they threw away their guns in the same fashion.

He had put these regiments on a strong point called Chatterton's Hill. He had seen them bedded down behind stone walls, with cannon protecting their flanks, the artillery consisting of two field pieces in charge of the boy, Hamilton. It pained the Virginian to be prodigal with his cannon, so few pieces were left after the losses at Brooklyn and New York, considering the pieces that had been set aside in the beginning to defend Fort Washington and Fort Lee. It seemed to him that every time his army was driven from a place, it left behind such a vast store of munitions and arms as could never be replaced; and then it was root and search and lay hands on some iron balls here, a few kegs of powder there, some old muskets, matchlocks, pikes, rusty bayonets. Each time, it was like putting together an army once more, out of nothing.

At any rate, Hamilton fought, whipping his gunners into standing by, loading the cannon, and firing them; but it took only a single man wounded in the thigh to make the Maryland men break and run. Then it was the old heartbreaking story, officers pleading and yelling for the men to make a stand and the militia running wildly, without purpose and direction from the close, precise ranks of attacking British. Once again, by the hundreds, the Continentals fled like rabbits, crawling into whatever shelter they could find, hiding themselves in the brush, in the tall grass, burrowing into piles of dead autumn leaves, climbing trees, crawling into the caves of animals.

General McDougall, a New Yorker, leading a regiment of New Yorkers, mostly placid blue-eyed Dutch boys, did manage for a while to stem his end of the retreat. He got his men to stand at a stone wall, but when the British sent a company of light dragoons to dislodge them, they broke and fled much the same as the others.

And again, there was darkness with its saving grace.

The Virginia squire was becoming hard. He didn't slump in his saddle, nor did all the world fall away in a broken ruin. The change in him had been slow and painful; nevertheless it had happened. He had watched his men run away, yet all the emotion those around him could see was a more definite set in his jaw. Lines were forming, around his eyes, around his mouth, and something vastly more eruptive was happening within him. He had no sympathy for the tears of anger young Hamilton shed, nor for the rolling, resounding curses of the slow-witted and earnest Putnam.

"We're still here," he said of his army, as if in accomplishing that they had achieved more than the British.

"Except five hundred or so who have run away today," Lee reminded him.

"They'll come back," he said grimly. "When it's dark enough and quiet enough, they will come back."

And McDougall could only groan, "Those bastards, those dirty, cowardly bastards—"

"I don't blame them about the horse," the Virginian said evenly and judiciously. "They're not used to horses charging. They'll learn about cavalry. They'll learn that a man on a horse can die as quickly as a man on foot. They'll learn other things."

His faith was no longer exuberant; it was grim, it was becoming slightly terrible, and even old Putnam was afraid of the gathering ice in his grey eyes. From day to day, they, his aides, his friends, his enemies, could not perceive what was happening to the big, shy farmer from the Potomac, who had once thought of himself primarily as a foxhunter and who had desired nothing more than the love of those around him; but they felt and saw the results, and sometimes they were afraid—and sometimes they were made happy with a desperate, lonely sort of pride. As for instance the time two days after the rout on Chatterton's Hill, when two of Rogers' Rangers were dragged into the Continental camp.

They were Westchester gentlemen brought face to face with one of their own kind, the foremost gentleman of Virginia, the aristocrat of the Potomac, the foxhunter; they, too, were foxhunters. A pink coat bound the three with chains that had been forged centuries ago, setting them up and over the world of little, frightened men; and therefore they swaggered a little until they began to realize what the stony set of his face meant. He asked them, "What are you?"

One was a handsome, tall, ruddy-faced blond man of thirty-five or so; he answered for the other, a thin-faced boy in a perfectly tailored suit of green buckskin.

"Captain Lacey of Major Rogers' Rangers, sir, and this is Lieutenant Albert."

"I don't know of a Major Rogers," the foxhunter said coldly.

They stared at him blankly.

"I know of a certain Rogers," the foxhunter said.

They waited, the older one cautiously feeling for an opening.

"And I hear he is an Englishman of sorts," the foxhunter went on. "But what are you?"

The older one blundered into this opening. "We hope and trust, sir, that you as a gentleman will give us the consideration that is our due. We are fortunate in addressing you instead of those—" He saw his blunder and stopped.

"What were you going to say?"

"Nothing."

"What were you going to say? What were you going to call my men?"

"Continentals, sir."

"We call ourselves Americans," the foxhunter said evenly. "You are not an Englishman, and I don't know what to call you, and that buckskin you wear, gentlemen, is less than dirt. I don't consider it a uniform and you were within our lines, so properly I have the right to hang you. But you called upon my consideration as a gentleman. Sergeant, take them away and give them two hundred lashes apiece."

In this time, directly after the Battle of White Plains, the Continentals stood upon the brink of an abyss, their backs against the Hudson, their front crumbling and awaiting the final stroke by General Howe. Why General Howe never delivered that blow, the Virginian was not to know for many years to come, and even then he was not certain he had the true answer. Perhaps Howe could not believe that an army of thirteen thousand men would simply fall to pieces if he prodded at its front.

The Virginian knew that it would, light as the prodding might be; in his heart and soul, he knew that he had come to the end of his rope, the final end and the single end, not as at Brooklyn and Harlem, where there was the alternative of retreat, not even as on that terrible Sunday morning when a whole division of his army, numbering thousands, had fled headlong through New York; but the end where there was no retreat.

There was no retreat, and this was the end, and if he dared to move his cowed Yankees the British would leap on them and destroy them. He had alternatives, but they were all the choices of a condemned man before the trap is sprung. His army had been split into three parts, one at Fort Washington in New York, one across the Hudson at Fort Lee, and the third part here in Westchester; and each of the parts was attempting with all the ability of the individual members, to desert him.

And what he did was the whole key to the change that had occurred inside of him: he went about his task as though he were a victor among victors; he inspected regiments; he punished deserters; he wrote letters to Congress; and in the evening with his men around him, he drank

Madeira and toasted, "The Congress, gentlemen, and a quick and happy victory."

There was a certain peace of mind in knowing so surely the road he had to travel, not the length of it, but the single direction it took.

Part Four

---❖{ *JERSEY* }❖---

12

THE FORT CALLED "WASHINGTON"

On the bright, cold morning of November 12, 1776, the Virginia foxhunter stood on the shore of the Hudson and watched the brown-skinned Marblehead fishermen expertly ferry a brigade of his troops across to Jersey. Life was good and the wind was in his face and two mugs of hot flip were under his belt, along with cakes and honey and a pot of tea, enough to bulge comfortably and give him the good, morning content of a man who has eaten well. He had read a letter from his wife and written one to her, and the night before with three bottles of Madeira inside of him, he had danced for three hours straight. It added up—with the sun and the wind and the crisp leaves and the cold, glistening belly of the river.

If he had love, admiration, respect for any body of his men, it was for these same Marblehead fishermen, for all their dispassionate New England efficiency and for all their very apparent contempt of him and his kind. He was as foreign to them as they were to him; he could imagine them gawking at the gracious Georgian beauty of Mount Vernon

119

and going into their cold Yankee rage at the sight of his Negro slaves in the fields. They had their ways, and their ideas were set; his own ideas had never been set, and he envied men who could go straight about their work with such certainty of purpose. Again, in a way, he was afraid of them, knowing that with five thousand like them he could sweep the British back into the sea—but not knowing, not even able to imagine what five thousand of them would do after they had finished with the British.

This morning he was in no mood to examine the future. His troops were on their way to Hackensack, in Jersey, where he had established his new encampment, and he looked forward to a brisk ride down the Palisades to Fort Lee. Behind him, dispositions had been nicely made, and it seemed that his position was better than it had ever been before. Two thousand men under General Heath were holding the upriver Hudson highlands, and another five thousand were in Westchester under the command of General Charles Lee. It was true that there had been a good many desertions, but in all he was wonderfully fortunate; for having had Washington completely at his mercy after the Battle of White Plains, Howe had hesitated to attack. The Virginian found no explanation of this course; it was so obvious to him that Howe had only to launch a frontal attack to have the whole American army fall to pieces. Like a doomed man, the Virginian had waited and waited, composing himself for an end that did not come. A few reports came to him from the British camp while Howe frittered away his opportunity; some said that Howe had not yet recovered from the terrible, bloody memory of Pell's Point; others speculated that he did not dare to end the revolt summarily, since feeling in England for the rebels grew higher and higher, and there was a possibility that the spark might leap across the Atlantic and set fire to the British Isles. But all of this was speculation; and when finally Howe turned around and marched his army back to New York, the Virginia squire knew that he was saved. But he had not and never would have any clear notion of why destruction had avoided him.

By now, he already had more than four thousand men in Jersey. When he had established himself at Fort Lee and given the fishermen the job of drawing off the garrison of Fort Washington, in Manhattan, he would have almost eight thousand men on either side of the river—and be in a posi-

tion to execute a pincer movement against the British, who
had been pinching him rather tightly.

All in all, it seemed that the tide had turned.

When they had crossed the river, the commander in chief
received a salute from his troops and watched them march
smartly away. They too were more cheerful, relieved at having the Hudson River between them and the English. He,
himself, with only two of his staff, cantered down the cliff
road toward Fort Lee.

All that day and that evening, the holiday spirit remained
with him. At the house where they stopped to spend the
night, a rambling Dutch farmhouse, there were two little
girls, one six, the other eight. It was almost their bedtime
when their shyness and the big Virginian's dignity had worn
off, but an hour was left for him to sit in front of the dining-
room oven and tell them stories while the loggerheads baked.
He was not a good story-teller; for all that he lived outside of
himself, his lips wet with the wind of the whole world, he
was not able to make a description alive nor an action ex-
citing, merely stating sedulously:

"Six Indians were hiding in the woods and we had to
shoot them to go through the woods, and then there were
ten more Indians hiding up on a hill, whereupon we shot
them—"

The little girls shivered, and the small one in his arms
crawled closer, and what he said didn't matter at all, he
was such a magnificent man, higher than a giant, with his
wonderful blue jacket and his buff trousers, and shadows
from the fire on the fascinating little pockmarks on his face.
When the story was over, the eight-year-old said simply,
"That was good. Papa says you're a good fighter, but you
drink too much"—all with her curious Dutch accent.

"What?"

"Why do you drink so much?" the girl insisted sadly.

"Not too much. Not any more than anyone else."

"Papa said," the girl persisted, still very sadly, "that when
you came here tonight, you would drink him out of house
and home."

He reached Fort Lee about noon the next day, and discovered to his amazement that instead of beginning to withdraw the troops from Manhattan Island, Greene had rein-

forced them. The Virginian said nothing until he had the handsome young Quaker alone in his tent.

"By God, Nathanael, what sort of damned insanity is this?"

"Insanity, sir?"

"Yes, insanity. Why didn't you make preparations to evacuate the fort? Why did you send more men into New York?"

"To hold the fort, sir."

"Hold it? It can't be held!"

"Good heavens, sir, why can't it be held? Because that damned renegade Englishman, Lee, told—"

"Greene!"

"I'm sorry, sir."

"It's not enough to apologize to me, General Greene," the big man said evenly. "I want you to understand now and for the future that General Lee is second in command to me in this army, and that his orders are deserving of all the respect—that a Yankee can muster."

Greene stared at him, and then shook his head dumbly. "My God, sir," he whispered, "What more can I say? Do you want me to kneel down at your feet? I will if you want me to." There was no mockery in his voice.

After that, after a minute or two of silence, the Virginian asked gently, "Do you think, Nathanael, that the fort can be held?"

"Forever!"

"Not forever. For a week, a month?"

"A month! Sir, please give us a chance! They've had New York, all of it their way; now only give us a chance."

"I'll give you a chance," he agreed.

Greene nodded, not trusting himself to speak.

That same evening, the big man rode west to where his troops were encamped at Hackensack, some five miles from Fort Lee at the top of the Palisades. At Hackensack, still crowing over the fine weather and the fact that the British army was some distance from them, the men were in good spirits, the more so since so many of them were Jersey men, and would no longer have to cross a mile-wide river if they decided to desert and go home. The mass of the Yankees had been left with Lee, and the slightly less-tattered Jersey men, eating better than they had for weeks and with no prospect of battle in the near future, had in some way come to the conclusion that they were a victorious army, a belief bolstered by the number of Passaic and Paterson girls who had already attached themselves to the new encampment. The troops clustered around the big man when he arrived, and cheered him more heartily than they had in weeks. Standing close to a cheerful, blazing fire, he told Knox about it.

"I like the looks of it, things were so much worse. They're better now. I was worried before because Nathanael pleaded to hold Fort Washington." He always said that name haltingly, feeling an almost childish pride in the fact that a place, a fortress of the republic, had been named for him, for an obscure Virginia farmer.

"You'll let him?" Knox demanded eagerly.

"Yes—but Lee—"

"Oh, damn Lee, sir! I'm sorry, forgive me, but you must let us fight, sir, you must!"

"Yes, if he can hold it, it may turn out to be a thorn in the side of Howe. Congress wants it held."

"Until hell freezes over, sir, believe me. We weren't beaten—we retreated, but we weren't beaten. Look at me, sir. I'm an officer of artillery, but where are my guns? In Brooklyn, in New York, at Fort Washington and at Fort Lee; but I swear to God, sir, that if I lose them all, it will be the same, we won't be beaten. We had no guns when we started—" The young bookseller was fairly dancing.

"Knox!"

"Yes, sir?"

"Go to bed," the big man said, somewhat morosely.

"Sir?"

"I said, go to bed," the big man repeated.

Puzzled, Knox stared at him, and then turned silently away; while the commander in chief began to walk through the sprawling, noisy camp. He walked slowly, with long, measured steps, his head bent forward slightly, his pale grey eyes barely open, barely reflecting the many lights of the fires. His long arms hung by his sides, and though he looked straight ahead of himself as he walked, he was conscious of the thousand and one movements all around him, the buzz of talk that died into sibilant whispers at his approach, the laughing groups of men and those who were not laughing, the mumbling and grumbling, the songs, mournful, lonely, haunting Dutch and Scotch and Welsh airs that had lingered in the Jersey hinterland for a century, preserved as they had been in the old country where they had been sung for five centuries. He saw the disorder, the ragged tents, the unkempt, fat, back-country wenches who giggled and tried to hide from him, the pigs that rooted in the piles of waste, dumped anywhere and everywhere by the soldiers, who made no attempt to dispose of it, the stacked muskets with bayonets rusted so that they could only be melted off the barrels, the few skinny horses that pulled the creaking provision wagons, and the unprotected mounds of food and ammunition.

And as he walked, the gay elation of the past few days vanished, and he was filled with a sense of foreboding. It was only through constant contact that he could forget what manner of an army he led; let him go away for a day or two days, and he would see it with new eyes, as he was seeing it now, and he would fall victim to the old and terrible hopelessness. It was no use blaming Knox and the others, he told himself; they did the best they could. They were brave and gallant—yes, gallant—men, even if it was not the gallantry of a Virginia gentleman but the buffoonish clowning of shopkeepers and artisans.

He turned back to his tent, and there, by the light of two frolicking candles, sat down to write a letter to his wife. But when he had spread out the paper and dipped his pen in the ink, he found himself suddenly attacked by a fever-like wave of homesickness. It was so sudden, so absolute, so imperious that he let go of the quill and sank forward over the table, his face in his hands, his breath sighing between his fingers, his whole inward mind concentrated lushly and pitifully upon Mount Vernon. At that moment, as he had never before desired anything, he wanted to be back in his home, living the life he was made for, the life of a farmer and foxhunter, rising in the morning and eating his first breakfast alone in the kitchen, having two or three cups of good strong tea, riding out over the fields when they were still wet with the night's dew, cursing his spotted dogs good-naturedly and contemptuously, out of sight and hearing of anyone, raising a fox perhaps and chasing it for a mile or two until it escaped and left his dogs with their tongues hanging and their small minds puzzled, returning to his house full and brimming with life, having a second breakfast with Martha, who was pettish in the morning, not gloriously alive as he was, going over his accounts, a meticulous business he secretly loved, gloating over his past two weeks' winnings at cards, momentarily angry with a neighbor who got the best of him in a deal with pigs, welcoming guests for lunch, listening to good talk, eating good food, drinking good Madeira, sipping good brandy, lounging on the veranda for an hour of politics, out over the fields and then two hours of cards before the change for dinner— the way a man lived, not too easily, yet not hard, bored a great deal with his own content and wanting an adventure, a single, great, glorious adventure.

He sat for a long time with his face in his hands.

Late in the afternoon of the third day after he had arrived at Hackensack, a messenger from Fort Lee drove into the encampment on a lathered and winded horse. The messenger brought news that the British had attacked Fort Washington and that General Greene thought General Washington should know the state of affairs.

"And what is the state of affairs?" the big man demanded.

"I should say very good, sir. I should say the garrison is most enthusiastic. There is no doubt that they have already taken a heavy toll of the British."

For just a moment, the big man stared at the sweating, grinning messenger, and then he strode abruptly to his horse, mounted, and cantered off along the road to the Palisades. When he reached the edge of the high cliff overlooking the Hudson River and Manhattan Island, it was already dark. From the direction of Fort Washington came the occasional dull boom of a cannon, and now and again little fingers of light reached out of the darkness. Certainly, it did not look like a general attack, and he could hear no sound of musketry.

"Where is General Greene?" he asked Major Galloway, who had been left in charge of Fort Lee.

"Across the river, sir."

"And General Putnam?"

"Also at Fort Washington, sir."

For about fifteen minutes the big man paced back and forth, nervously and anxiously, peering at his watch again and again, straining his ears to hear some sound from across the Hudson, and his eyes to make out what might or might not be a battle. At last he could stand the suspense of waiting no longer, and he demanded of the major, "Is there a boat down at the landing?"

"I believe so, sir."

"Then get me someone with a torch to light the way down. I'm going across."

"Yes, sir—if you think it advisable."

"Damn it, major, I don't require your doubts concerning the advisability of my actions."

Meekly, the major crept away, returning with a militia-man, who carried a blazing pine torch. In its ruddy, dancing glare, the big man climbed and stumbled down the twist-ing path to the boat landing. He woke a sleeping boatman, climbed into the sternsheets, and pushed off from the shore himself. He sat in the stern, and when the oars poked at the water, roared at the boatman, "Damn you, row!"

They were halfway across the river, when the Virginian heard the creak of oarlocks and the lap of water. "Who's there?" he called.

"American!"

"American!" his own boatman shouted back.

"Hello, who's there?"

"Nathanael, is that you?" the Virginian asked.

The two boats drifted together, the boatmen hooking the gunnels, and the big man was able to make out General Green and General Putnam. Putnam's lined and rather sour face nodded in greeting, while Greene grinned happily and reached across the boat to take the hand of his commander.

"I'm glad to see you, sir," he said. "I'm terribly glad to see you."

"What happened over there?" the Virginian demanded im-patiently. "Have the British attacked?"

"Not yet, sir, not yet—just shooting a cannon or two to keep us on edge, and we had a poke or two back at them to keep them on the same edge. No, they haven't attacked, sir, and just listen to this—it's glorious, I tell you, sir, it's glorious. Howe sent in a man to ask Magaw for surrender; you know, sir, the way they drawl and look down their noses, some matter like this: 'Sir, Colonel Magaw, General Howe offers you gentle and generous terms of surrender; but if he should be forced to carry the place by assault'— assault, sir, *your fort* by assault—"

"Go on, Nathanael."

" 'If he should be forced to carry the place by assault, then he cannot promise to hold back his men from ex-tremities.' 'Assault?' Magaw answered, talking down his nose the same way. 'Really, sir,' Magaw said, 'I can't believe that His Excellency would carry out a threat so unworthy of himself and the British nation.' And then, sir, Magaw said, 'But give me leave to assure His Excellency that, impelled by the most glorious cause that mankind ever fought in, I am determined to defend this post to the last man, sir—to the last man. Tell His Excellency that.' "

"I never suspected Magaw of such a turn for rhetoric," the Virginian murmured.

"But isn't it glorious, sir? I must write it down and send it to Knox for a time when the history we are making is already made."

Putnam coughed, and the foxhunter said, "Tell me about the fort and leave go of the rhetoric for a while, Nathanael. I'm worried—"

"No, please, sir, don't worry; it's all right. We have them this time, and they'll batter their heads against us until they've broken them. I tell you, this is the turning point we've been waiting for."

The Virginian shook his head wearily, but Putnam said, "I think Nathanael's right, sir."

"We've had to retreat before," the foxhunter murmured. "There's no retreat out of there. How many men are in the garrison?"

"Almost three thousand by now. They'll do the retreating, not us. I give you my word, sir."

"We'll see, Nathanael. I wanted to go across tonight, but I suppose—" He shrugged. "Boatman, row back to Jersey." He sat in the boat, silent, humped over, until they reached the landing under the Palisades.

The geography of the tiny finger of land that comprises northern Manhattan Island is neither complex nor difficult to understand, the finger itself being less than a mile in width and no more than four miles from its northern tip to where it broadens into the fat belly of the island. In peculiar American terminology, it is called a panhandle.

The defense of this panhandle had been obvious to the foxhunter, to Greene, to Knox, to Magaw—to any one of the amateur soldiers who had wanted so desperately to hold on to some little bit of Manhattan; not only obvious but enticing. The place seemed made for defense; it appeared destined for a last-ditch stand; it spoke aloud to the reeling, beaten revolutionists:

"Come to my bosom and fly your colors; and so long as a man remains alive, I will stand by you."

Deep in their hearts was plain knowledge of the futility of their struggle. The officers and the men under them wanted to stop running; they wanted a place where they could stand and fight for a cause, which if hopeless, was nevertheless all they possessed. They wanted to take a toll; they wanted to hit back; their thoughts said:

"God damn you, come and get me! Here I am! I can't run away, even if I want to. But every step you take, you'll pay for! Every rock you climb, you'll make slippery with your blood. This won't be easy; this won't be Brooklyn and New York and White Plains all over again! If you want the wolf, come and dig him out of his lair! And it won't take you a day nor a week nor a month."

That was the way their thoughts went, and their resolutions. They had had enough of running away. Some three thousand of them primed their guns and set about holding the panhandle until hell froze over.

From the Hollow Way, which had been the line of the American army in Manhattan, and which was some five miles from the northern tip of the island, the ground sloped up steadily for about three miles, and then divided into two ridges, one extending along the Hudson River and the other along the Harlem River. These two ridges were about the same height, each a few hundred feet above sea level, each with rocky, steeply sloping sides, and between them the land sloped down sharply to Spuyten Duyvil Creek, the trickle of water which connected the Harlem River with the Hudson. The two ridges did not extend to the end of the panhandle, but stopped abruptly, just a mile south of the creek. A deep gash furrowed the panhandle at this point, and north of it was a third hill, just about the same height as the other two.

Each of these three hills was magnificent from the point of view of defense, yet each suffered from the same deadly drawback—that if one went, the other two would become untenable. The fort named after the foxhunter, the single and splendid tribute of an obscure provincial confederation to an obscure farmer, sat on the Hudson River ridge, a small stone structure which at its best could hold two or three hundred men comfortably. As with Fort Lee, across the river, a steep and rocky path led from the fort to the boat landing below.

Colonel Magaw, who was in charge of the fort's defense, had realized how difficult it would be to hold Fort Washington and no more than the fort. Two or three hundred determined men behind the stone bastions might hold the place for a week or two; but cut off and surrounded, they would sooner or later be starved out, and all the while they would be hammered by cannon placed on the other two hills. Knowing that and knowing the fort's drawbacks, Magaw had evolved the grandiose scheme of holding the whole panhandle until such a time as the Virginian might feel strong enough to attack New York and drive the British back into the sea. He had talked Greene and Putnam into his way of thinking, and had got them to pour more and more men into northern Manhattan.

On the night that Greene and Putnam rowed across the Hudson River, Magaw had three thousand men under his command, and these men had already been placed in their various defensive positions. Spreading a map in front of the two generals, he triumphantly pricked off position after position, challenging them to find a loophole in his scheme.

"Here"—he explained, drawing his finger across the panhandle, some two miles to the south—"are the Pennsylvanians, eight hundred of them. Let the lobsters come up from the south, and we'll have a merry welcome for them." Magaw was a little man, with bulging eyes and round cheeks—and a great awareness of his destiny. "And here"— he went on, pointing to the hill that overlooked Spuyten Duyvil—"are the Marylanders. Riflemen," he explained, as if they had not known that. "Baxter is over the Harlem, with his militia, but they won't come that way. Anyway, I think I've covered everything."

"No one covers everything," Putnam said sourly.

And Greene remarked, "It will be all right, if we don't run away."

He was getting old, thought the foxhunter. He had awakened in the cold morning full of little aches and pains and discomforts, and when he tried to raise his left arm, the joint groaned and stabbed like fire. If he had been at home, Martha would have sent him to bed and kneaded the shoulder herself with smelly bear grease; but here he had to pretend to ignore it. If Billy were here, then perhaps he could confide his woe to the Negro; but Billy was at Hackensack, and the Virginian could have no more called in an orderly and asked him to massage his shoulder than he could have walked naked in front of his assembled men.

He dressed alone, awkwardly, standing barefoot on the ground in his long woolsey underwear, pulling on his clothes, struggling with his high black boots, groaning as he bent the arm to get into his shirt first and then his jacket. His toilet was messy and miserable, and no matter what he did he felt unkempt; and when he left his tent, it hurt him to hold himself straight.

Though it was hardly light, Greene and Putnam and Mercer were already dressed and waiting for him; and he got some small satisfaction out of reflecting that they had slept no better than he had. It was a constant drain on his conscience to know that he was so troubled with countless fears when all the men on his staff were dashing and gallant, never troubled by the dark horror of death or mutilation. He sat down with them to have his breakfast, but throughout the meal he said nothing and hardly ever lifted his eyes from his plate. He knew that if he said anything, it would be in the way of worried supposition about the three thousand men on the other side of the Hudson. So he sat at the camp table with his back toward Manhattan, and all through the meal resisted the impulse to glance behind him—although he knew well enough that the Manhattan shore was shrouded in mist.

His silence tripped and presently halted the conversation of the others. Mercer, never loquacious, said practically nothing, and Putnam, whose puffy face was rather yellow, complained morosely about his liver. Greene kept quiet until the meal was almost done, and then he observed, "See, sir, the mist is lifting!"

"It usually does," the big man agreed, restraining himself from an impulse to glance over his shoulder.

"The flag is flying," Greene nodded with proud emphasis. The flag was a battered old rattlesnake banner that had been dyed a violent purple, but Magaw was inordinately proud of it, and swore he would keep it at mast until the cloth rotted.

Mercer agreed in respectful silence. He was one of the strangest characters in all that strange army, a withered Scotsman and old professional soldier, silent, gloomy most of the time, but with a fire of rebellion burning deep and quiet inside of him. He never spoke of liberty, of freedom, of any of the catchwords; his purpose was never verbal, and the only hint of his thoughts was a certain glitter in his grey eyes.

After breakfast, the commander in chief embarked on a

tour of inspection, striding purposefully through the camp, finding fault with a dozen things, which was never difficult, giving two captains and a lieutenant a bitter tongue-lashing because they had not shaved for three days—in all killing an hour before he allowed himself to return to the cliff-edge and look at the farther shore of the Hudson. Greene, who had been waiting, handed him a spyglass, and the big man had to concentrate on the steadiness of his hands as he focused it. In the glass, a doll's world came to life, the little star of the fort, the flag rippling in the sunlight, the tiny figures of men. It all seemed so secure and so orderly that for the first time in three days his mind was put at ease.

"It's a good fort, sir, believe me," Greene said.

The big man shrugged and continued to stare through the glass.

By eleven o'clock there was still no sign of a British attack. The Virginian felt he could no longer control himself if he did nothing but stand here on the wrong side of three-quarters of a mile of water, waiting and watching. He knew that his presence at the fort could serve no purpose, yet he had to indulge in some sort of action. He remarked casually to Greene, "I think, Nathanael, that we ought to go across and see how things are."

"Good, sir! You'll be pleased. Will you want General Putnam?"

"Let him come if he wishes to."

On their way to the boat landing, they were joined by Mercer, who gloomily asked whether he alone would have to watch a "leetle show" from the wrong side.

"You can come, general. There's nothing likely to happen over here."

They reached the foot of the Palisades and climbed into a boat. The two Marblehead men at the oars, quite overwhelmed to have four generals to ferry across, spat on their hands and rowed manfully, cocking their ears for juicy bits of gossip that might be repeated later. But all they got was a mumbled and tiresome complaint from Putnam about the state of his liver and an old Highland recipe from Mercer: a cup of barley, the jelly of a sheep's hoof, and four fingers of whiskey, divided in three parts for three meals—said to be very good for the liver. Greene said nothing, and the commander in chief kept his eyes on the Manhattan shore.

They were halfway across the river, when a furious roll of cannon split the air, the sound like a blanket of thunder all over the shore and the river.

"They're at it!" Greene yelled, and the big man snapped at the boatmen.

"Damn you, why don't you row?"

"We be rowing," they answered stolidly.

As the boat grounded, the Virginian leaped into the water and led the rush up the steep path to the fort. Halfway there, his heart was pounding, his breath coming in short gasps. He forced himself to go more slowly, knowing that he should present a calm and unworried appearance when he entered the fort. As he neared the fort, Magaw bounded out to meet him, saluting and grinning, raising his voice to talk over the rumbling cannonade.

"Well, they're at it, sir!"

"I can see that, colonel. Are your men holding?"

"By God, sir—they'll hold until doomsday! Of course, the fort itself isn't under fire yet—your fort, if I may say so, sir, in the manner of a toast. They're butting against the outposts, and they'll butt a long while before they knock them off those two hills. We're prepared to sell our lives dearly, every one of us, to the last man."

"I don't want lives sold," Washington said wearily. "I want the fort held."

"It will be, sir."

"I want that path down to the boat landing defended very actively, both as a line of communication with Fort Lee and as a means of retreat if that should be necessary."

"It won't be necessary, sir!"

"Nevertheless, Colonel Magaw, I want you to understand the importance of keeping that path open. If necessary, after darkness tonight, if we find the tide of battle not sufficiently in our favor, you may call upon me for reinforcements."

Magaw could not refrain from rhetoric. "Believe me, sir," he said, "my only desire is to give them such a knock that they will go reeling back out of New York and free our beloved soil of their presence."

"Holy God," Putnam said, "he's worse than Knox."

The Virginian shrugged and walked into the fort. The men cheered him. They were Southerners, most of them, and they yelled that it was time they were given a chance instead of the God damned Yankees. They waved their muskets and their hats and they danced on the battlements, yelling:

"Come on, you bloody lobsters! Come and get it! Come on, you God damned bloody lobsters!"

It was not the sort of thing the foxhunter approved of, not when there might be cold and bitter work to be done in just a few hours. There was no reason for them to feel certain that the fort was invincible, that it would be a lark to defend it. He reflected that these men had been too long outside of his command, but he also realized that this was not the time for discipline.

He climbed onto the battlement himself and looked through his spyglass at the two hills that were under attack. On the one directly across from him and facing the Harlem River, he could make out men moving through the woods, but as yet there was no sight of the British scarlet or the Hessian green. The other hill, the one to the north, was too heavily wooded to reveal anything of action that might be progressing there. From south of the fort, where the eight hundred Pennsylvanians were attempting to hold the whole neck of the panhandle, there came the sound of intense musketry, but there too the battle was hidden by a screen of trees.

He had been on the battlements for about ten minutes when Greene climbed up beside him and said somewhat nervously, "Sir, I think we should be going now."

"Why?"

"No one believes more strongly than I that this place can be defended, but if they should cut that path to the river, you may have to be here for a week or a month."

"I was determined to see some of the action, Nathanael."

"Please, sir. I will remain here if you want me to."

The big man shrugged; there was good sense in what Green proposed. "We'll all go off now," he agreed, "and have some dinner across the river. If we wish to, we can return tonight."

Before he went, he shook hands with Magaw, who clasped his big hand fervently and promised again to hold the fort for six months, if that had to be.

As they got into the boat, the commander in chief twisted around to look at the fort again.

"What is it, sir?" Green asked.

"Nothing."

And Putnam said, "They're too damned sure, too damned sure."

They all sat facing the Jersey shore, except for the two boatmen, who now that they had been given no orders to hurry pulled slowly, with long, powerful sweeps, a rhythm, now, now, now—until suddenly it was broken, and with his oar poised in the air, the boatman nearest the commander stared back at the shore they had left, popeyed. And so, slowly, the foxhunter, Greene, Putnam, and Mercer turned around, and the boat, loose on the tide, began to swing broadside. And they didn't speak because what they saw was the impossible and incredible, the place they had just left, the boat landing occupied by a guard of redcoats and a long file of redcoats climbing up the path to the fort, the path that would be kept open, that had to be kept open, come what might.

The boat rocked, a little less than halfway out on the Hudson, but far enough out for them to observe the whole sweep of the shore of the panhandle, the meadows that led up to Fort Washington from the south and the big wooded hill to the north. From the north, men were slipping and sprawling headlong down the hill, in a frantic effort to get back to the fort before they were cut off by a division of redcoats marching through the gorge with beating drums and flying banners, the Continentals unaware that they were already cut off by the British who had taken the path and the boat landing.

The big man reached out, and someone—afterwards, he never knew who—put the spyglass in his hand.

In the south, it was more horrible. The Hessians were there, attacking the eight hundred Pennsylvanians, and the Pennsylvanians were running, and the Germans were running too. The big green-clad Jagers were having a field day. Over all the other noises of battle floated their wild warcry.

"Yonkee! Yonkee!"

The Pennsylvanians ran as if all the devils of hell were behind them. Many were Germans themselves, simple peasant folk who had come to America many years ago to put the Prussian specter behind them; but here were the terrible green-shakoed Jagers, with their long broad-blade bayonets, come three thousand miles to inflict their vengeance, yelling as they cut into the backs of the Pennsylvanians, spitting them like pigs. For the four generals in the boat, it was near and real and tragic, lit by sunlight the way a theater stage is lit by footlights; and they could do nothing but sit and watch the slaughter.

And as if the Jagers knew that four generals of the Continental army were watching, the performance became more terrible. The Pennsylvanians were flanked; they were butchered; they were pinned against trees; they were driven screaming into the river, while the Hessians hung over the bank and pot-shotted them.

Putnam began to curse. He stood up in the boat, roaring, "You bastards! You dirty bastards! You filthy, murdering bastards! God damn you! God damn you! God damn you!"

Greene put his face in his hands and began to sob.

Mercer whispered, "The poor bonny, bonny lads."

And one of the Marblehead fishermen said, "The Lord is my light and my salvation; whom shall I fear? The Lord is the strength of my life; of whom shall I be afraid? When the wicked, even mine enemies and my foes, came upon me to eat up my flesh, they stumbled and fell—"

The foxhunter said nothing, his face so white that the pockmarks stood out like scars of the damned.

The boat, swung broadside by the tide, swayed and tilted, while little whitecapped waves lapped at its hull. The Palisades, covered with autumn colors, stood like a wall of flaming glory, and all the broad beautiful Hudson was splashed with golden sunlight.

The second act now began. All the outposts, all the carefully planned defenses devised by Magaw, were crumpling; and the Continentals fled toward the tiny fort that could hold no more than two or three hundred persons. They scrambled up the rocky sides of the gorge to the north, they spilled out of the meadows to the south, and they fled from their lines on the hill over the Harlem River. Some of this the men in the boat could see, and some of it was hidden from them; but the whole tragic purpose of what was happening was evident enough. More and more men poured into the fort, five hundred, a thousand, fifteen hundred, two thousand. They were packed in like cattle, unable to move, unable to sight a gun, unable to fire a cannon for fear of killing a hundred of their comrades—and still more Continentals came, clawing over the stone walls.

At last a point was reached where the fort could hold no

more, where the panic-stricken late arrivals could not reach the walls through the press of bodies, where they fell back and made a second wall of human flesh.

There was never a question of defense. Like a ripe plum, almost three thousand men of the American army fell into the lap of the British. The net tightened. The grinning, triumphant Hessians swarmed in from the south, the light infantry breasted the eastern cliffs, and close-ranked redcoat troops marched stolidly up from the river. And from the north, the dragoons pushed their panting horses over the wooded hillside.

In another hour, it was all over; the purple rattlesnake flag hauled down and the British Jack up in its place.

The big man lowered his spyglass, pressed it together, and in a harsh whisper told the boatmen, "Row across—"

Greene couldn't look at him. The handsome young Quaker sat hunched over, his arms hanging limply, his whole body racked with sobs.

Putnam had become an old, old man. When he lifted a hand, it shook violently; when he tried to speak, his voice cracked and broke; when he turned to the fox-hunter, his face bore the deeply grooved imprint of pain.

"My fault—" he was trying to say.

Greene looked up.

"My fault," Putnam repeated, with miserable insistence.

"No, no," Greene said brokenly. "I wanted it, I wanted the fort to be held—all the time I wanted that."

The Virginia foxhunter said, "You, General Greene, and you, General Putnam, and you, General Mercer—when you go ashore at Fort Lee, you will remember that you are officers in my army, you will remember that you have a duty both to yourselves and your men, and you will strive to present an appearance compatible with your position."

Knyphausen, the Hessian, with his grinning Jagers behind him and in front of him, clearing a path, pushed into the fort.

"Wo ist Euer Hauptmann?"

The Continentals, pressed back at bayonet point, stared sullenly.

"Euer Hauptmann!" the Hessian roared.

A trembling backwoods Pennsylvania German answered,

"Dort," pointing to Magaw, who stood with the unseeing eyes of a man destroyed, body and soul.

"Er spricht Deutsch," Knyphausen smiled, adding, with all promise for the future, "Schurke!"

Magaw stepped forward, head nodding dully.

"Wie heisst Er?"

Magaw looked around him slowly, at the Jagers, at the bayonets, at his packed, beaten men.

"Wie heisst Er?" Knyphausen repeated.

Through his misery, Magaw comprehended the intent, if not the meaning of the words. "Colonel Magaw," he whispered.

"Sein Rank?"

Magaw nodded helplessly, and Knyphausen, pointing to Magaw's sword, barked, "Hundsfott, geb er den Degen!"

Magaw slowly shook his head, while the Jagers roared with laughter.

"Den Degen," Knyphausen repeated.

Now, at last, Magaw understood, and trying to keep himself straight, erect, as befitting an officer of the republic, unbuckled the sword that had been bought with the shillings of his friends and the pennies of their children, and presented to him in a little white church by a pastor who had enjoined him to go out and do his duty by God and his conscience. He handed it over, ashamed of the tears in his eyes, and Knyphausen, receiving it, nodded slightly and said, "So!"

Even the Jagers did not laugh now.

Greene, plunged in blackness, scraping the bottom of hell, had hidden himself in his tent where he would not have to present an appearance compatible with his position and lay on his bed, face down, trying to realize what a man does when he has ruined not only his own life but that of his best and dearest friend, and when he has almost singlehandedly destroyed his country. For Greene could see no future; nor could he see the tattered, ragamuffin little army recovering from this devastating blow.

Whether others were to blame or not, he blamed himself, knowing that it was almost entirely on his insistence and pleading that the Virginian had overruled his own and Lee's decision to abandon the fort. And now all was gone: hope and future and the revolution itself. He thought to himself, if only he had died, if only he had remained at the fort, if only he had gone out with the Pennsylvanians and spitted himself on a Hessian bayonet, if only he could go into the darkness that had been the reward of so many better men—

He heard the sound of someone entering the tent, and rolling over, he saw the high, bent figure of the foxhunter silhouetted against the flap, but only a black shadow without expression or intent. He got off the bed and onto his feet.

"Sit down, Nathanael," the foxhunter said.

Greene sat down and waited, steeling himself for the inevitable blow.

"It's been hard, Nathanael, hasn't it?" the foxhunter said.

"Sir?"

"I think it will be harder."

Greene stared at the tall man, trying to make out his features, his expression, trying to glean some evidence of his feelings.

"This is only the beginning," the Virginian nodded gently. "God only knows where we are going or what we are making or what the end will be; but we go on."

"Sir?"

"Do you understand, Nathanael, we go on?"

Greene got to his feet, found the other man's hand, and held onto it as if it were the only real thing in a bizarre world of nightmares.

"Sir—" He was glad the foxhunter could not see the tears in his eyes.

"Always, Nathanael."

"Always, sir."

Down the dusty road to New York City marched 2818 men of the Continental army, strung out over a mile of the way, feet dragging, arms hanging, and faces miserably white under the dirt and blood. On crude stretchers they carried their wounded and dead, and inside of them were all the dead hopes of a nation. And as they marched the Hessian drums ruffled and the British fifes sang; the wind blew the brown autumn leaves from the trees and fluttered the rattlesnake flag, carried by a group of triumphant Jagers.

As they neared the city, more and more curious, laughing citizens packed the roadway and hundreds of trulls and sluts ran along the Continental line, shrieking their opinions of the defeated men, cursing and spitting at them, darting between the redcoats who tried to fend them off. Small boys showered the Continentals with clods of dirt and rocks, and they began the cry that was presently taken up by all the citizens:

"Where is Washington? Where is Washington? Where is Washington? Show us Washington! Who is the great George Washington? Which one? Where is he? Show him to us! Show us the rich man! Show us the richest man in America!"

They chorused: "A hunting we will go, a hunting we will go, we'll catch a fox and put him in a box, and then we'll let him go."

"Washington!" they demanded.

"Show us Washington!"

"Who caught the fox?" they sang. "Who caught the fox? Who caught the fox?"

They swirled around every officer who wore the buff and blue of his commander, laughing and screaming.

"Washington! Washington!"

Again and again, the redcoats beat them off, and again and again they were back with "Give us Washington—we want to celebrate his great victory!"

The fifes and drums of the Jagers took up the tune of *Yankee Doodle,* and the trulls sang:

> *Yankee Doodle went to London,*
> *Riding on a pony,*
> *Stuck a feather in his cap,*
> *And called it macaroni. . . .*

Over the noise of all this, a British quartermaster sergeant was trying to report to his colonel on the spoils, reading monotonously:

"146 of cannon pieces.

12,000 of shot, shell and case.

2800 of muskets.

900 of pikes.

1400 of bayonets (bent and rusty, a shame to see, sir).

400,000 of cartridges.

270 of swords—" and adding:

"Sorry, sir, this bloody uproar—"

Walking on the high cliff of the Palisades, that night, he held it all inside of himself, the bereaved, the lonely, the terrified; he who had failed and always would fail, a dull Virginia farmer, a man who held water and sand in his fingers, but never anything solid or substantial, a man who had loved the wife of his best friend and held the love inside of him, like a charge of explosive, and then had seen her go away to add hopelessness to pain, a man who had loved an idiot stepdaughter and then kneeled by her bedside, pleading and whimpering for her not to die, a clown without wit or laughter, a clown without grace or hope of salvation.

13

HOW THEY WENT INTO JERSEY

Riding from Hackensack to Fort Lee, a few days after the British capture of Fort Washington, Henry Knox sought for words to say to the tall man beside him. Knox had been at Hackensack when the fiasco at Fort Washington occurred, and the first definitive news of it he had was a note from Greene, a confused, hopeless confession. Knox liked Greene, as a man and as a friend—aside from the fact that the two of them, along with Mifflin, Putnam and Mercer, constituted almost all the support the commander in chief had. Now Knox wanted to say something in defense of Greene.

"A man makes a mistake which any man could make," he began.

"Sir?" The Virginian glanced at him curiously.

"Any man, I mean, sir, any man. I had a note from Nathanael, and my God, sir, I wonder that he hasn't killed himself—"

"Harry, don't be a damned fool!"

The tall man rode on, looking straight ahead, and Knox, feeling he had said too much already, could find no more to better it. He was not an imaginative person; he had to look a fact in the face, and the fact now, to all intents and purposes, was that the revolution had finished itself. Even a well-trained, well-supplied army the size of this could not stand the shock of the loss of three thousand men with supplies, guns, ammunition; and they were not a well-trained, well-supplied army.

"I'll stay," the bookseller thought to himself, wondering just how long it would be, whether three weeks or three months.

Putnam wasn't a young man like the others, but a Yankee farmer fifty-eight years old and not in the best of health, wanting peace and security, but security especially more than anything else on earth. There were no fires in him; he was old and dry, and he wanted a roof over his head.

For him, the reasons toward rebellion had been neither tangible nor furious. With his hired man he had been building a stone wall on his farm, his back aching as he chipped the rocks and set them in, his mind concentrated, if on anything, on that old New England dictum that good walls make good neighbors—when a rider had pounded up with news of what had happened at Lexington and Concord.

"I don't like it," Putnam said, shaking his head.

"You remember old Shep Featherlee, he's dead, they shot him."

"They shouldn't have done that," Putnam said, knowing already that old as he was his peace and security were both gone, that he would have to drag his aching bones somewhere and do something, not a rebel and not a democrat, but standing by the dictum that good fences make good neighbors. And here, now, a year and a half later, it had washed out, the revolution, the crazy comic-opera war, the dirty, frightened Yankees—and he wondered whether there was anything else but to go back to his farm and grow old and rotten inside.

A long time ago, not in months nor years, but as time goes, in changes of many things, they were organizing the militia in Rhode Island, and young Nathanael Greene had been made a general—by virtue of the book he was always reading, *Military Tactics as Practiced in Continental Lands, with a summary of those virtues which go into the making of a competent officer*. He had drilled the militia with the book under his arm, to the complete admiration of a knot of giggling, fascinated girls. He was handsome as a devil, only thirty-three, and he was a self-made man.

There was an old friend of his father's, a Quaker, who had taken him aside one afternoon when the drill was over, and said, "I would have a word or two with thee, Nathanael."

"Yes?" Greene still smarted from the fact that without being permitted to say a word on his own behalf, he had been disowned by the Quakers. Now he stood stiff and impatient in his new uniform.

"Thee are going to war, Nathanael?"

"Yes."

"And thee will make thy peace with thy conscience?"

"I know what I have to do."

"Thee knows, Nathanael; but have thee considered that never since this world began came good out of evil."

"I'm not concerned with good and evil," he said, thinking of other things he might, but somehow could not, say to the old man, not the rights of man, the freedoms, the liberties, but the glorious adventure that promised a future without limit.

Now, thinking back over the months to what that old Quaker had said, seeing no future without limit, but instead one sharply defined and tragically proscribed, he tried to make for himself some plans, some intentions; he tried to relate himself once more to the Virginian and to the army of liberty.

Reed, the adjutant, sitting in front of a fire at Hackensack after the foxhunter had ridden away with Knox, thought about the past and the present and found nothing to hope for in the tall, awkward, blundering Virginia farmer. It seemed to him that he was living through the more or less historic moment when a movement dissolves, and his delicate fingers crept anxiously around the veins and muscles of his neck. Hanging would not be pleasant; and in the flames every wisp and twist of fire took the shape of a gallows.

A little while before, he had seen five hundred Vermont farmers march calmly out of the encampment, not as deserters, but as clearheaded Yankees who knew that the jig was up and were going home while their heads were still on their shoulders. They were the last of the Yankees on the west shore of the Hudson, and behind them they left only sullen, discontented midlanders, Pennsylvania and Jersey men.

Reed sighed, rose, and went to his tent. He took out quill and ink and paper, and began to write, addressing himself to General Charles Lee:

". . . I do not mean to flatter or praise you, at the expense of any other; but I do think it is entirely owing to you that this army and the liberties of America, so far as they are dependent on it, are not entirely cut off. You have decision, a quality often wanting in minds otherwise valuable, and I ascribe to this our escape from York Island, King's Bridge and the Plains; and I have no doubt, had you been here, the garrison of Mount Washington would now have composed a part of this army; and from all these circumstances, I confess, I do ardently wish to see you removed from a place where there will be so little call for your judgment and experience, to the place where they are likely to be so necessary. Nor am I singular in my opinion; every gentleman of the family, the officers and soldiers generally, have a confidence in you. The enemy constantly inquire where you are, and seem to be less confident when you are present. . . ."

When Knox and the Virginian arrived at Fort Lee, Greene had alarming news for them. About six thousand British soldiers had crossed the Hudson five miles north of Fort Lee and were already advancing inland in a broad circle which was intended to cut off the fort and surround the encampment at Hackensack.

"They want to make a whole end of us," Greene said bitterly but hopelessly. "They know they can do it, and by God, I see no way to stop them."

"Have you started to evacuate the fort?" the Virginian demanded.

"How can we evacuate? We have no horses, no wagons. I thought if we could hold them off for a time—" He and Knox stared at each other, and then Greene said helplessly, "My God, where will the end be?"

"Evacuate the fort," the tall man said.

"My God, sir, the tents, the provisions, the cannon—what are we going to do—"

"Evacuate the fort, General Greene. Immediately."

"And leave everything?"

"Everything."

"By tomorrow perhaps we could have horses for the cannon," Knox pleaded.

"Now!"

The foxhunter sat on his horse and watched the men stream out of the fort. They left behind them the tents stand-

ing, the big iron camp kettles cooking on the fires, the
cannon primed and loaded. He rode behind them as they
fled toward Hackensack; he drove them as a cattle herder
drives stock. When they showed signs of slackening, stumbled or fell, he roared at them and whipped them with his
quirt. It was a wild and grotesque race, hundreds of men
running, panting, walking, running again down the road
to Hackensack. The birth of a nation became a foot race with
a tall, pock-marked farmer bringing up the rear, and the
audience was four Dutch children—who stood along the
road and watched with charmed detachment, munching
curds and bread—and a light dragoon who watched from a hill
and then rode back to Lord Cornwallis to report.

"Too late, sir."

"They left the fort?"

"They're running down the road to Hackensack as if the
devil himself were behind them."

He wanted his men counted, he told Knox.

"Sir?"

"Counted! My God, Knox, do I have to repeat an order
seven times?"

"No, sir, only the desertions—"

"I'm not blind. I know there are desertions."

"But, sir—whole regiments."

"I want them counted."

It only took Knox a few hours to make the count. He
came back and reported. "Two thousand, nine hundred and
eleven, sir."

The tall man stared at him, and Knox said, "I'm sorry."

"You're sure?"

"I'm sure, sir."

And then the tall man nodded.

It rained as they plodded from Hackensack to Newark, not
gently, but a strong, steady, cold pouring. It turned the road
to mud, and there was no sound except the constant slop,
slop, slop of their steps. They walked hunched over to protect themselves, their heads bent, their arms crooked
around their muskets. The front ranks mashed the mud, those
behind dug deeper, and when it came to the end of that
mile-long column, the road was a bog. The foxhunter was
at the head of the column, with Reed on one side of him
and Putnam on the other; they were all three of them soaking wet, but Putnam, the old man, shot through and

through with rheumatic pains, suffered most. Farther down the line, Greene straddled a sorry nag. Knox walked with Captain Hamilton and the fragment of artillery left them, while Mercer brought up the rear. Mifflin had gone the same day to Philadelphia, to plead with the frightened Congress for more men.

As they rode along, Reed asked the Virginian, "Where will we camp?"

"Newark, perhaps."

"And then retreat?"

The tall man shrugged.

"For how long?"

"I don't know."

"We can't retreat forever," Reed said.

"We can, I think. Almost forever."

"Where?"

"Pennsylvania."

"And if they follow us there?" Reed insisted.

"Westward."

"Where?"

"Across the Alleghenies."

It ended in a blank, a vast, unexplored wilderness, a million square miles of wild, dark forest that was incomprehensible to Reed, that meant pain and more pain to Putnam—but which, to the foxhunter, was only a continuation of a road that went in one single direction.

Whenever a horse could be found and spared, reasonably strong, sound of wind, it was dispatched with a pleading letter to General Charles Lee, who was in Westchester with more than five thousand New England Yankees. The letters were all of the same tone, begging Lee to come across the Hudson and join the Virginian with his army. But Lee had plans of his own.

Even for a mercenary soldier, there was a difference between thirty thousand dollars and destiny; and day by day, destiny had been coming closer and closer to Charles Lee. Destiny sat on his shoulders when he looked at himself in his mirror and contemplated his long, unattractive face; destiny was with him when he crooned at and caressed his pack of dogs. Destiny was in the letters he received from Joseph Reed and so many others who were dissatisfied and impatient with the blundering Virginian.

Lee had cast his fortunes with this crazy revolt of farmers

and mechanics and tradesmen, and now the whole insane
structure was tumbling. To run out would be too simple
and too unprofitable; there was nothing waiting for him at
the hands of the British, only contempt and dishonor. But
suppose he were to rescue the almost inert carcass? Not
mutiny; for one thing, he had been born and bred a soldier, and to mutiny against a mutiny was not only against
his nature, it did not make sense. But suppose he waited
patiently until the ripe fruit fell into his lap? The pattern
of the future was clear enough; the foxhunter's army was
dissolving like wet sand. It might hold together for ten days,
for twenty days, for thirty days; thirty days was the limit
he put on the business. Thirty days would see the army
on the west shore of the Hudson gone, and the foxhunter in front of a British court martial. For his part, he had
only to wait and to put off the Virginian with excuses, and
in a month or less he himself would be commander in
chief of the Continental armies. Certainly, there was no
one else suited for the place, and certainly his army would
be the only rebel army of any size left in America.

The Virginian could not forget the simile of the sand.
Again and again, he stared at his big hands, fumbled with
them, opened them and closed them. His hands were too
big to hold a quill comfortably, even if he had been a
scholar, even if he could have handled words, spelled them,
reared them into intelligent sentences. It was agonizing pain
for him to write, yet he sat in his tent at Newark, his candle burning, writing and writing, to Lee, to the terrified
Congress, to the governors of the colonies, pleading for men
and supplies, for cannon, stopping very often to feel at his
neck and wonder what it meant for a man to be hanged for
high treason and how it felt when the trap dropped and the
rope tightened. Once he would have been sick with humilia-
tion at the thought, but now it was merely a way for a
man to end, and he managed to smile grimly as he rubbed
his long, creased, sunburnt neck.

His thoughts now turned very often to Mount Vernon, to
a part of his life that was drenched with sunlight, to little, fat Martha, to the white buildings and the green fields,
memories harder to regain now that winter was approaching.
It was strange, but the fact—which he now accepted—that
he would never again see Mount Vernon, did not discon-
cert him too greatly. No one knew better than he how in-

credible his present position would have been to the man he was five, or even two years ago, the beaten commander of a fast-vanishing army, a lank bewildered man in a shapeless, faded uniform—sitting in a leaky, torn tent with a broken-spirited, dirty rabble of New Jersey and Pennsylvania boys around him. But he was not that man; that man couldn't have had such lonely, terrible pride, now the only thing left to him—pride in something that had not existed for him then and which he could not well put into words even now, which he could think of only as certain rights of man.

The tattered army fled out of one end of Newark as the British entered the other end of the town. Knox and Hamilton and a few others loaded a twelve-pounder with grape and flailed the streets with metal in a frantic bid for a few moments more of grace; and then they ran, leaving the cannon behind them. The whole army was running, sprawled out over the road that led to New Brunswick. The advance guard of the British was too small to attack the Continentals, but the dragoons climbed up on the Newark rooftops and cheered the army of liberty on its way.

Marching down to New Brunswick, they had their first brief flurry of snow. It had been summer when they began the retreat from Brooklyn Heights, and now it was almost the end of November, and they still wore the same clothing. If anything, they had less, for here and there along the way they had dropped this and that—a knapsack, a blanket, a jacket. Their stockings had long ago worn through, and there was no hope of replacements. Dirty toes poked through their shoes, and the shredded soles, where they still existed, were paper-thin. Wool, the manufacture of which had been forbidden in America, was almost unknown among them; their shirts were linen, their breeches homespun, neither material very warm nor lasting.

Winter came slowly, but now at last it was here, the damp, bone-penetrating winter of the Jersey flats, cold and wet and nasty; and on the muddy or frozen Jersey roads they began to leave their trademark, their insignia and single sign that marked them from all others for years to come. It was an ooze of blood, a stain from a thousand dragging feet, a dark spotting on the road that advertised: "Here walked the army of liberty"—for all who wanted to see or cared to read.

It was not only the cold. They began to feel the dull ache of starvation in their bellies, for the fields were gleaned clean, the cattle were driven away, and the barns were locked against them. The good Jersey citizens had taken a lesson from the good citizens of New York; this was not their army, this rabble, this bastardly conglomeration of foreigners, children, and madmen. The Jersey houses were shuttered tight, and the Jersey farmers had their guns loaded. More men of the army of liberty during that time died at barn doors than before the guns of the British; and deserters, tens and hundreds of deserters, made crazy with hunger, had their brains blown out when they approached houses to beg for food. How it had happened, so suddenly, the poor devils themselves did not know; themselves, they were Jersey and Pennsylvania men, yet suddenly they were an alien army in an alien land, every hand turned against them, every door closed to them, every window barred to them, and death waiting if they should venture only a few hundred yards from the main army.

As much as they wanted food and clothing, they wanted answers, desperately. There was only one man who had any; he was a small, ugly Englishman, with a long, pear-shaped head. His name was Tom Paine.

He had fire in his eyes. He walked with them, with a musket slung over his shoulder, and the musket was almost as big as he was. He shared their food, and he sat around the fire with them. He was sick with them and lousy with them and tired with them and dirty with them. And he had answers.

He preached; they would have hated him if he were clean and handsome, but he was dirty and ugly. They were never quite sure what he was; they couldn't make out whether he was an officer or a private; sometimes he was one and sometimes the other; he was neither when he stood up at the fire in the evening and said, in his curious Thetford accent, "Patriots, listen to me! Come and take comfort, for I swear to you there is comfort to be taken!"

They would come out of the corners and press around the fire where he stood, nudging each other, grinning a little self-consciously. "Tom Paine," they would tell each other, and nod.

He would single one out of the crowd and demand. "Patriot, what is your name?"

"Burk Hopper."

"Burk Hopper, why are you fighting with this army?"

"Damned if I know!"

"Then let me tell you—then let me tell you for a sign and a banner to lead you in the fray. Let me tell you that there is nothing on this earth more glorious than a man's freedom and no aim more elevated than liberty. . . ."

If it had been anyone in the world but Tom Paine, they would have laughed or cursed or killed him. But the words came out of Tom Paine like a prayer and a benediction, and there was fire in his eyes. They were martyrs, and he let them know it, drawing an inner stuff of fierce wonder from beneath their rags and filth. So they crouched and listened to him, picking their noses, spitting, pulling the little knotted hairs from their beards, nudging each other.

"That makes sense."

When he asked them, "Am I superstitious?"

"No! No!"

"Am I a damned Salem Puritan?"

"No!"

"Have I ever condoned the persecution of Jew by Christian, of Catholic by Protestant?"

"No!"

"Then you can believe me when I say to you as a man, only a man, no more than a man, that there is a God!"

Then they waited expectantly, knowing what was coming; for they had been told it a dozen times before.

"I say there is a God Almighty who will not give up his people to destruction by tyrants!"

Then there came an intellectual discord. "Now wait a minute, Tom—looka here. I ain't making to doubt you, but looka here at the lot of us, dirty, lousy—do we look like God is with us? Are we winning or are we losing?"

"I say that we are winning!" he thundered. "I say that should the ground open up and swallow us to the last man, we would still have won, for the world will not forget! We are a peaceful people, a humble people who took up arms only for the sacred rights of man! Be damned with who wins the battles on the field, my triumph is here!"—striking at his thin chest.

There was one night when he sat with a long, battered drum between his bony knees, tilted so that the top of it would catch light from the fire, using it as a desk and writing furiously, one devoted soldier beside him to hold the ink and another to sharpen the quills he bent and ruined in his rush of thought. In the place where he worked, a dead silence reigned; for word had gone around that Tom Paine was at it, and there was only the resonant mutter of the drum as the quill scratched back and forth.

As he wrote, more and more men crowded around the fire, until finally looking up, he saw the reddened burning eyes of more than a hundred fixed on him. Then he began to read what he had written, bending over the drumhead, his low voice beating back like a roll call down the ages:

"These are the times that try men's souls. The summer soldier and the sunshine patriot will, in this crisis, shrink from the service of their country; but he that stands it now, deserves the love and thanks of man and woman. Tyranny, like hell, is not easily conquered; yet we have this consolation with us, that the harder the conflict, the more glorious the triumph. . . . Heaven knows how to put a proper price upon its goods; and it would be strange indeed if so celestial an article as FREEDOM should not be highly rated. . . ."

And the foxhunter sent letters to Lee, pleading for help, for a thousand, for even a few hundred of his Yankees, for— if nothing else—the regiment of fishermen. Only now, with the desertions increasing daily in spite of Tom Paine's roaring, with the British hounding him day and night, did he realize what a store he had placed on Glover's men, what it would mean to know that there were six or seven hundred long-faced fishermen who would not run away. His councils of war were now almost wordless, himself facing Knox and Greene and Putnam and Mercer, the order of the day always the same, retreat; all that coupled with his desperate insistence that they should make counts so he might know how many or how few men were left.

At New Brunswick, two whole brigades of Pennsylvania men had announced their intentions to return home. He told Greene to have them surrounded by what loyal men he could muster and Knox to load a cannon with grape. He himself didn't know what he would do if the Pennsylvania men refused to lay down their arms. The midlanders began to walk, their bayonets level, their faces set with a desperation they had never shown against the British, and Greene looked helplessly at the Virginian. In that moment, the whole torn fabric of revolution might have dissolved in bloody ruin, but the tall man shook his head and the two brigades marched out of the encampment with no opposition.

The tall man couldn't retreat inside of himself. He pleaded with old Putnam afterwards. "What should I have done?"

"I don't know."

"Would you have fired?"

"I don't know. A man goes the way he sees a thing."

"And if he doesn't see anything—?"

He trusted Reed and was able to say to him, "You know how near the end we are, Joseph."

Reed nodded.

"I've written to Lee again and again. God knows what he's doing—he's a wise man and a good soldier, I can't criticize him. But he won't help us. Perhaps he can't help us."

There was a curious, half-frightened expression on Reed's face.

"Go to Burlington," the foxhunter said hopelessly. "Tell them we need men. Tell them it's the end, the real end this time; let them feel their necks the way I've been feeling mine."

A frightened Jersey legislature sat at Burlington. "It won't do any good," Reed protested.

"Go anyway, Joseph. It's the only straw I can catch at."

Reed had not been gone long when the letter came from Lee, addressed to Adjutant-General Joseph Reed. The dispatch rider gave it to the commander in chief, whose first impulse was to send it on after the adjutant. Then it occurred to him that this letter might contain the ray of hope he had been seeking. There was no letter for himself from Lee, and since Reed had been taking care of a good deal of the correspondence, this might serve the same purpose. He opened it and read.

"*My Dear Reed*—I received your most obliging, flattering letter; lament with you that fatal indecision of mind, which in war is a much greater disqualification than stupidity or even want of personal courage. Accident may put a decisive blunderer in the right; but eternal defeat and miscarriage must attend the man of the best parts, if cursed with indecision. The general recommends in so pressing a manner as almost to amount to an order, to bring over the Con-

tinental troops under my command; which recommendation,
or order, throws me into the greatest dilemma from several
considerations. . . ."

He continued to read, his mind blundering down a narrow
black passageway, endless and without light. He stared at
the salutation, repeating it to himself over and over again,
My Dear Reed, My Dear Reed. He put his finger upon the
signature: Charles Lee.

" 'Lament with you,' " he whispered to himself.

He stood up, an effort which required almost all his
strength, and paced miserably back and forth between the
dirty curtains of his tent. He groped for the shaking world
and tried to place it upon an even keel. Reed was his friend,
his adjutant, his companion; Lee was a servant of his Congress. The letter was a false and rotten lie, forged to create
dissension, served to him just at that precise time when Reed
was away on a mission to Burlington.

"A damned lie!" he cried, and his voice brought the sentry's head into the tent.

"What is it, sir?"

"Nothing—"

His hands were shaking as he read the letter over a second time, wearing his glasses now, peering at every word.
No—that painful scrawl of Lee's could not be forged; he
knew the handwriting as well as he knew his own. Lee
had written this letter in answer to another letter of Reed's,
"obliging, flattering." As his army dissolved, his officers
plotted against him, the men he had loved and trusted; and
now whom could he trust? Greene? Greene would die for him,
but he might have said the same of Reed. Mifflin?—why had
he gone off to Philadelphia so eagerly? Who knew what was
behind Mercer's brown mask? Putnam? Knox?

"Oh, my God," he whispered.

Hour after hour he paced back and forth in the narrow
space of his tent, staring dumbly at his colored servant when
the man came in to say that dinner was ready, nodding without hearing to a message Knox sent him, walking and walking and prodding with his bony shoulders at the walls
which confined him. There was no salvation, no solution,
only a direction; and the direction was fixed, a thing without change, a focus for his life that would never be any
different. He felt tired and frightened, because he knew now
how completely alone he was; but once more his feet were

on the ground and he knew they would remain on the ground until he came to the end of his road, whatever that end might be.

He sat down and wrote to Reed:

"The enclosed was put into my hands by an express from White Plains. Having no idea of its being a private letter, much less suspecting the tendency of the correspondence, I opened it, as I had done to all other letters to you from the same place and Peek's Hill, upon the business of your office, as I conceived and found them to be. This, as it is the truth, must be my excuse for seeing the contents of a letter which neither inclination nor intention would have prompted me to. I thank you for the trouble and fatigue you have undergone in your journey to Burlington, and sincerely wish your labors may be crowned with the desired success. With best respects to Mrs. Reed, I am, dear sir, &c.
                                       "GEORGE WASHINGTON"

14

HOW DESTINY SAT
ON GENERAL LEE'S SHOULDER

Men who knew and liked Charles Lee complained that he should have been born a king, and indeed in his ugly features and consistent melancholy there was something both kingly and devilish. He hadn't, like the foxhunter, gone blundering into destiny; destiny had been inside of him from as far back as he could remember, and as far back as he could remember he had been conscious of that destiny. Yet in one way and another, that destiny had eluded him; now, for the first time, it perched on his shoulder.

And on his shoulder he was determined to keep it. He knew only too well what a potential lay inert in the sprawling American settlements, numbering as they did almost three million souls, and he had quite come to the conclusion that he was the man to awaken that fire. He was not worried

about his ability to drive off the Briitsh; that would come
later. He already had his army, and all that remained was
to obtain supreme command.

On the fourth of December, deciding that he had waited
long enough, he had the Marblehead fishermen ferry his
army across the Hudson. The British, in Jersey, were between
him and the foxhunter; obviously, his army was the best-
equipped and the strongest, and just as obviously, the British would leave him alone and concentrate their force upon
destroying the foxhunter. All this he had carefully thought
out in advance, and he was so satisfied with his work that he
could afford a rare smile, lying back in his boatload of dogs
and crooning to them while they made the air hideous with
their yapping.

If Charles Lee loved nothing else, he loved his dogs;
he saw them into the boat as carefully as a man would
shepherd his children, and on the Jersey shore the fishermen
stared in amazement as he lifted the dogs out one by one,
standing in the water himself, and carried them onto land.
The army had already started its slow march under the second in command, General Sullivan, who had been exchanged
recently, after being made prisoner at Brooklyn, but Lee
wouldn't move a step until the dogs were fed. As meat was
brought, he examined each piece carefully, threw some aside
in disgust, and raged and ranted until food to suit his choice
was produced.

The army turned down the Jersey shore in the general
direction the Virginian had taken some two weeks before,
but Lee's progress was so sluggish that even the New Englanders complained about their marching. Ten miles a day
was unusual; sometimes it was only five or six, and sometimes they sat around for days and did nothing but sleep
and eat. Sullivan, who suspected that things might not be
going too well with the forces of the commander in chief,
began to grow uneasy, but since he was denied the privilege
of reading Lee's dispatches and papers, he had nothing concrete to base his suspicions upon. The rank-and-file Yankees had no knowledge at all of what had happened to the
New Jersey and Pennsylvania men; as far as they knew, the
earth might have opened and swallowed them. For their
own part, it was a peaceful and lazy march, and they were
not moved to object too violently, the more so since the

horror of Brooklyn and New York was still vivid in their memories.

Seemingly, the war had lost all plan and purpose, and as the weather turned colder, the New Englanders began to desert in increasing numbers. By the time a week had passed, Lee and his army were at Morristown, but in the march from White Plains, he had lost almost a thousand men through desertions. Now he was close onto the rear guard of the British, and therefore he slowed down his already snail-like pace. On the twelfth of December, Lee marched his troops out of Morristown, eight miles to Vealtown. His moment of destiny had almost arrived. Each successive pleading dispatch from the commander put the tall Virginian in a slightly more desperate position. A week more, Lee estimated, and there would be both a new Continental army and a new commander in chief.

For one thing, Lee was sick of the stench of camp, of his doltish troops, of the boredom of a week's tedious marching, of the constant and uninspired questions asked by the members of his staff as to where they were going and what they intended. Glover, the leader of the fishermen, didn't like Lee, and he lost no chance to make it plain. If Lee threatened him, he threatened back, and when Lee cursed him, he cursed back. For the time being, Lee intended to do nothing; he wanted command first, and when he had that, he would give his troops a taste of discipline.

But now he was sick to death of the whole thing; after the troops had encamped at Vealtown, Captain Gunnerson told him about the tavern, and Lee was in a proper mood to respond.

"How far is it?" Lee asked.

"Three miles. But it's worth it."

Why not? Lee asked himself. A man can go crazy without a little relaxation.

"A blonde?" Lee asked.

"No, she's dark." Gunnerson made motions with his hands, and Lee felt his body tense with desire.

"Her name's Anna," Gunnerson said.

Lee said, "You know, I suppose, captain, that a man can go far with me, a man with discretion."

"I pride myself on my discretion, sir."

"Continue to!"

The captain nodded, staring at the thin, ugly, sorrowful man who in a day or a week would be the leader of a nation. He felt neither love nor repulsion and thought that he would have been better satisfied with a handful of shillings than with Lee's promises for the future.

Lee went in to his dogs, a tentful that stilled their yapping the moment he entered, rushed at him and climbed onto him to kiss and welcome him. He knelt down so that they could get at his face, and he became almost womanly with tenderness.

"Babies, babies," he crooned.

They crawled into his arms and licked his face and hands.

"Little babies," he crooned. "Be quiet. Be still. Lie down."

They lay down obediently, and he fished sweets out of his pockets. One by one, he gave them the favors, allowing them to lick his face in thanks.

"Tomorrow, I'll see you, babies," he said.

They knew he was going away, and they lay quiet and looked at him out of their big, melting eyes.

"Tomorrow—"

The tavern was at Baskingridge, three miles away, and Lee rode there with six men as a guard. He would have preferred to go alone, but he realized the unimpressiveness of a general arriving anywhere without a guard.

The guards pushed into the inn behind him, grinning, clasping their big muskets clumsily and self-importantly. The Jersey farmers rose, bowed in return, but awkwardly, and retreated to one side of the room. A little innkeeper rushed out of the kitchen, bowing, rubbing his hands, licking his lips.

"A patriot, sir. You have entered the house of a true and loyal patriot."

Lee smiled as he noticed the girl behind the bar; she was all that Gunnerson had promised.

"And I welcome you to my humble house, Your Excellency."

"All right. I want dinner and a bed, a featherbed, do you understand?"

"Completely, Your Excellency."

"And a place for my men."

"In the carriage house, dry and snug and warm, too. May I say, Your Excellency, that never before in twenty-two years of keeping a decent and honest house, have I been so honored?"

"You may." Lee nodded magnanimously.

"Our food is simple, but tastily cooked. You will not be disappointed in our food."

Lee threw off his coat and slumped into a high wing-chair by the fire. "Bring me a bottle of wine, now."

"Claret, Burgundy, Madeira, Port?"

"Claret," Lee decided. He was warm; he was comfortable; he was being treated with dignity. The girl brought the wine, and as she stood between him and the fire, hidden from the rest of the room by the high wing-chair, Lee ran his hand lightly across her thigh. She almost dropped the tray, giggling and rolling her big black eyes.

"Oh, Your Excellency."

"Pour the wine," Lee said. "My dear, pour the wine."

As she bent and poured the wine, he caressed her again, and the feel of warm, smooth flesh under his hand made him shiver with desire.

After two bottles of wine, he was ready for dinner, and by then the inn was empty except for himself, the landlord and the girl. Whether she was the landlord's daughter or a servant, Lee didn't know; whichever the case, the landlord urged her on him. She served the dinner and stood by the table while Lee ate. And along with the dinner, which consisted of a fine roast duck, a meat pie, and a pudding, there went a bottle of Burgundy and then an earthenware jug of homemade peach brandy.

Not in many months had Lee felt so completely at ease, so mellow, so little put-out with the world. He had never been a very successful person with women, yet he had made enough advances already to know that the girl would be his without any fumbling courtship. When he asked her to sit at the table, she giggled and refused, but she arched toward him and rubbed her full breasts against his shoulder like a big, purring kitten.

He was full, bloated, his belly tight against his waistcoat, when he got up from the table and slipped into the wing-chair by the fire. The girl was preparing a rum flip for him, and he sighed with content as she plunged the red-hot loggerheads into the pitcher. And then, while Lee sipped daintily at his mug, she pulled off his boots and set his feet on a footstool. By now, in Lee's eyes, she had lost all her grossness; she was delicate and dainty and precisely what he had always dreamed of in the way of a woman, and even her giggle as he stroked her hair was like musical laughter.

"Ah, my dear," he said, "you're very good to me."

"It ain't like we have a general every day," she simpered.

"No, my dear, nor does a general always have a princess to ease his weariness."

"Go on," she giggled.

"A general's life is neither a bed of roses nor a path of glory."

She continued to giggle.

"He has the weight of an army and the destiny of a nation upon his poor shoulders."

"I seen a British colonel once," she remembered.

"Our enemies, we must treat them honorably, but harry them sharply."

"He had white britches and a red coat. He was pretty." She frowned and recalled: "He had a perook."

"My poor army fights in rags," Lee sighed.

"They stink," she said bluntly, thinking of how the six troopers had pawed her when she showed them their beds in the barn.

With his third mug of flip, his mood became melancholy, and all the miseries and wants of his life rose up to plague him. "The path of glory," he said, "is a lonely road. I am a miserable man, a lonely man, an ugly man. I have no friends but my dogs, and by God they're better than men. They're my babies, they love me, they trust me. You look at glory, my dear, because the buttons on my uniform glitter, glitter, but I'm a miserable man, a lonely man. No warm hearth for me and no roof over my head, and no sweet wife to say farewell to me, and no little children to call me papa, no, for me the camp kettle is all and I must dip into it like a brute along with the other brutes and lay my head on the ground. . . ." Maudlin tears rolled down his flat cheeks and his under lip drooped and his head swayed from side to side.

"Come to bed," she smiled.

"Bed with a whore," he mumbled. "That for the new commander in chief of the army of liberation."

She continued to smile as she helped him upstairs.

It was four o'clock in the morning when a pounding on the door of his room woke him. The room was black and his head ached violently and his mouth was huge and rank and leathery.

"Who's there?" he muttered.

The pounding continued.

"Who's there?"

"Major Wilkinson."

"Who in damnation is Major Wilkinson?"

"Messenger from General Gates, sir."

"Who?"

"General Gates."

"Go to hell and be damned. There's time for that in the morning."

"This is very urgent, sir."

Lee felt the soft, yielding presence of the girl, but the night before was shrouded in the mystery of countless glasses of wine and flip. He dragged her from under the covers and tried to make out her face in the dark, frightening her until she whimpered like a bewildered kitten.

"Who are you, you bitch?" he demanded.

"Anna."

"Who?"

She broke into a frightened explanation of the night before, but he exclaimed, "God damn you, you bitch, get out of here!"

She started for the door, sobbing, but he caught her in the dark and whispered, "Under the bed!"

"What?"

"Under the bed, God damn you!"

Still sobbing, she crawled under the bed, and Lee opened the door. The man called Wilkinson stood there with the little innkeeper, who was clad in a long nightshirt and held a candle in his trembling hand. Wilkinson was a boy of nineteen, smirking, his eyes full of nasty knowledge he had wheedled from the landlord.

"Well?"

"This letter, sir," Wilkinson explained, holding it out to Lee.

"Who sent you and what the devil does this mean?"

"General Gates. He's with four regiments up by Wallpeck."

"You're crazy! He isn't a hundred miles of here!" He plucked at the letter and held it under the candlelight. "This is addressed to Washington!"

"My God, sir," Wilkinson said with mocking dismay. "I don't know where General Washington is. Neither does General Gates. Neither does anyone in this whole cursed country. Schuyler sent Gates down with four regiments because he heard Washington was bad. But the general couldn't find him, and I couldn't find him. I been riding around all night, sir. I'm so stiff I can't move."

"All right," Lee said, tearing the letter open. "All right. Get out of here. Put a blanket somewhere and go to sleep."

Not until after he had crawled back under the covers did a series of pitiful wails remind Lee of the girl.

"Come out," he said. He had taken the candle back into the room with him and now he was able to see something of her, her swollen face and red eyes and stringy hair down to her waist.

"Who are you?"

"Anna," she sobbed. "Anna."

He rubbed his eyes and pulled air down his tortured throat, and bit by bit something of the night before came back. He groaned and said, "Can you get rum?"

She nodded eagerly.

"Bring me a drink."

She came back with a can of the stuff and he gulped it, almost choking with the hot fire in his throat, but feeling better once it was down. The girl, dressed only in a thin shift, had seated herself composedly at the foot of the bed, from where she regarded him with curious wonder.

"General Lee," she said.

"What?"

She made a face and then giggled and rubbed her belly.

"Get out," he groaned.

She went to the door, giggling and glancing across her shoulder; Lee rolled over and buried his face in the pillow.

The candle burned out and dawn filtered through the dirty little windows. Lee sat up in the bed, staring ahead of him, hating himself, wretched, with a splitting headache and a sour stomach. He belched slowly and regularly, and his outstretched hands were yellow against the bolster. It was almost eight o'clock before he felt the strength or inclination to get out of bed, poke his feet into his slippers, and stumble across the room to where his coat hung. The very thought of the effort of dressing sickened him. He managed to get the coat on over his nightshirt, and without washing he opened the door and went downstairs.

Wilkinson was waiting, warming himself by the fire; when he saw Lee he grinned and stared as if his eyes were deceiving him.

"What are you looking at?" Lee demanded coldly.

"Nothing, sir," Wilkinson said, licking his lips.

"Me?"

"I'm sorry, sir." The apology was insultingly meek.

"Don't be sorry, damn you," Lee said, taking some small consolation out of the knowledge that Wilkinson was looking at the next commander in chief of the Continental army. He got over to the wing-chair and dropped into it, telling the boy more gently, "Get me a drink, major."

"Rum?"

"Rum," Lee nodded glumly. Pulling the chair closer to the fire, he drained the goblet and then toasted his hands and his bare feet. The innkeeper approached to ask about breakfast, but Lee growled and swallowed several times, shaking his head.

"About that letter, sir," Wilkinson began.

"Damn it, where do you think Washington is?"

"I don't know, sir—across the Delaware, perhaps."

"Well, I don't know either. I don't know whether he's alive or dead or whether he has an army. I don't think it matters. Damn you, don't look at me like that! I said I don't think it matters."

"Yes, sir. I'm inclined to agree with you." He grinned again, ingratiatingly.

"Get your breakfast if you want to."

"I'm not very hungry, sir."

"Well, damn it, don't stand there staring at me!"

Lee was still sitting apathetically by the fire when Colonel Scammel, his adjutant, arrived. It was after nine now, but the inn, being off the main road, had no customers, and Lee was the only guest who had spent the night there. The girl had hidden herself in the kitchen and all the squeaky threats of the landlord could not bring her into the parlor where Lee sat bare-footed, his coat over his nightshirt.

Scammel was as surprised as Wilkinson at Lee's appearance, but he controlled himself somewhat better and remembered to salute.

"What is it?" Lee demanded, returning his gaze to the fire after a single glance at the adjutant.

"General Sullivan wants his marching orders, sir."

"Marching orders?"

"Yes, sir."

Lee frowned at the fire. "Why does he want marching orders?"

"I suppose, sir, that he didn't think you intended a permanent encampment at Vealtown."

"No? Well, damn it all, Scammel, where does he want to march to?"

"I don't know, sir. That's up to you."

"I won't have your damned insolence, Scammel!" Lee cried, turning fiercely on the adjutant, who met his glance evenly, but said softly, "I'm sorry, sir. I did not intend insolence."

"I'm sorry," Lee muttered. "My head is splitting."

"Is there anything I can do?"

"No—no. Have you a map?"

Scammel nodded and went outside to fetch the map from his saddlebag. When he came back, he spread it out on the table, and Lee dragged himself from the wing-chair to look at it. The letters, lines, rivers and towns blurred before his eyes. He tried to focus, supporting himself over the table with both his outstretched hands, until Wilkinson brought a chair and helped him into it. Gradually, the places on the map came into focus and outlined themselves; and with Scammel and Wilkinson standing over his shoulders, Lee traced a wavering line from Vealtown to Pluckamin. There his finger stopped, and Wilkinson and Scammel exchanged glances.

"Pluckamin," Lee said.

Wilkinson grinned knowingly.

"It's not more than seven miles, sir," Scammel pointed out.

"What!"

"I said it seems to be a very short march, sir."

"Why should it be a long one, Scammel?"

"No reason, sir. But General Sullivan is under the impression that we should be moving to join General Washington."

"Tell Sullivan we'll move at my own damned pleasure! Tell him that, Scammel!"

"Very well, sir." And Scammel swung on his heel and walked out of the house.

Lee stared after Scammel, and then he turned to Wilkinson and demanded querulously, "Did you see my army? Did you see their shoes? Did you see their clothes?"

Wilkinson nodded. Lee appeared full to the brim with self-pity, his red eyes becoming moist, his lower lip trembling. "Join Washington," he said, aggrieved and asking for pity. "Did you see their shoes? And how do I know where Washington is? Does anyone know?"

The major shrugged and sat down at the table, where the landlord was spreading the breakfast dishes. Lee, who had not been hungry before, now began to eat ravenously—eggs, pancakes, bacon, stuffing his mouth with chunks of bread as if he had been starving for a week. The girl came out of the kitchen and stood at the bar, giggling, her hands on her hips, her eyes reaching toward Wilkinson, who grinned at her and winked lewdly.

"Damned hussy," Lee muttered. He felt better now that he had eaten.

"Who is she?"

"Yours," Lee said, giving with lordly satisfaction. He pounded on the table, calling for the landlord to give him pen and ink and paper. "I'll burn the ears of your General Gates," Lee told Wilkinson. "By God, there's a new order coming, and I can make or break a man, Wilkinson, understand that!"

"Sir?" the boy smiled innocently, and then added, "I hope to be included. For me, sir, the old order's a filthy bitch."

"Make him or break him," Lee said pointedly. Wilkinson rose and walked to the window, and Lee grabbed the quill and began to write furiously:

"The ingenious maneuver of Fort Washington has completely unhinged the goodly fabric we had been building. There never was so damned a stroke; *entre nous*, a certain great man is most damnably deficient. He has thrown me into a situation where I have my choice of difficulties: if I stay in this province I risk myself and army; and if I do not stay, the province is lost forever. . . ."

Wilkinson had been staring out of the window, from which point he could see something over a hundred yards of the road. When a party of British dragoons appeared from around the bend and dashed down on the inn with their pistols drawn, it was neither inconsistent nor impossible; it was the bad end of a bad little drama, all of which had given Wilkinson the impression of being inside a nightmare.

Lee had just finished writing his letter, and he was signing it when he heard the roll of hoofs. "What's that?" he asked Wilkinson, without turning around.

"British cavalry," came the strangely calm answer.

Lee finished folding his letter, and then suddenly leaped out of his chair and whirled around. "What?"

"British cavalry," Wilkinson repeated calmly.

"Where? My God, how?" Lee stood there in disheveled impotence, one slipper off, his arms hanging tragically, his bird-like head thrust forward. "Where's the guard?" he moaned.

Wilkinson was already starting up the stairs.

"For God's sake, Wilkinson, where are you going?" Lee cried.

"To save my hide," the boy said cheerfully. "I'm quite fond of it."

The guards had stacked their muskets on the shady side of the house, and then, becoming chilled, had gone around to the sunny side to warm themselves, leaving the muskets stacked and on the other side of the inn. While they were basking in the sun, the girl came out with hot flip, and after they had finished the rum they caught her and almost came to a battle over which should keep his hands on the best parts of her. She was screaming with laughter and they were in the process of dragging her across to the barn when the British dragoons appeared. They let go of her and stared stupidly, while she stood poised in wide-eyed admiration of the gorgeous horsemen.

Then they broke and ran in every direction, the dragoons after them, riding them down and beating them with sword-flats.

Lee was standing by the fire, holding onto the wing-chair, when Colonel Harcourt of the Royal Dragoons entered the inn, and afterwards Harcourt said that he had never in his life seen anything all at once so funny, tragic, and pitiful. They were old acquaintances, and back in the years when Lee had been a British officer, the dragoons had been his own regiment. And now it seemed to Lee that some terrible, woeful irony had planned his whole stay at the inn, culminating it with this. Looking at Harcourt as he would at a ghost, Lee tried with a trembling hand to button his coat and hide the dirty, wrinkled nightshirt.

Harcourt smiled and nodded. "Pleased to see me, Lee?" he asked.

Lee sought for some sort of dignity, letting go of the wing-chair and drawing himself up, trying to hide the bare foot, swaying a little, feeling faint and nauseous. Captain Harris, whom he also remembered, pushed into the inn; Harris was young and handsome and immaculate. He regarded Lee with disgust.

"What are you going to do with me, sir?" Lee whispered.

"Hang you, I suppose," Harcourt replied callously.

"No—no. Oh, my God, no."

Harcourt took a perfumed handkerchief out of his pocket and sniffed at it delicately.

"You can't hang me," Lee whispered.

"What shall I do with him, sir?" Harris asked.

"Take him out and put him on a horse."

"You don't want him to dress, sir?"

Harcourt stepped back a pace, allowing the handkerchief to dangle and measuring Lee carefully from head to foot. "No—really, I don't think so," he drawled. "Really, I don't think so, he's so attractive as he is. Don't you think so, Captain Harris?"

"Sir," Lee pleaded, "for God's sake, let me put on my uniform."

"Aren't you wearing your uniform, Mr. Lee?"

"Give me the dignity of my rank."

"You have no rank," the colonel said harshly. "Take him out of here, Harris."

Wilkinson came out from under the bed and went to a window. The dragoons, with General Lee in their midst, were riding down the road in the direction of New Brunswick. Wilkinson brushed the dust from his uniform and went downstairs to the parlor, where the landlord was moaning that Lee had not paid his bill. "Two pounds," he told Wilkinson. "I'm a poor man. Seven dinners, eight breakfasts, feed for the horses, two pounds."

"Oh, go to hell," Wilkinson said to him.

He went outside. The girl was there, and she smiled at him and began to edge toward him. Some of the guards, wretched and bedraggled, were shuffling back toward the inn. The girl was very close to Wilkinson now, but she saw his face and stopped and pouted. The guards were sheepish and forlorn, one of them with a long, bleeding cut over his ear, and they kept eying Wilkinson, trying to gauge what his temper was. Now the girl came on again until she was close enough to put her hand on Wilkinson's arm. At that he whirled and slapped her brutally across the face.

"You slut! You dirty slut!" he shouted.

Sullivan, the general left in command of Lee's army, had only recently been a British prisoner. Taken at Brooklyn, he sat in a British jail until the Virginian got hold of a British officer who could be exchanged for him, and since then he had been serving with Lee in a not too cordial relationship. Suspecting Lee's intentions, he felt that the outcome would not only be the ruin of the commander in chief, but the end of everything that was left of the revolution. Nevertheless, for the time he could do nothing but obey orders, and when Scammel appeared with his weird tale of what had taken place at the inn, Sullivan shrugged and gave orders to break up the encampment and start off toward Pluckamin, thinking that a seven-mile march was better than no march at all.

It was about two hours after that, when the army was already on its way, that Wilkinson appeared. He had met Sullivan the night before, when he had come to camp looking for Lee and had been directed to the inn. Now Sullivan nodded brusquely, and Scammel said, grimacing at the memory, "You left our general in good health, I presume?"

Wilkinson smirked, licked his lips, and glanced with calm calculation at the two officers. A born plotter, completely egotistical, Wilkinson, superficially at least, was hard as rock; for all his nineteen years, he had plunged headlong into the wild scramble of ambitious men to make the revolution their own ladder to glory. The fact that Lee had been captured bothered him not one bit; he considered Lee a brute and a fool, stupid enough to be boiled in his own fleshpots, and therefore better out of the way. What troubled Wilkinson was a certain doubt as to how deeply Scammel and Sullivan were implicated in the widespread if loosely jointed conspiracy to ruin the Virginian, a conspiracy which until now had had Gates and Lee as its chief supporters. Watching them keenly, Wilkinson let his news fall deliberately and baldly.

"In good enough health," he smiled, "but in the hands of the British."

They had been walking their horses slowly with the army, and now as if by spoken agreement, their horses came to a standstill, Scammel blinking, but Sullivan staring at the boy with hard, cold blue eyes. Sullivan dismounted, never taking his eyes off Wilkinson, and Scammel and the boy followed.

"That's not funny, you little brute," Sullivan said, unable to swallow his contempt of Wilkinson.

The three stood close together now, and beyond them the shuffling Yankees made an endless, drab panorama.

"You can go to hell, damn you, it's true!" Wilkinson said shrilly.

Sullivan turned to Scammel and asked, "What is this young bitch talking about?"

"I don't know, sir. I told you how I left Lee a little while ago and what he said. But he was all right then."

Wilkinson shouted, "You've got no right to talk to me like that, damn you, mister! I'm a major! I won't take that from you!"

"Shut up," Sullivan said, taking the lapels of the boy's coat in his hands, glancing sidewise at the marching men. "Shut up or I'll kill you, you dirty little son of a bitch."

The look in Sullivan's eyes cowed Wilkinson. "What happened to Lee?" Sullivan demanded, not letting go of the boy's jacket.

"Someone called the dragoons and they took him."

"Who?"

"I don't know."

"Who, Wilkinson? I'd as soon kill you as not!"

"Not me!" the boy protested. "My God, why should I want Lee out of the way? Why should I want the dragoons to take him?"

Sullivan let go of him. "Yes, why—" he said thoughtfully.

Wilkinson was almost in tears now. "I tried to help him," he improvised. "It was just me against all those dragoons—his damned guard ran away. I took a pistol in each hand and stood at the door and told them I'd shoot the first man who entered the house—"

Scammel laughed and Sullivan asked quietly, "Why didn't they take you, too, Wilkinson? Or didn't the dragoons have any use for you?"

"Lee gave himself up, and when I saw it was hopeless, I went upstairs."

"You're a dirty liar," Sullivan said.

Wilkinson managed to stay silent, but the look he gave Sullivan defined his feelings. His thin lips, white and pressed together, trembled slightly, and Scammel thought, "Some day he'll put a bullet in Sullivan's back, unless he's killed first, which is not impossible."

"Go on with your story," Sullivan nodded.

Wilkinson told the rest and then gave Sullivan the letter, explaining, "Lee was writing this when they took him away. I saw it on the table afterwards." He studied Sullivan's face as the general read it, seeking some indication of his reactions and finding none. Sullivan glanced up.

"Do you know what's in it?"

"No," Wilkinson lied.

Sullivan handed it to Scammel, who read it and handed it back without a word. As Sullivan maintained a thoughtful and somewhat worried silence, Wilkinson gained confidence and began to bluster.

Sullivan gave him the letter. "Take it to General Gates," he said shortly.

Grinning once more, Wilkinson demanded, "And what shall I say General Sullivan intends to do?"

Scammel and Sullivan exchanged glances, and then Sullivan said softly and dangerously, "Give him the letter, and then tell him, Wilkinson, that I'm marching to join General Washington. Tell him that anyone who disagrees with my course of action can go to hell and be damned. Tell him that."

Somehow, the news that Lee had been captured got out and through the army, perhaps from Lee's guards who drifted back to their regiments, perhaps from the officers who had to be told the news and why the direction of the march was being changed. At any rate, only a few hours after Wilkinson brought the news, the whole line was alive with speculation, and the change of mood and intention was instantly apparent. Sullivan, still unable fully to comprehend the fact, asked Scammel almost pathetically, "But how would they know he was there at the inn? Unless that little bastard— yet he's in it up to his neck, with Gates and Lee, so why should he—?"

"Why shouldn't they know? Everyone knew. This country is filthy with Tories."

"I should have broken his dirty back!"

"I don't think he did it," Scammel said. "Why should he?"

"God knows."

The marching army seethed and boiled, and early in the afternoon came the first eruptive consequence of Lee's capture. Two hundred Massachusetts men marched stolidly out of the line. Sullivan spurred after them and reined his horse across their path, but they marched on around him and past him, their eyes fixed on the ground and straight ahead, their ears closed to his exhortations and cursing.

An hour later, one hundred men from Maine turned out of the line. Sullivan was a Maine man himself, and he begged them to wait only two or three days. He got off his horse and walked along with them, pleading, but it was no good.

The Jersey men went off by tens and twenties, by ones and twos and threes.

Sullivan knew what the Marblehead men had done at Brooklyn and Pell's Point, and now he asked Glover, "Will your men fire on deserters if I order them to?"

Glover shook his head sadly. "I don't reckon they will."

"Will they stand by me?"

"That's likely," Glover considered. "But they don't lean to slaying their own kind."

At six o'clock, a band of eighty Connecticut cavalry rode off into the night.

And during the night, almost two hundred Vermont and a hundred more Virginia men marched away. It took a regiment of Pennsylvanians a night's discussion for them to make up their minds, and in the morning they too marched away, three hundred strong. Sullivan didn't sleep that night; he went from regiment to regiment, pleading with all the tattered medley of captains, colonels, majors, lieutenants by the score, even those who called themselves generals. He wrote orders; he threatened; he raved until he was hoarse. He went into his tent, drank almost a quart of rum, and wept tears of pity for himself, his country and his destiny. He woke Scammel.

"My God, what am I going to do?"

"I don't know."

"What can I do?"

"You can take what's left and order them to shoot deserters."

"That's no good—they won't. They're all thinking the same thing."

"How many have gone?"

"Close to a thousand, I reckon."

"I don't know what you can do," Scammel said, thankful that he was not in command. "I wish I did, but I don't know."

And the next day, a haggard, bleary-eyed Sullivan saw

the same process continue. Massachusetts men, Rhode Island men, Connecticut men, Jersey men, New York men, Maryland men, Virginia men, they trickled off, they went off by regiments, by brigades, by ones and twos and threes.

15 🏴 🏴 🏴 🏴 🏴 🏴 🏴 🏴 🏴 🏴 🏴

HOW THE FOXHUNTER
BECAME A DICTATOR

The nursery rhyme, learned by the foxhunter so long ago when he was six or seven or eight, had lingered down the long passage of years, framed in its crusty hornbook with its steel engravings of little men with big feet and big noses, the way some small, unimportant things linger:

> *Run, run, run away,*
> *Run, run, run away,*
> *Because, because, you should know when,*
> *Again, again, again, again,*
> *You will run, run, run away.*

At Brunswick he had wanted to pause and rest and breathe a little and see if he could find some flour and warm clothes, and linger in the hope that perhaps here at last Lee and his five thousand would join him—and maybe give the militia a chance to come in. That hope, that phrase, "to come in," had become so forlorn and rusty. Congress liked to use it; Adams, Hancock, Franklin, Jefferson—they all liked to use it; it gave in a broad sense such a stirring picture, the farmers, the countrymen, the mechanics, the clerks, all dropping their ledgers and plows and tools and picking up their guns and marching proudly and forthrightly to drive the enemy from their land and establish liberty and freedom and justice for all time. But the empty, hollow actuality was barred doors, shuttered windows, a sullen musket warning: "Keep off, damn you beggars!"

New Brunswick, which meant at the least a rest for aching feet, a pause to look at themselves and count themselves, came to an end on December 1st, when Captain Peter

Mendoz, nineteen, drove his starving, skinny nag up to the house where the commander in chief was quartered and yelled, "They're here, sir!"

He came out in his shirt, his long bony shoulders hunched inquiringly, a piece of bread in his hand. "Who?"

"The British, sir!"

He finished the bread in a mouthful, and then Billy was behind him helping him struggle into his jacket. He said, "Get off the horse, captain, and talk sense."

The boy explained frantically. "About a mile away."

"How do you know?"

"I saw them," the boy wailed. "My God, sir, I saw them."

"How many?"

"Oh, sir—the whole army."

The foxhunter began to run, with his long, loping, swaying strides, seeing Greene and calling, "We're marching, Nathanael!"

"When?"

"Now."

"Where?"

"Out of here."

"Where?"

"Tell Mercer and Stirling to start the brigades!"

He saw Knox, a fat whirl of excitement and evidently aware of what had happened, and called to him, "Can you knock down a bridge, Harry?"

"Bridge?"

"Damn you, Harry, haven't you any sense? The bridge across the river."

"I never tried, sir."

"Well, knock it down, Harry. Put some guns there if they should try to cross—and knock down the bridge."

The bookseller had a pair of lungs like a foghorn; he rolled along bellowing, "Brigades on the march! Brigades on the march!" The whole encampment had become a maelstrom of men running for their equipment, officers shouting senselessly at them, and drivers trying to load up their wagons with whatever they could lay hands on. Through this Knox pushed his way, roaring for his artillerymen, wondering where he could find crowbars and hammers. He had never torn down a bridge, and the heavy wooden structure across the Raritan did not look as if it would collapse with just a little prodding, and all he could think of at this moment were hammers and crowbars. At any rate, it was small and short salvation, for most of the Raritan was no more than knee deep. He spied Hamilton and yelled.

"Alex, where are your guns?"

"On the river, sir. I was looking for horses."

"The hell with horses! Drag them over to the bridge and keep the British from crossing!"

"Yes, sir."

"Have you seen any crowbars?"

"Sir?"

"Crowbars! I have to knock down that damned bridge."

He shook his head helplessly and Knox went running on. A while later, when he had picked up a dozen men with axes and bars and hammers and gotten them to the bridge, Hamilton was already there, the cannon loaded and waiting. Knox led his men into the icy water, where they sneezed and shivered and attacked the piling and planks. Meanwhile, over their heads, the guns began to explode. It was about twenty minutes before the end of the bridge gave way.

On the bank again, shivering, dancing clumsily to warm himself, Knox saw the British drawn up on the other shore, just out of cannon shot, in precise and orderly rows of red and green. At the other end of the bridge lay the bodies of three light infantrymen, caught by grape as they tried to storm across. A British officer, whom Knox thought later to be Cornwallis, doffed his hat in a half-mocking, half-respectful salute, while the Highland pipers paraded back and forth, screeching an off-key version of *Yankee Doodle.*

"Damned, bloody, kilted savages," Knox muttered, and Hamilton ground his teeth in impotent rage.

"I suppose we'll have to spike the guns," Knox said.

"Unless we can drag them away after dark."

"Without horses?" Knox was thinking that by dark the British would have crossed the river and gotten in behind them, and wondering how it would be to sit in jail, rid of all this nightmare. When he turned around to look, he could just make out the last of the Continentals, racing down the road toward Princeton.

Toward evening of the next day, the shambling remnant of the army of liberty reached Trenton. As a gesture, a pleading gesture that he should not be driven out of New Jersey without making some sort of a show, the Virginian left some twelve hundred men at Princeton, under Stirling, who had been exchanged, along with Sullivan, since the two of them were taken by the British at Brooklyn.

"But what will I do, sir?" Stirling asked, looking at the ragged, shivering, half-armed, half-starved brigades.

Almost wistfully, the tall man said, "Maybe some Jersey militia will come in if they know we are trying to defend their land."

"Defend them? Christ, sir, they hate us."

The tall man winced.

"Defend them," Stirling said. "The richest land in America, stuffed with food, and we starve in it."

"They don't understand," he whispered.

"They understand well enough how to keep their own bellies full."

"I know."

"And if the British come?"

The tall man shook his head.

"Twelve hundred men—look at them, sir! And the British have ten, fifteen thousand of the finest troops in the world."

"I know."

"But, sir—"

"Do the best you can," the Virginian said.

He sat in his tent at Trenton with Mifflin and Greene, and it seemed an eternity ago that he had flown into a rage at Mifflin at Brooklyn Heights and more than an eternity ago that he had once raced after hounds through the lush meadows of Mount Vernon. He could study that tall, handsome, aristocratic foxhunter of the Potomac with all the detachment that a man living has for one a long time dead, not with regret, but with the painful, certain knowledge that a whole world had died, as worlds died before, as they would again, leaving no future but only a dark and weary present to men who traveled a road between them.

He said to Greene, "I would like the men counted, Nathanael."

"There's no use doing that, sir," Mifflin said bitterly.

"Why?"

"The New York militia walked off today. We have less than a thousand left, between eight and nine hundred, I think."

"That can't be," the foxhunter said softly, unbelievingly.

"It is," Greene remarked stolidly. "Mifflin's right. The New

York militia walked away. It was no use trying to stop them. We're too thin. If we had tried, the rest would have walked away with them."

"Eight or nine hundred," the foxhunter mused.

"I hate to think that it's the end, sir," Mifflin said miserably. "I hate to think that."

"There's Lee's army," Greene reminded them.

"If we ever see Lee's army again."

"We'll see them," the foxhunter said, but with no confidence, the way one speaks of all the goodness and forbearance of Providence.

"It seems only yesterday," Greene said, "that we were in New York with twenty thousand men."

"Yesterday's gone," the foxhunter said. "I want you to go to Philadelphia, Mifflin, and I want you to come back with men, all the men you can get. I want you to go in front of Congress, because they don't read my letters; or if they read them, they put them away where neither their memory nor their conscience will be troubled; but go in front of Congress, threaten them, bully them, plead with them if you have to—but come back with men."

"Come back with the moon," he might as well have said.

Knox, returning from holding the British at the Raritan River, little the worse except for a hacking cough, told the Virginian about the proclamation issued a day or two before by General Howe. "It commands all persons in arms against His Majesty's government to disband and return home," he explained. "It offers a free pardon to those who comply within fifty days."

"I expected something like that," the Virginian nodded.

"Will it hit us hard, sir?"

"Can we be hit much harder?"

"I don't know—word's running like fire through the countryside. They used to be afraid to admit they were Tories, but now they're damned proud of it. It's worth a man's life to travel alone in Jersey."

Almost at the end, the end was put off for a little while. Mifflin performed a miracle; he came back from Philadelphia with fifteen hundred militia, not soldiers, but at least men, white-faced Philadelphia clerks and storekeepers, bookbinders and drapers' assistants and carpenters and tailors. They were frightened, tired and aching from their march; the two-

thirds who had muskets held them awkwardly and somewhat fearfully, and the rest were armed with pikes, swords
which had but recently hung over mantelpieces, and ancient
blunderbusses. They were raw, and their drilling and marching had been all a game until Mifflin threatened and bullied
them into coming up to Trenton. Still they were men.

The Virginian shook Mifflin's hand, and something in his
eyes disclosed how near he had been to the end. "How
many are left?" Mifflin asked cautiously.

"Six hundred—"

Mifflin whistled.

"It was very close," the tall man admitted. He looked weak
and tired, and his face had a yellow, sickly sheen. But a
better evidence of his state was his loquaciousness; for explaining, he said more to Mifflin than he ever had before.
"I tried not to let them know—they would have bolted, all
of them. I broke them into small groups, and I kept them
moving, anything at all in the world except to let them see
that none of them were left. And general—I prayed—" He
broke off, flushing, self-conscious; a little ashamed of himself, he turned brusque. "Have them enrolled with the adjutant, and then march them off to Princeton. Greene is
there, and I'll be along later with what's left of mine." He
turned and eyed the new militia:

"And, general, march them by twos—let these damned
Jersey Tories see that we have an army, only—don't let them
fight," he added.

He went back to his headquarters and called Billy, and
when the Negro came, demanded, "Have you any Madeira
left?"

Billy nodded.

"How much?"

"Six bottles."

"Bring them all," the foxhunter said.

He had never really been drunk, and this time the wine left
him cold and miserable and tired. He drank mechanically and
quickly and hopelessly, not to forget, but to remember, to
unfasten the tight-packed, tight-locked patterns that had
gone to make up his life.

It was no use, for he found it as impossible to remember as to make himself drunk. Mount Vernon was a faint
dream, and no more than that, and the foxhunting Virginia
squire that he had been at Mount Vernon was part of the
dream. All that was gone, lost and unobtainable; and on the

bleak road he now traveled a fortitude was required that could draw no sustenance from the past.

All that mattered now was to exist, as an army and as a movement and as a cause; they ran, dodged, hid, and twisted; they stumbled, fell, crawled, but moved on somehow, and they no longer spoke of striking back. Not so long ago, the Virginian would not have run away; bursting with pride, he would have battered his handsome head into a bloody ruin; but now his pride had become something else, even as ends and values had changed.

On his way back to Princeton, to join his army, after he had sent the Philadelphia reinforcements on ahead, he met the vanguard of a fleeing mob. But the difference was that instead of becoming a raging madman, as once he had, he now observed his troops with cold and measured detachment, and when Greene appeared, asked him calmly, "What is it now, Nathanael?"

Greene was tired and pettish, having no sympathy even for his commander in chief. "The same thing," he groaned. "My God, what else would it be?"

"The British are in Princeton?" the tall man asked softly.

Greene nodded hopelessly.

"There was no chance to hold on for a little while, Nathanael?"

"No—no, don't you think I wanted to hold on? If we had been an army of regulars, we were still outnumbered three to one. But my word, sir, did you see what that Philadelphia militia was?"

"I saw," the big man nodded, and then asked fatalistically, "How many desertions?"

"Only three hundred."

The Virginian sighed with relief, nodded, and swung his horse after the retreating army. Riding behind him, Greene demanded, almost savagely, "What are your orders, sir? Or are there no orders? What am I to do now?"

"Nothing, Nathanael, except to take hold of yourself."

"But what are you going to do?"

The Virginian shrugged. "Cross the Delaware, I think."

"And then, sir?" Greene asked shrilly.

The tall man smiled, rode on without answering, and then when Greene spurred desperately up alongside of him, said, "When there is only one road, Nathanael, you don't need maps."

"For God's sake, sir, don't talk in riddles!"

"Then without riddles, Nathanael, we will go on retreating. How far?" The Virginian shrugged. "Do you think the British are patient? Will they follow us across the mountains? Then we will fight them through the forest. Beyond the forest—I don't know. No one has ever been there. Perhaps we will be the first, Nathanael."

They left their signature for all time. It was snowing lightly as they marched down to the Delaware River, and suffering from cold, from hunger, from fear, they left their trail of blood in the snow. Cornwallis would need no hounds to follow; to his dying day he would remember, without exultation, how he knew where the Continentals walked.

"If the fishermen were here," the Virginian thought, watching his freezing men awkwardly and hopelessly try to ferry themselves across the swift-running river. They stumbled and struggled and fell into the icy current. They rolled the guns onto boats, and then shed tears of futile rage when the boats overturned and tumbled the guns to the bottom of the river. They soaked their powder and their muskets, and if the British had come on them then the revolution would have finished quickly and painlessly. They cursed and whimpered; and even Knox, up to his waist in water for hours, became a raging two-hundred-and-fifty-pound blob of anguish.

Yet they moved across, slowly, painfully, bitterly; somehow they dragged most of their guns across, some of their wagons, some of their few remaining horses, and most of their pitifully small stock of food.

This time, the Virginian needed leeway and rest too desperately to take any chances. The Delaware was not fordable at this time of the year for a good distance; if he removed all the boats for twenty-five or thirty miles in either direction, he might hold the British back for a while—for how long he didn't know, yet a week would be redemption and two weeks would be grace from heaven. With this in view, he sent small parties of men up and down the river, and wherever they found a boat, they took it across, or if that was impossible, destroyed it.

They got over the Delaware, and this time, as on the Raritan, they escaped only by a hair's breadth, for the last boatload had hardly left the Jersey shore before they heard the skirling of the Highland pipers. The freezing militia built fires on the west bank, and crouched around their fires, they saw Cornwallis' redcoats, kilted Highlanders, and green-clad Hessians marching down to the spot they had just quitted. For the cold, hungry, half-naked, completely fright-ened Continentals, it was a terrible and awesome sight: the thousands and thousands of brightly uniformed regulars, the wonderful precision of their marching, the matter-of-fact way in which they deployed along the bank, the hundreds of pieces of artillery that rumbled down after them, black and ominous under that cold and cloudy winter sky, the seemingly endless train of supply wagons, the white tents rising up everywhere like mushrooms, and the pipers strut-ting along the bank, skirling defiantly and mockingly:

"Yankee Doodle went to London, riding on a pony."

And then, as the sun went down, the clouds broke open, and a long, slanting ray of light filtered through onto the massed British, making the whole brilliant picture impos-sible and unreal.

Knox, standing with the commander, with Greene and Put-nam and Mifflin and Mercer, remarked, "In all my life, I've never seen anything like it."

"It's very beautiful," the tall man said quietly.

"Yet we go on," Mifflin mused.

"I never realized before what they meant," Knox said, a good deal of awe in his voice. "It's so long now that we've been fighting with them and running away from them, but I never realized before what it was. I never knew it was so big and so terrible. I didn't think about it."

"It's no good to think about it," Mercer said sourly. "They've a canny way, to put themselves like that in front of us, but it's no damned good to think about it."

"It's not a cheerful thing for them to see," Greene re-marked, nodding at the men, who had left their fires and crowded forward to the bank.

"No," the Virginian agreed. "We'll encamp at least a mile back from the river."

"Yet I'm glad I saw it," Knox said thoughtfully. "I think it's better to know what you're fighting—or what you're running away from."

The next morning, Greene and the Virginian rode up the river about ten miles, paralleling the path of British patrols in search of boats.

"They won't find any," the tall man said, with some satisfaction.

"No, but if they march up to Frenchtown?"

"That's a long march. They don't like the cold any better than we do."

"Still, they can't go away and leave us alone."

"Some of them might, and some of them might not."

"They can't cross," Greene reassured himself, and then added uneasily, "But God help us if they do."

The Philadelphia patriots, those who had supported the revolution, either by word or deed, were becoming frightened. This city of brotherly love had been anything but that for a long time now, and in spite of the fact that the Continental Congress sat there and the Declaration of Independence had been signed there, the city was far more Tory than rebel. The Tories, with some exceptions, ran to two extremes: on one hand the wealth and aristocracy, the people of family and blood and substance, and on the other the dregs and scum, the useless, the vile and degenerate. The Quakers remained aloof or were—again with a few exceptions—Tories; and holding for the revolution, in between, were the middle class, the artisans, the smiths and masons and shopkeepers and printers and sailors and small merchants and wheelwrights and cabinet makers and plumbers and glazers and drapers and millers and carpenters and brewers— and along with them, smugglers, pirates and privateers, a swashbuckling, hard-drinking, hard-speaking blot on the Delaware waterfront.

Until now, the Tories had quietly waited their moment, knowing that it was only a matter of time before the British swept away the Continental rabble. They were without organization, while the rebels had their militia, whatever it was worth. But now Mifflin came from the Virginian's beaten army, exhorting, threatening, and finally carrying away with him fully half the militia. And that was all the Tories needed.

Suddenly and boldly, knowing that their time was approaching, they proclaimed themselves. They barred their doors, closed their shutters, armed their servants and all of the dregs and scum who would sell themselves for a mug of rum and a silver shilling. The disorganized militia, bereft of half their number, realizing that the Continental army was crumbling, were afraid to take any definite stand against the Tories. If, as rumor had it, the British fleet sailed up the Delaware and took the city, what then would become of them, their homes and families? Thus, the city split into two armed camps, each unable to attack or dispose of the other; and the members of the Continental Congress, looking at each other, saw nothing but condemned men and mass hangings. Suddenly, they reversed the procedure; they had been importuned constantly by the Virginian, and now they turned and sent him frantic appeals for help.

"What can I do?" he asked Putnam. "I have no men to send them. You must go there, Israel, and see what you can make of their militia."

Putnam was old and tired and sick; at night he dreamed about his farm and groaned in his sleep.

"Who else can I trust?" the tall man demanded petulantly. "I know you're tired, Israel. Perhaps in the city you can rest."

"It won't be a rest," Putnam said morosely. "I know what it will be—it will be hell. From what I hear, they are all crazy with fright, and what can I do?"

"Whatever you do, it will be better than nothing."

"And if the British come?" Putnam asked sourly, already giving in.

"Take what men and supplies you can and retreat."

"I'm tired," Putnam complained. "You have troubles, but you haven't got rheumatism."

"I wish to God things were brighter," the foxhunter said gently. "For your sake, Israel. You're not as young as the rest of them. I'm not so young either. I know what it means, that feeling when your body won't listen to you any longer."

"It started so easily," Putnam said ruefully.

"It always begins easily."

Putnam rode away, sighing and grumbling, but he had hardly arrived at Philadelphia before the Congress loaded what government remained into a wagon and left for Baltimore. Putnam sat down painfully and wrote to his commander in chief.

Greene found the Virginian sitting in front of a fire, a woolen muffler around his neck, his glasses perched loosely on his nose, and an old stocking cap on his head. It was almost impossible to warm the shack he had turned into his headquarters, and the tall man, eyes red and nose even more brilliant, sneezed constantly.

"Sit down, Nathanael," he said, motioning to a battered ladderback chair, which with a rickety table composed all the furnishings of the room.

"Flip, sir, is the best thing I know for a cold," Greene said.

"How much flip can a man drink? I've had a quart, and it hasn't helped."

Greene nodded his sympathy and sat gingerly in the chair. He was very cold and sat so close to the fire that the frayed threads on his knees began to singe.

"You'll burn yourself," the tall man warned him.

"Thank you, sir. The winter in these parts is uncommonly wet." He sat with his knees close together, his hands clasped on them, waiting to hear why he had been sent for.

"Congress has gone away from Philadelphia," the tall man told him.

"What!"

"They did right. The revolution exists only so long as a government exists. It's better for them to flee than to be taken."

"Where have they gone?"

"To Baltimore, I think. It isn't that—" Greene had never seen the Virginian look so old, so tired, unsure even, his big hand trembling a little as it groped in his breast pocket for a letter. "I don't know how to tell the others—Congress has changed things. Sometimes, God help me, I'm afraid they've given up."

He had never spoken like this before; every last vestige of authority, of aristocratic pride was gone from his voice. Greene asked hoarsely, "Who, sir?"

"Congress—"

Greene shook his head stubbornly.

"They've given it all over to me," the tall man said miserably.

"Given what, sir?"

"The government. I never asked for that, never wanted it. How much can I carry on my shoulders alone?"

Greene stared at him.

"This is the way it is," the tall man said, peering through his glasses at the letter and reading: ". . . until they should otherwise order, General Washington should be possessed of all power to order and direct all things relative to the department and to the operations of war. . . ."

"If it were anyone else I would be afraid," Greene protested. "But it's you, sir. Don't you see?"

"No—" The tall man shook his head miserably. "What's the difference who it is? What are we fighting for—for one man to rule a people?"

"I'm not afraid of that, sir, I swear to God, believe me, but why did they do it?"

"They think it's the end and they are grasping at straws."

"Do you think it's the end?" Greene asked softly.

"I don't know," the tall man said. "I don't know."

They were sitting around him in the cold room for a council of war: Greene, Mercer, Knox, Mifflin, Stirling, and John Cadwalader, the last a young man of Philadelphia who had come under Putnam's sour but strangely moving influence and had marched up from Philadelphia with a band of volunteers, and who was still shaken by what he had seen on the banks of the Delaware. Aside from Cadwalader, whose suit was fresh from a Philadelphia tailor, their clothes were threadbare, patched, their uniforms, once carefully made in imitation of the commander's buff and blue, now mostly replaced by old breeches and secondhand, ill-fitting home-spun coats. Cadwalader had seen the horrible, dirty, broken thing they called their army, and it was like a grotesquely humorous dream that they should sit here in what they called a council of war.

The Virginian had just finished explaining the situation that had turned him into a dictator, and now humbly, almost pleadingly he was saying:

"Gentlemen, I never looked for this, believe me: I never wanted it. I consider our Congress a noble and courageous body, to whom I am responsible for all my actions." There was no hint of mockery in his voice. "I remain responsible to them; nothing can change that. The splendid purpose to which they are working can only command our respect, and their army, which I have the honor to command, must be worthy of that purpose. Yet there are certain actions which I must embark on of my own account, for the time only, since it is almost impossible now to have our Congress consider them.

"We have been retreating only for one reason, to preserve our army, and through it, our country; but we have come to a point where further retreat will only destroy the little that remains to us. We must strike back, and whether that blow will be the beginning or the end of all we have fought for, I don't know. But strike we must, for in a little while it will be too late."

They stared at him, as though he had gone suddenly mad; they looked at each other; he went on:

"Our country and Congress, unfortunately, has little money; most of what they had is spent. Perhaps if more of the wealthy families of this land were inclined toward our cause, the situation would be different; but most of the people in our ranks are poor in worldly goods, and many have given all they can. I am counted a rich man, and I believe I can find some money; some of you, perhaps, will be willing to help, although I know only too well how little you have. Nevertheless, we must offer bounties and rewards of various kinds, so that men will be persuaded to enlist. I do not have to impress on you how unfortunate our situation is; even with the timely arrival of Colonel Cadwalader, we may, in another few days, have less than two thousand men. I don't think, gentlemen, that is a reason for despair, but rather evidence of a need to exert ourselves to even more strenuous effort—"

He paused and looked from face to face. Mercer was staring at the table. Knox's eyes were wet, and Greene was making a dogged effort to keep his face set and purposeful, while Stirling gazed blankly ahead of him. In Mifflin's eyes there was the dull despair of complete frustration.

"You are old comrades in arms," the tall man said softly. "I thank you, each and every one, for all the dark days you have borne with me." And then he rose and walked out.

Greene came to Knox, bursting with the first news of Lee's capture; and after the initial shock, Knox said, "For my part, it's good riddance to bad rubbish. I hate the swine."

"Are you going to tell him that, Harry?" Greene asked.

"I couldn't tell him."

"And where's the army, five thousand men, good men, the fishermen—Christ, Harry, you remember what the fishermen did at Pell's Point. It's all we have to remember. Where are they?"

"Didn't the express say? Wasn't he from Sullivan, if Sullivan's left in command?"

"He said Sullivan was going to try to cross the river, north of here."

"How long ago was that?"

"A few days. They should have been here, unless Cornwallis cut them off. If that happened—" Greene shrugged.

"Who was with Lee at the inn?" Knox asked.

"A filthy little wretch called Wilkinson, one of Gates' men. I know him. He's just a boy, but no good. He says he tried to fight, but I'll swear it's a lie. If he was there with Lee, I can guess why."

"How did he take it?" Knox wanted to know, nodding toward the Virginian's headquarters.

"How do you think, Harry?"

"I don't know—he was worried about the army, I suppose."

"No," Greene said bitterly. "He was worried about Lee, not only worried, but broken, you hear me, broken, Harry. Broken up because he had lost a comrade in arms, a noble leader, an unselfish patriot. He sent an express off immediately to Cornwallis demanding that Lee be exchanged, offering almost every prisoner we have, offering anything and everything and threatening God only knows what if Lee is hanged."

"Why?" Knox asked simply.

"I don't know. I've given up trying to understand him. If I were in his place—"

"Do you suppose they'll hang Lee?"

"They may. He was a British officer, you know."

Four days later, on the twentieth of December, the tattered, suffering remnant of Lee's army arrived at the encampment on the Delaware. Less than two thousand were left of the five thousand Yankees Lee had commanded at White Plains, and even the poor beggars who made up the foxhunter's army were moved to pity at the sight. Blue with cold, their clothes in rags, their feet cut and bruised and bleeding, the Yankees dragged themselves into the encampment, some stumbling blindly toward the fires, others dropping down and going to sleep almost instantly. For a week they had dodged the British in a stubborn, twisting flight, and it was more than a miracle that they had got through at all. The only sign of order or hope among them was the company of the Marblehead fishermen, still together and some six hundred strong, their blue jackets worn thread-bare, their shoes gone, but their lean, long Yankee faces grimmer and harder than ever.

Sullivan, swaying from weariness and lack of sleep, a week's growth of whiskers on his face, his eyes bloodshot and staring, stumbled over to the Virginian and said, "I must ask your forgiveness, sir, for certain men of faint heart who dropped out along the way."

16 🏴 🏴 🏴 🏴 🏴 🏴 🏴 🏴 🏴 🏴

AND HOW HE CROSSED THE DELAWARE A SECOND TIME

Once again, at long last, Glover and the Virginian sat opposite each other, a pitcher of hot flip between them with full glasses on hand, Glover rested and shaven, the fox-hunter leaner than ever, hollow of cheek, with deep, dark circles under his eyes. Each man saw the change in the other, and each accepted it with new and humble aware-ness. Some of the down-east cold had gone out of Glover; he had seen men stripped bare to the soul, and it was harder to take, even, than what he had seen at Pell's Point. As with the foxhunter, he had chosen his road and was de-termined to walk down it for as long as it went. Both of them the same age, they were as alike in some ways as they were different in others; Glover saw that the aristocrat was gone, and he accepted the fact, sensing if not realizing the strange new pride and purpose in the man sitting across the table from him. They were both lonely men, and even from each other they could take no comfort to ease that loneliness; but in their loneliness they comprehended each other.

The foxhunter, sipping at his glass, said, "I'm glad to see you, colonel. It was a long time."

Glover nodded and smiled a very rare smile.

"I never considered fishermen," the foxhunter mused, half humorously. "I never thought that my life, my army, and my country's cause might depend upon them so much."

"That's good of you, sir," Glover said, a trace of a flush creeping into his wrinkled, weathered face.

"We owe you much."

"Very little, I would reckon," Glover remarked uneasily.

"At any rate, the point is that you're here. I am not much good at compliments."

"Nor I at holding on to them, sir."

The foxhunter drained his glass and said, "I had a plan in mind—"

The Yankee leaned forward.

"Cumbersome, insane—" He poured new flip for each of them, and staring at the hot, strong rum, said, "I needed you; it was no use to think about it otherwise."

"Crossing the Delaware," Glover said softly, not incredulously, but with matter-of-fact awe.

The foxhunter nodded.

The Marblehead man, smiling, murmured, "I reckoned that. It had to be that. What else could it be?"

"The British went away," the Virginian said, speaking with singular rapidity for one usually so slow in marshaling his thoughts. "They went away to the firesides of New York and left the Germans sitting on the bank. That's how they despise us. It's just as well, and we owe the Jagers a great deal!" It was the first time Glover, or indeed any of the others had seen this side of him, a gush of passionate eloquence. "They left the Jagers, men who fight and kill and murder, not because their country is at war, not because they have anything to defend, not because they hate or oppose hate, but because they are hirelings and mercenaries! Knyphausen is there, and we have a score with Knyphausen!" He broke off suddenly, the effort leaving him spent and coughing.

"When do you want to cross?" Glover asked.

"Christmas Day," the tall man answered quietly, the spell broken, his old, calm, almost rigid self come back again.

Reasons were not something Glover cared to discuss; he leaned back, eyes half closed, considering the execution of the matter, as if for a beaten, half-starved, half-armed rabble to attack an encampment of Prussian-trained mercenaries was the most commonplace occurrence in the world.

"How many men?" he asked.

"We should have almost five thousand by then."

"In one night?"

"In a few hours, I hope," the tall man said.

Glover whistled softly, closed his eyes entirely, and sipped at his rum. His fingers drummed on the table, and with his eyes still closed, he asked, "How would it come out, actually, sir?"

"I want them embarked, taken across, re-formed on the other side, and marched from the landing places to Trenton, and I want the attack undertaken, from beginning to end, in darkness."

"It might be done," Glover speculated. "At the same point?"

"At three points, as far as I've planned it, one nine miles upriver, another a mile below here, and the third at Burlington."

"That makes it harder," Glover said. "What kind are the boats?"

"I'm not seaman enough to judge," the foxhunter said. "They're up and down the river for miles, but all on this side. There are enough, I think, for we took every boat on the river that we could move." He stared anxiously at Glover, who leaned back again, eyes closed, fingers drumming nervously.

"How do you think?" the foxhunter asked him.

"I think we can do it," Glover answered slowly. "If you want guns, it will mean barges; we'd be all night working them across in dinghies. But I think we can do it."

"I can count on you?"

"You can count on me, sir," Glover said, and then they shook hands, each leaning his long length across the top of the rickety table.

Things were a little better. The Virginian ordered a count, and it showed almost five thousand men, although not the full number were actually fit for duty. General Gates had come down from Schuyler's army in the north, starting off with four regiments, but losing half his men along the way from desertions. But when Gates heard about the plan that was brewing, he went to the Virginian and said, "I should like to have leave—to go to Philadelphia, sir."

"Philadelphia?"

"I find, sir, that there is a certain degree of madness I cannot fall in with."

"To Philadelphia or to hell, you are welcome, sir," the tall man said quietly. "It's one and the same with me."

"If that's your attitude," Gates replied, "I think you understand mine."

Wilkinson had come along with Gates, and now he strutted through the camp, telling, with much embroidery, how with a pistol in either hand he had stood off a whole company of dragoons when they came to take Lee. He talked endlessly and incessantly; he let hints drop that perhaps the commander in chief himself had connived at Lee's capture. Grinning knowingly, he let it be heard about that soon there might be a new commander in chief, and it would not be surprising if the name of the new leader was Gates. He pointed out what a great many letters had passed between the foxhunter and Howe, and how certain disaster which had befallen the army might not have been either chance or circumstance; but rather a part of a plan.

Captain Hamilton sought him out one day. "I want a word with you, Wilkinson."

"Major Wilkinson," the boy said.

They were the same age, both of them nineteen, Hamilton a little taller, a little slimmer, his violet eyes glowing strangely, a crooked smile on his face. "Major Wilkinson," he agreed.

"What do you want?"

"I want to kill you," Hamilton smiled. "But I don't think I will—not yet."

"Are you crazy?"

"No, I'm very sane, major. You'd better go away. Go to Philadelphia with General Gates."

"If you want to duel—" Wilkinson began furiously.

"I don't want to duel, I want to kill you," Hamilton said, turning on his heel and walking away.

The following day, Wilkinson left for Philadelphia with Gates.

"If this is insanity," the Virginian was saying solemnly, "it will be our last insanity, gentlemen. I haven't come to this decision easily; it has cost me many hours of thought and struggle with myself. I haven't lightly considered and used those powers which our Congress gave me, but only after much resolve and equal necessity. How urgent the necessity is, I don't have to point out to you. The game is up. I said once that if needful I would retreat a thousand miles to the west, so long as that would keep our army intact and our Congress in existence. But we have broken faith with our Congress, gentlemen; because we cannot defend them they have had to leave their city and run as we have been running, and were we to retreat not a thousand miles, but a hundred miles, there would be nothing left of our army."

They were all there, facing him, Greene and Sullivan and Knox and Mercer, Stirling, Putnam, Mifflin and Glover. Reed and Cadwalader were at Burlington, but they had already been informed of the plan. The men who were left with the commander listened gravely to what was, for all purposes, a summons to destruction.

"I have chosen for the time," he went on, "Christmas Day at night, one hour before the next daylight."

They stared at him curiously.

"Because the Jagers will be drunk," he explained in a matter-of-fact way.

"Can you count on that, sir?" someone asked.

"We can't count on anything, nor can we hope; we are moving, gentlemen, because our need is desperate."

"Cannon, sir?" Knox asked.

"You have sixteen pieces?"

"Eighteen, sir. General Putnam found two twelve-pounders that could be spared from Philadelphia."

"You will try to put them all across, Harry," he said. "Colonel Glover here has found barges and you will begin to embark the guns the moment the light fades. That will be soon after four o'clock. We will try to take across horses as well, and if possible will mount a group of men on the other side. General Putnam will return to Philadelphia, where there are signs of an insurrection, but the rest of you will be with me. Tomorrow, you will set your watches with mine, so that even if we are apart in the night, we will be able to operate in accord."

They nodded gravely, their fear gone, their faces set, not with hope, but with the realization that this was either a beginning or an end.

"Colonel Cadwalader," the foxhunter said, "has been good enough to present us with some Madeira. I will have it broken open, gentlemen, and we will drink a toast."

By noon on Christmas Day, the whole camp was stirring, the Continentals, wrapped in every rag or piece of blanket they could lay hands on, nervously forming into files, the officers glancing at their big, round watches, everyone stamping, moving, clapping hands to keep warm, the vapor of their breath steaming into the air.

It was a sharp, grey day, clouds banked up in the sky, the still air promising a snowfall before long. It was not very cold, but cold enough for the poor devils, who with all their rags piled on were still half naked. Even now, they did not know exactly what they were going into, except that it would be with the Jagers, a word that rose and fell like sounding notes through their ranks, in anger, in hatred, in sudden terror, a band of south-German volunteers from the Pennsylvania back-country sickening at the thought of going to face the Prussian devils, all they had fled from and feared, their dread baked into them through countless generations, the New Englanders thinking of that raucous battle cry, "Yonkee, Yonkee," of how it might feel to be pinned by a bayonet to a tree or to go into a Hessian jail, poked and prodded along like beasts, the Jersey Dutch remembering a terror that had always loomed over the low country across the sea, the Pennsylvanians recalling stories of eight hundred other Pennsylvanians stabbed and cut and butchered as they fled up Harlem Heights to the poor security of Fort Washington. They were not brave, but mixed with their fear, there was an aching and terrible determination.

Hamilton was a tonic for Knox. He wouldn't leave the battery of eighteen guns, not giving the gunners a chance to think, but keeping them busy greasing the axles, cleaning the bores, chipping rust off the sighting screws, and making careful packages of the loads. Knox thought back to the time, not so far past, when they were twenty thousand strong in New York and when they could count the guns by the hundreds. Things had changed, just as he had changed from a bookseller who had once dreamed of being a publisher like Ben Franklin. That was gone and out of his life, left behind and somehow already too far behind to ever be reached for or regained; and he would never sit and gloatingly correct manuscript for a book that might sell a hundred or even a hundred and fifty thousand copies. He had liked comfort and ease so much, the good things of life, a house tastefully furnished with imported Chippendale, the best books by the wittiest English writers, the round comfort of his wife in bed at night, children he could look at always, mold, filling them with the good, civilized smell of printer's ink. He was only twenty-six, but he felt old, washed clean of every purpose but one, to stalk along with the Virginian on a lonely road that led to nowhere.

And Hamilton scampered around the guns like a thin-faced, violet-eyed imp.

Looking at the woefully scant ranks, the foxhunter asked Mercer, "Have you the count?"

"Twenty-three hundred and seventy-two."

"And about eighteen hundred with Cadwalader," the foxhunter said, almost to himself.

And then he and the little Scotsman looked at each other.

Greene came over to the fat colonel of artillery and asked him, "What do you think, Harry?"

"I don't know; it's better not to think. If he wanted to go into hell and bait devils, I suppose I would go along with him. There's nothing else, is there?"

"I suppose not."

"What time have you?"

"Twelve-twenty."

Knox wound his clumsy, silver-shelled timepiece, and then set the hands. "This isn't much good," he complained. "It goes off about five minutes on the hour."

"So long as you know if it's fast or slow."

"Slow, sometimes more, sometimes less."

"I hope it doesn't snow," Greene remarked.

"It will."

"I hate to think of those poor devils in that water."

Knox shrugged and grinned.

"When are you going to start the cannon?"

"Soon."

"There's ice in the water," Greene said.

"There would be," Knox agreed ruefully. "There would be every damned filthy thing today."

"Well—good luck, Harry."

Ice, breaking from the shelves and shallow creeks in the north, was fast filling the river, big, nasty slabs, not very thick, but sharp and like knife-edges in the swirling current. Watching it gather through the white veil of his breath, Glover shook his head ruefully.

"I don't like it," he told Captain Purdy of Gloucester. "We'll have to count on poling."

"If the bottom don't fall away."

"At any rate, we'll slip downstream more than we thought. I figure we ought to look for a likely spot up about a mile."

"It's too late, and we can't get the guns into the boats without the ferry landing. We'll do what we can."

The foxhunter, now mounted on a bony chestnut, galloped along the freezing, shivering line, calling, "General Greene! General Greene!" His big cloak was thread-bare and flapped loosely about his long figure; his nose was bright red, his eyes watery; and he coughed and sneezed as he demanded, "General Greene!"

"What is it, sir?"

"What time is it?"

"Just about half after one."

"Well, what are you waiting for, Nathanael? Start the men for the ferry. Can't you see they're freezing cold?"

"I thought I would wait just a while longer."

"No, start them off now!" And then he wheeled away and was spurring his horse down to see how Knox and Hamilton were doing with the artillery.

It made Greene's heart ache to watch the half-frozen men shuffling along on their way to the river. They had known an hour of dreadful anticipation, but by now their fear had been whipped into a stolid, dogged determination. Their cockiness was gone and their boasting was gone, but in its place had come a silent, somber intent. Many of them believed that this was the end of their tragic, short-lived revolution; arguments and reasons had vanished; they were men going forward to die because they had committed themselves to freedom, and now, when everything else was gone, there remained only that commitment.

They did not sing nor did they talk as they moved along; they gripped their big, clumsy flintlocks with deadly earnestness; and their eyes, for the most part, were set straight ahead: and they did not know that the cold shuffling sound of their steps would echo undyingly.

And Greene, also treading a blank path, thought to himself: "They are brave, and that is something I will remember. Even if they run away, I will always remember that they were brave at this time."

Greene had once fought a battle with himself; he was a Quaker, and the edict was stern and straightforward: Thou shalt not kill. But if ever there was vindication, this was it, on Christmas Day, the day a man came into the world to preach Peace on Earth, Good Will toward Men—and incongruous as that was, strange as that was, Greene knew that he was not defiling the day, that he was keeping a rendezvous with men of good will. As faint of heart as the rabble that marched beside him, he was nevertheless proud and humble.

Leaning over his saddle, the foxhunter asked Glover, "How are things now?"

"As well as can be expected, sir."

"You have the boats ready?"

Glover nodded, but pointed to the spinning ice cakes.

"You can get us across?"

"We'll get across," Glover said. "Maybe a little more time than we reckoned on, but we'll get across. When do you want to start?"

The tall man looked at his watch and then at the sky. He thought that in about twenty minutes it would be dark enough to veil their movements from the other shore.

"Men first, then the guns?"

"A little of each," the tall man smiled.

He rode along the line of his men. They were crouched on the cold ground, and as he went past a succession of white faces turned in the dusk to look at him. He thought that it would have been the right thing to say something to them, but looking at their faces, there was nothing for the life of him that he thought mattered enough to put into words. He wondered whether they felt, as he did, the crashing insanity of this last desperate move. And what did they think of him? Did they hate him or did they love him, or did they follow him as sheep follow a leader? Was the stake, the intangible something called freedom, big enough? Was it worth the suffering, the starving, the cold and the hunger?

He didn't know. Once he had been sure of many things, but now he was sure only of the dark, singular path he must travel. He was lonely, and he knew that regardless of what happened, regardless of what came out of this, victory or defeat, glory or ruin, there would never be compensation nor relief from that loneliness. Still, he was not unhappy; often, he had said and written that he would not undergo this again for any reward on earth, but now he was not quite certain of that fact. He had learned something terribly difficult for an aristocrat, for a foxhunter, for the wealthiest man in America; but now that he had learned he would not have been willing to unlearn. Wanting more than anything else to be loved and respected by others, he had found a strange peace in giving out of his own troubled heart.

For hours and hours the infantry had been standing and crouching motionless in the cold; now, at last, the order came to move. Their limbs were stiff and their joints creaked as they walked; they clapped their hands and beat their knuckles against their muskets. They stumbled and fell and got up again, feeling their way in the darkness; and they laughed, somewhat hysterically, at the way the Marblehead fishermen sang out, "Step smart there! Step lively!" They jostled against each other, and some of them slipped and fell into the icy water, and then were fished out shivering and cursing. The grinding crunch of the ice cakes and the constant thud against the frail sides of the boats made their throats contract, but they didn't hold back. They went into the inky blackness slowly but certainly.

For all the cold, the artillerymen poured sweat as they put their shoulders to the cannon, and strained and heaved them onto the barges, some of them standing waist-deep in the ice-cold water, others fighting the cannon on the rocking boats as if the big, insensate pieces of metal had suddenly come alive, others staggering under the weight of cannister and iron balls. And the fishermen, groaning at the clumsy, butter-fingered landsmen, cursed and directed and pleaded. Knox, his huge voice drowning out all other sound, roared commands.

"Come at it there! Stand to it! Put your shoulders to it, God damn you! Put your shoulders to it!"

A barge overturned, spilling three horses into the water, creating a sudden maelstrom of confusion as the frightened beasts fought the current, neighing shrilly. Sullivan, whose horse was among the three, shouted, "Get them! Get them! For God's sake, don't let them drown!"

The foxhunter, stumbling through the dark, looking for the harried, tireless Glover, came up with Knox and grasped both his shoulders, demanding, "For God's sake, Harry, it's past midnight! Why can't you get the guns loaded?"

Knox was soaked with sweat and river water, alternately

feverish and chilled, his boots full of icy slush, his hat gone, his coat split down the back. He looked at the tall man pleadingly, shaking his head, "I'm doing my best, sir, I can't do more than that. It's the ice. The boats can't go across to where they want to go; they have to float downstream and then be dragged up. And I've been trying to get powder and shot across, sir—in case we want to use the guns in a hurry."

"Well, get them across, Harry! Get them across! And call for Glover. My voice is gone—call out!"

Knox roared and bellowed like a bull, but when he turned around again, the Virginian had gone off into the dark.

At two o'clock in the morning, most of the army had already been ferried across the river. Working like demons, the fishermen had once more accomplished the impossible; they had pushed the army and guns through the black night, the ice and the current, to a point on the other bank some nine miles distant from the Hessian encampment at Trenton. Glover, coming to report, found the foxhunter standing with Knox and Greene.

"I think that you had better go across now, sir," Glover said. "The worst part of it is over."

Washington nodded, and Greene took his arm to help him down into the boat. But he stood aside and said, "Get in, Harry. I'll feel safer once you're set."

For Knox, the reaction was close to hysteria. He climbed into the boat, bellowing laughter until the tears ran over his cheeks. He sat down, and Greene followed him, and then the Virginian, helped by the steadying hand of Glover, stepped in. He looked around for a place to sit, and then poked the fat colonel of artillery with his toe, telling him:

"Shift your weight, Harry, and trim the boat."

The fishermen pushed off from shore, their hard laughter breaking for once the wall that had been between them and the tall Virginia farmer; and Knox, still shaking with mirth, felt a great happiness and a great pride, for next to him, on the same seat, and close against him, was the man he loved more than any other. He looked at Washington, and saw how the light grey eyes were searching the darkness; and Knox knew, and Greene knew, with fierce joy, that this was not the end, that for their kind there could never be an end, but only new beginnings.

AN AFTERWORD

Some books end with the last page; this one does not, for the sound of the bleeding feet that marched on Trenton rose in a crescendo that echoed and re-echoed across the world, and that today is not lost, and that will not, God willing, be lost for all time to come. How the poor, shivering rabble came on to Trenton and captured the place, taking over a thousand prisoners, is too well known to need retelling here.

But the man who had set out across the Delaware as a Virginia farmer, as a foxhunter, became on the other shore something else, a man of incredible stature, a human being in some ways more godly and more wonderful than any other who has walked on this earth. For he became, as with no other man in history, the father of a nation that was to be peopled by the wretched and the oppressed of every land on earth. As simple, as burnished as this sounds, it is no use to plead otherwise; the stamp of George Washington is indelibly and forever set upon America—and for the good. All the debunking in the world cannot change the facts of his wonderful simplicity, his complete unselfishness, his humble respect for those who had asked him to leave his home and fight a revolution. Given power, he spurned it, thereby giving to America for all time the ideal of leaders who serve a people but do not rule them. And whether this ideal is forgotten at times or not, it is there, stamped in the soul of a nation.

It is a pity that toward the end of the eighteenth century, the writing of history was still a mixture of homilies, lies and legends. Today, the truth is very hard to find; and Americans as a whole do not know what George Washington suffered during the eight years he led the revolution nearly as well as they know what Lincoln suffered at a time when history had become a somewhat more exact science. Those who gilded the American Revolution, preserving it in a glass case for the D.A.R. and the S.A.R., hiding a noble and courageous effort of mankind, also gilded the man who led it; and that coat of cheap and tawdry varnish has led millions of Americans to reject with a smile all that was George Washington. Because the cherry-tree story was an invention, they came to regard all of George Washington as an invention, as well they might when one considers the windbags, the loud-mouthed enemies of all democracy who fling his name to the four winds today.

This book is an effort to restore the man and the men around him, not as tin gods, but in some measure as I believed them to have been, as human beings clinging with steadfast purpose to a cause that might certainly be called lost. None of these men, with the exception of Alexander Hamilton, was brilliant, and none of them, again with the exception of Hamilton and of course Washington, played much part in constructing the nation that came after the war. They were in a time between two eras, making the change, but divorced from what had been before them and from what came after them. They were revolutionists. They gave to others, and though after the giving there was nothing for them, they were not regretful. Many of their names were forgotten, and I don't think they would have regretted that either.

When I set out to write this story of the New York campaign and the subsequent retreat as a piece of fiction, I knew well enough on what delicate ground I was treading. There are no fictional characters in this story; for each name, a man lived, playing his part much as detailed here. But I wanted them to come alive, feeling that at such a time as this there is need for those half-forgotten men to live again and do their deeds once more, and join in the battle of all men of good will against the forces of evil. And therefore I put thoughts into their minds and let them speak words of which there is no record.

I will say that I tried faithfully to keep to the character of each of these men, to use recorded speech wherever I could, changing only the stilted form, to give them words that they might have said and thoughts that they might have had. As to the historical events, regardless of how far they depart from the writings of the great army of historians who up until the recent past have done their best to obscure facts of our revolution, I believe them to be true. At least,

I have earnestly tried to keep them as near to the truth as anyone can after one hundred and sixty years of deliberate obscurity. As this is a work of fiction, I feel no need to include a bibliography, although I must express a great debt to the almost numberless biographies of Washington, the best and the worst, particularly Rupert Hughes' splendid work.

ABOUT THE AUTHOR

HOWARD FAST was born and educated in New York City. He traveled around the United States, working as a laborer in a lumber camp, a shipping clerk in a New York factory and a page boy in the New York Public Library. He studied art at the National Academy of Design. He finished his first novel at seventeen and sold his first story in 1932. His first published novel, *Two Valleys*, appeared in 1933, but it was not until 1937, when his novella "The Children" was published, that he was able to give up his other jobs and devote himself full time to writing.

Mr. Fast's most successful work, both critically and commercially, has been in the field of historical fiction: *Conceived in Liberty, The Last Frontier, The Unvanquished, My Glorious Brothers* and *Spartacus*. His novel *The American* was a Literary Guild selection, and *Freedom Road* has been translated into twenty-one languages.